Linda—
Sorry for the bush league insert of chapter 4. Our publisher has been a nightmare. Warning: it's edgy spiritual + the lead character is vain + profane until... well, you'll see.
        Enjoy (maybe),
            Dave

David Mills Hay

Worthless
A Tale of Unlikely Redemption

Copyright © 2018 David Mills Hay

All rights reserved. No part of this book may be used or reproduced by any means, graphic, electronic, or mechanical, including photocopying, recording, taping or by any information storage retrieval system without the written permission of the author except in the case of brief quotations embodied in critical articles and reviews.

This is a work of fiction. All of the characters, names, incidents, organizations, and dialogue in this novel are either the products of the author's imagination or are used fictitiously.

Archway Publishing books may be ordered through booksellers or by contacting:

Archway Publishing
1663 Liberty Drive
Bloomington, IN 47403
www.archwaypublishing.com
1 (888) 242-5904

Because of the dynamic nature of the Internet, any web addresses or links contained in this book may have changed since publication and may no longer be valid. The views expressed in this work are solely those of the author and do not necessarily reflect the views of the publisher, and the publisher hereby disclaims any responsibility for them.

Any people depicted in stock imagery provided by Thinkstock are models, and such images are being used for illustrative purposes only. Certain stock imagery © Thinkstock.

ISBN: 978-1-4808-5400-0 (sc)
ISBN: 978-1-4808-5401-7 (hc)
ISBN: 978-1-4808-5399-7 (e)

Library of Congress Control Number: 2017918661

Printed in the United States of America.

Archway Publishing rev. date: 07/10/2018

Dedication

This book is dedicated to the memory and eternal spirit of Bertram W. Salzman.

Acknowledgements

As is often the case, this book was many years in the making and it is no exaggeration to say that it would never have made it to the publication stage if it wasn't for the help of three individuals.

The first is Christina Dudley, who converted what was originally a long and rambling screenplay into this concise novel. Her polished writing and editing skills--as well as her excellent judgment on what to include and what to excise—were essential in seeing this project through to completion. Christina has had several books published and I would encourage you to go online to check out their reviews—and then order one!

Secondly, I want to express deep gratitude to another fellow writer, Mark Joseph Mongilutz, who has spent countless hours over the last two years helping me refine the story and coaching me through the publication process. To say that, as a first-time author, I needed his support and advice is a massive understatement. His autobiographical book, tentatively titled "Solemn Duty in The Old Guard", which is to be published in early 2018, is a moving description of his years serving his country at our armed services' most sacred of final resting places, Arlington National Cemetery, as well as his time spent overseas in support of Operation Enduring Freedom.

Lastly, I was blessed to also have the guidance and encouragement of the late Bert Salzman, who passed on to his new life almost exactly a year prior to the publishing of this book. In addition to having been my great friend and spiritual mentor for over 25 years, Bert was an Academy Award-winning film director. Bert also wrote the autobiographical book, "Being a Buddha on Broadway". Though Bert was a Buddhist and I am a Christian, we were kindred spirits from virtually the moment we met.

Introduction

While much of Worthless is fictional, much is not. For example, the Jubilee Youth Ranch actually exists and is located between the Tri-Cities (famed for developing the atomic bomb during WWII) and Walla Walla, well-known in its own right for its prolific and highly regarded wineries. Additionally, several of the characters are based on real individuals from that area whom the author has come to know over the years and who have made Jubilee into one of the nation's finest facilities for at-risk young men, at considerable personal sacrifice in both time and money.

As you will read, the land itself plays a crucial role in the story. For non-Northwesterners, the striking topography featured on the dust jacket may seem incongruous with their general perception of Washington state, as might the weather patterns described herein (abundant sunshine and colder, periodically snowy winters). The contrast with the more familiar lush terrain of the Seattle area—with its wet, typically temperate climate—are accurately conveyed and a key reason the Walla Walla Valley has become a worthy runner-up to the Napa Valley as America's finest wine-producing region.

It is my hope that a close reading of these pages will evoke a desire within some to personally visit this breathtakingly scenic corner of the state and, especially, the extraordinary venue that is the Jubilee Youth Ranch.

With humble gratitude,
David Mills Hay

Walla Walla General Hospital
Present Day

Was he alive, or was he dead?
He couldn't tell.
He was lying there listening to steady beeping and a hum. There were attachments of some sort sticking in him. So, he was alive, then. But he couldn't raise his arms or open his eyes to investigate further.

He felt something or someone trying to reach him, like a faint call down a hallway that stretched out of sight. He listened as it came closer, expecting who knew what. A nurse, maybe. God. Sarah.

But it turned out to be something closer at hand—his own thoughts or voices. A memory.

This is what he remembered.

1

"I spent most of my money on booze, (babes) and fast cars. The rest I just wasted."
— George Best, Northern Irish soccer legend (1946-2005)

The boys were at the river. The summer weather was as hot as an open furnace, but it was a dry heat that desiccated you slowly. And if you ever got too hot, there was always the water. The mighty Columbia, coursing down from the mountains of British Columbia, was vast enough to power dam after dam, deep enough to irrigate almost infinite acres of wheat, and cool enough to keep the reactors at Hanford from going "China syndrome" on them.

The two boys were fishing below the bluffs. Or one was fishing. The taller one had thrown his pole off to the side and was kicking at the banks, looking for rocks to skip.

"This is boring," he said for the fifth time. "We haven't caught anything, and I'm hot. Let's do something else." He let one fly: one, two—damn! It sank a few yards out.

The boy with the dark hair didn't answer, not even to say, *Would you quit throwing rocks in? I'm trying to fish here!* He scratched at his T-shirt, which was white, without one single hole in it.

The taller boy wiped his hands down his own ragged shirt. "I know, Nate—let's race our dirt bikes along the river trail."

"You know we're not supposed to do that," Nate said.

"Come on! It'll be fun, and your dad'll never know. Besides, it'll cool us off."

"So would jumping in the river," Nate pointed out. But he was reeling in his line all the same.

"Thought your dad said we should watch out, swimming," the other jeered. "'Cause the river's so high with them letting out that water from Grand Coulee."

"I didn't say swim, Jason," Nate retorted, his lower lip sticking out. "I said *jump* in."

"We do that all the time. We need to do something more exciting."

He could tell Nate was weakening, so he turned and grabbed his dirt bike off the bank. Before Jason even had the motor started, Nate's own fishing pole clattered down, and he was running for his. Gunning his bike, Jason yelled, "Race you to Painted Rock!"

God, it still made his teeth ache to think of that trail along the river. Calling it a trail probably glorified it. It was no more than a track half carved out. It was all moguls and gravel and trying not to let the seat nail him in the nuts as he bounced along. Dust was flying, and the whine of Nate's bike dropped as he put distance between them.

"I'm beating your chicken ass!" Jason crowed over his shoulder, the roughness of the ride slamming his jaw shut and almost making him bite his tongue. "Beating your ass just like at basketball!"

That must have used up his hubris allowance, because while his head was still turned, his bike hit the Everest of moguls. Next thing he knew, he was airborne, the bike rolling over him in a kaleidoscope of sky, dirt, and metal. And then there was no bike at all—just him, flying.

He hit the river like he'd belly-flopped from the top of the bluffs. Then the brick-hard surface parted and dissolved into water that grabbed him with icy arms and swept him downstream.

Head spinning, limbs flailing, and trying to fight the current, he noticed one arm wasn't doing much of anything to obey his commands, and what was left of rational in his brain went missing. He screamed, he thought, with his mouth full of water, or maybe the screaming was all in his head. Nate had jumped off his bike where Jason went in, but when he saw how fast his friend was moving away from him, he scrambled back on and throttled it, trying to keep up.

There wasn't a chance. At the speed the current moved, Jason thought he'd probably get puréed by a McNary Dam turbine in fifteen minutes.

The river slammed him up against a boulder, tore him off again, and sent him rolling bass-ackwards away. Icy numbness took hold of his hands and feet. Part of him fought it—the one working arm, the head trying to stay clear to gulp in breaths—but as fatigue and pain stalked him, the other part of him almost welcomed it as a mercy. Did it hurt to drown if you couldn't feel it?

Before he could puzzle over this question, the river bashed him on the head with another rock. He heard Nate shout; he saw the sun dip crazily and wink out. And then there was only darkness and silence.

Count to a hundred, maybe.

Then light returned. Gradually. Not the sun, but a spinning whiteness that approached and intensified. He wondered where he was. Though he had been terrified only moments earlier, his panic was gone as if it had never been. He wasn't afraid.

The light was pulling him in, whirling faster and faster. And with his advance toward it, a sense of joy and wholeness filled him—overwhelmed him, like nothing he'd ever experienced. Like the best he'd ever felt and multiplied to the nth power. No—even that didn't do it justice.

Hours could be flying by. Or days.

He had always been here, in this nowhere-everywhere place. He had always been bathed in this light and made welcome.

He was almost there. The spin of the light was so fast now he could barely catch its movement, but it did move, and he moved to meet it.

He leaned in.

He reached to take hold.

"Twenty-six. Twenty-seven. Twenty-eight …" God Almighty, someone was looming over him, pumping his chest up and down with hands locked. "Twenty-nine. Thirty."

A mouth came down to cover his, driving air into him and driving away the crazy, unreasoning joy, the spinning light. Back came cold and weariness and raw, scraped skin and shooting pains from his arm and a throbbing head. He vomited out mud and what felt like a gallon of the Columbia.

It was Jess, Nate's dad, giving him CPR.

The bastard.

Jason would never quite forgive him for bringing him back.

Nate said Jason had snagged on a fallen tree right after he passed out. He thought about wading into the rapids to get him, but instead he went hell-for-leather for his dad. They found him floating face down, human limbs tangled with tree limbs. Jess had to rope him up and haul him in. Then he did CPR for what felt to him like a month.

And it was the Carsons who took him to the hospital to get his arm set and to check if the time in the water made him "any more brain damaged" than he already was. "What the hell were you two thinking?" Jess demanded. "That track is all of two feet wide and rougher than an alligator's back. You almost met your Maker today."

Jason didn't say anything—not about his idiocy or about whatever or whomever he really did meet. No one expected him to, and he wasn't about to open his mouth and tell them about the spinning light and the happiness that flooded him and how he would have gone with it—almost had gone with it—wherever it led. He could never tell Jess or Nate about that dream, vision, or whatever it was. He could never tell anyone.

For one thing, no one would believe him. Hell, did *he* even believe himself now, under the harsh green fluorescents of the clinic? Or worse, they would laugh at him. He might only have been twelve, but he already knew that out of the things he hated worst in the world, being laughed at was right up there with his mom.

And God, did he hate his mom.

Suffice it to say, his childhood home was a few notches below idyllic. How he lasted as long as he did there was anyone's guess, one of those great mysteries of the universe...like why ice floats.

The day when he finally got the hell out appeared on the surface to be nothing special, except it was too much like every day that came before it, and Jason didn't want to stick around to see if it was going to be par for the course for every day coming after. It was about a year after he had cheated death at the river. He must have been about fourteen.

Despite their high-sounding name, the Knightbridges lived in a dump of a singlewide in the Whispering Breezes Trailer Park. You could look up "poor white trash" in the dictionary for a family portrait.

Most kids in the Breezes were getting beat up by their alcoholic dads, but at 42 Elysian it was Jason's mom who ruled the roost. She was twice the size of his dad, Leon, for starters—not just physically, but personality-wise too.

He could picture her that day: tall and powerfully built, wearing that stained old pink bathrobe with the fuzz worn off, a cigarette hanging off her lip. Leon was scrawny and cowering because he'd blown it again.

"Now look, Mama," he said, whining, "I just ran into a little misfortune at the Indian casino on the way home from work."

Jason's mom could take it to DEFCON 1 before anyone else even clocked in, and she was letting Leon have it. "Where is your goddamned paycheck?"

He held up his hands. "Like I said, just a little—"

That was all he got out before she was on him, fists wheeling, one connecting with his jaw and throwing him against the table. The whole trailer shook. Then a dish came flying, slicing the air like an Olympic discus thrower had hurled it. Leon ducked with surprising agility—but then his plate-avoidance skills were well-honed—and the dish shattered when it hit the wall. Jason didn't know whether to whistle in admiration or shake his head when the idiot decided to charge her. His mom was ready: she head-butted him right in the chest, the cigarette not even detaching from her lip, and that did the trick. Leon went reeling back into the wall, smacking it with his head and sliding down for a happy landing on his ass, eyes gone wide.

"I'm gonna kill you," Jason's mother snarled. "You spineless little bastard."

Leon didn't have the wherewithal to respond, but her blood was up. Jason had made a soft *huh* sound, and in a flash, she was turning on him. "What're you laughing at?"

He could tell he was next on the agenda. Usually he would've muttered, "Nothing," and tried to lay low, but on this day, he couldn't—or wouldn't.

She came closer, and when that woman moved slowly, she was even more dangerous, like a leopard preparing to pounce. "I said, boy, *what are you laughing at?*"

This was it. He took a deep breath and said, "You."

Then he busted out of there, charging past her and flinging the screen door open so hard it broke off one hinge before slapping back to strike her. Roaring, she slammed it out of her way, breaking it off the other hinge and leaving it to rattle to the ground.

"You think you can run out of here?" she bellowed, coming for him. "Yeah—go on—get out, you ungrateful little parasite.

You're as worthless as your goddamned worthless father, and you're gonna turn out just like him—worthless."

She threw a right cross at him, but his moment had come. He was taller than she was now, and they both found he had grown stronger too. But more than his body, what had grown even bigger and more powerful was his hatred of her. His hand shot up and caught her punch in midair. She was so stunned that she froze, and the wilted cigarette finally lost its purchase and dropped away.

"I'm going," he said, panting. "If I don't get out now, one of us is gonna wind up dead—and it's not gonna be me."

Like a snake wrestler who had caught one about to strike, he kept his eyes on her and slowly released her fist. With a cry, she lunged for him, but he dodged her, and her momentum sent her past him, where she tripped over a corroded sprinkler head in the dirt.

"Get your worthless ass outta here!" she shrieked, leaping back up. "Get, before I grab my gun and shoot it off. *Worthless!*"

He didn't need to be told twice. He went. He had nothing with him but a duffel bag he'd kept stashed behind a rusted-out air-conditioning unit. He just started walking.

His head didn't tell him where to go, but his feet took him there anyway: the Carsons'—a mile down the road and a world away, in their Norman Rockwell ranch house on the bluff above the river.

Nate was at the top of the driveway, shooting baskets. His dad, Jess, was in the garage, under the hood of the pick-up truck. They both stopped what they were doing when they saw him. Maybe it showed on his face.

It wasn't like the Carsons' place was a mansion. He and Nate had to share a room, in fact. But they took him in all the same. Nate and his dad, who'd pulled him out of the river, and Nate's mom, Maria. And if they ever argued about it or were sorry they did it, Jason never knew it.

They gave him a bed and food and a roof over his head—and

something else. Every night, Nate and Jason stayed up as late as they could watching old movies on Channel 13. It was the only station Jess would allow the boys to view being a right Christian man and properly offended by the "trash" displayed nightly on TV in the late 1970s. So, Nate and Jason inadvertently became old film buffs. They would take turns imitating their favorite male actors, like Cary Grant, Errol Flynn, and, of course, the long dead star (who, coincidentally, was enjoying an international popularity renaissance in those days) Humphrey Bogart.

When their friends at school would make sexually implicit remarks about the foxy women on *Charlie's Angels*, Nate and Jason had no idea who they were talking about. Now, if they had brought up Lauren Bacall or Marlene Dietrich, they might have contributed a choice comment or two of their own.

These evenings in front of the old black-and-white TV, watching the classics, and feeling the approach of another night's soothing slumber—those were among Jason's fondest memories of his years with the Carsons. He felt safe—safe and loved, two feelings he'd never had before, and, as life would unfold before him, he wouldn't have much of them in the future—through no one's fault but his own. But of all the things he loved about those evenings, the best of the best was when Maria would come in, turn off the lights and the TV, and bend down to kiss a snoring Nate on the forehead. Then, she would go over and do the same to Jason. He pretended to be asleep—always—but the truth was, he never did go to sleep until he had that kiss. Because it was the cherry on top of the chocolate sundae.

Before Maria, he couldn't remember ever having been kissed. Hit, plenty...but never kissed.

2

A year went by.

Another hot, dry summer took hold. The sun arced over the vast sky, and the river ran on. On this side of the Cascade Mountains, there were no evergreens crowding the horizon, no sullen cloud blankets leaking drizzle—just the wide-open land, seemingly stretching forever, carpeted-in brown and tan, punctuated with tumbleweeds. Apart from the wind, which kicked up every day with the heat, there was silence.

He and Nate were playing cards in the den, where the house stayed coolest. Jason sprawled on the fold-up chair, his knee jogging up and down. He shook his glass of ice to get the cubes unstuck and tipped it back, seeking that last drop of lemonade.

Outside, a car came growling up the road below the Carsons'. The boys heard a door slam and a rumbling voice, answered by Jess's soft one.

Jason frowned at Nate, but Nate was calculating his odds and ignored him. He threw down a jack of spades and snorted in disgust when Jason trumped it.

"Who's that guy talking to your dad?"

A shrug.

If he was interested, Nate didn't have to wait long to find out, because next thing was the screen door flying open and

Jess's tread in the hall. "Come on out here, Nate," he said when his head appeared around the door jamb. "Someone to see you."

He said not one word to Jason, who tipped his chair onto its back legs and threw his cards on the table. Maria was always telling him not to do that—she thought the chair would fold up under him, but Jess said more likely Jason's size and weight would just bust the thing, and he'd get impaled on a steel leg, and it would serve him right.

He had almost gotten the chair balanced when Jess's voice came hollering for him. "Jason, you get out here too. Somebody wants to meet you too."

The same somebody hadn't given a lick about meeting him a minute ago, but Jason dropped the chair back to four legs, ripped his thighs off the seat, and got up.

The screen door was propped open, so he stopped a second before he went out, hanging onto the top of the frame. He'd grown plenty in the last year, his body lengthening and muscles sculpting him like some Walla Walla County David. Like the David, he had the same oversized hands and arresting good looks, the same furrowed brow, taking in the scene.

There was Jess, frowning, and Nate was frowning too, like he was doing an imitation of his dad. And there was some old guy, maybe in his fifties. Tall, with just the beginnings of a gut, he was chewing on an unlit cigar and leaning against a white Cadillac convertible that ticked in the heat. The car's red leather interior made Jason think of the mouth of a beast.

That was his first look at Sam Steele.

When the old guy saw Jason, he got a big grin and came at him, hand outstretched. "Hey there, son. I'm Sam Steele. Old acquaintance of Jess's here." He wrung Jason's hand and then, without letting go, grabbed his other one. "Look at the mitts on you! Yep—you're the one I heard about, the one with the fourth finger joint. I never did quite believe such a thing existed, outside Spencer Haywood of the Seattle Supersonics." Dropping

Jason's hands and shaking his head, he looked toward Jess again. "You mind if I ask these two boys to have a go at it, one on one? I see you got a hoop that's seen plenty of use."

Jess's face was still wary, but he made one of those be-my-guest moves and nodded at the boys. Jason looked at Nate, but Nate gave another of his shrugs and went to get the ball out of the garage. Even though they played nearly every day, they were awkward with an audience, at first. Or Jason was awkward. Nate was always quick with his feet and hands, and he seemed to have something to prove to the visitor. When Jason had the ball, Nate kept darting at him, knocking the ball away and making Jason scramble for it, until Jason got pissed off enough to forget the stranger watching them. Recovering the ball one last time, he grasped it like a grapefruit and slammed it down in front of Nate, making it bounce clear over his head. When Nate flinched, Jason lunged past him and grabbed the ball one-handed. Leaping, he more than cleared the rim, and his dunk slammed the backboard so hard it shook for almost a minute afterward.

Sam Steele's cigar tumbled from his mouth.

"I'll be damned. I've never seen a kid from these parts who could do that with a ball." A slow smile spread across his face. "How'd you like to go with me, son, and see some of the world?"

No longer embarrassed, Jason grinned back. "You mean in that old beater?"

"Have a little respect. That would be a seventy-three Cadillac El Dorado—the last year they made before they put all that emissions bullshit in 'em. Listen up: I was telling Jess and Nate here that coaching select basketball is my passion."

"*One* of them, at least," said Jess dryly. "Seems you took up plenty of pastimes after the war."

"That's right," said Sam, eyeing him. "*One* of them. Surviving Bastogne and the Battle of the Bulge gives a guy a hell of a will to live life to the fullest." He turned again to regard his new discovery. "I've got plenty I could teach you, Jason. If you're willing to learn, we could show this valley how the game of basketball is meant to be played."

At that stage of his young life, school wasn't one of Jason's favorite things, though his high grades said otherwise. He wasn't short on brains—just patience. Not that it mattered much. He suspected what Sam Steele would teach him had nothing to do with the four walls of a classroom.

Select basketball was only the beginning. After that summer afternoon, Jason and Sam Steele were together almost all the time: at practice, at tournaments, traveling. As predicted, Jason excelled at the sport, and when the season ended, Sam Steele showed no inclination to lose Jason's company. They traded basketball for golf, the court for the green, fast breaks for chip shots. Jason started with caddying, but pretty soon Sam was teaching him the game, and not long after that, Jason was breaking eighty.

The other thing regularly breaking eighty was Sam's Cadillac, heading down the road to faraway places any time Jason didn't have school. And he was right about doing life with Sam—it was an education in itself. The geography of the West. The physics of motion. The foreign language of Sam's vernacular. And then, more enlightening than any home economics class, there were Sam's special recipes.

"Jason, go inside and get a Coke while I fill up," Sam told him one day at a gas station somewhere outside Sacramento. He shoved a five-dollar bill at him. "Keep what's left."

When Jason got back in the El Dorado, he made to hand over the Coke bottle, but Sam shook his head. "Now drink it down fast."

"But I'm not thirsty."

"You just got thirsty. Hurry up."

Shrugging, Jason popped the lid and guzzled it. He got three quarters of it down before Sam grabbed it away. "Attaboy.

Perfect." Slipping a flask from his pocket, Sam tipped it into the Coke bottle, filling it carefully back to the top.

"A little mother's milk for the road. I hate driving naked."

"Naked" or not, they drove a lot. Jason was torn between squinting in the glare and goggling at things he'd never before seen. He was too young and too dazzled to wonder what went into making a man like Sam. There were hints thrown out here and there, but what teenage kid ever picked up on those? No, Jason didn't much care where Sam had been. He was more interested in where Sam was going. Sam always had a cigar clenched in his teeth. In Jason's memory, the cigars had the diameters of baseball bats, and they were as much a part of Sam as his car, his flask, and his old black leather bag.

"Why do you use this ancient thing?" Jason asked once when they pulled up at a hotel. They must have been in Vegas or Reno because he remembered the flash and blink of lights reflected in the dull sheen of the bag. "It's like you're some old-time doctor making house calls."

Ignoring him, Sam held up a hand to fend off an approaching valet. "Hold on there, son. Only *I* carry that bag. It's got some very precious cargo in it."

When they got to their suite, Jason sprawled in an armchair and kicked his sneakers off, watching his mentor place the bag delicately on a table by the in-room bar. He'd been on enough trips with Sam by now to know what was coming, but he watched in fascination nonetheless. Sam proceeded to remove and arrange the black bag's contents with the precision of a surgeon preparing a tray of instruments. There were the cigarettes, the Cohiba cigars, the bottle of Maker's Mark, and Sam's 101st Airborne lighter, all set precisely on the surface, as if their positions were predetermined. Maybe they were. It could have been superstition on Sam Steele's part: everything in its place for good luck because, God knew, Sam spent a lot of time getting lucky.

There were always the women at the tables, drawn by the sound and smell of money, leaning into him in their slinky, low-cut gowns. "Come on, honey," Sam would say, sweat beading on his forehead, giving the dice to one of them. "Blow on 'em. Don't be bashful. Luck be a lady tonight!"

Bending forward to oblige, the chosen woman would give him a slow, heavy-lidded look that said, win or lose, those dice wouldn't be the only things getting blown that night.

Jason spent so much time with Sam that, when he hit fifteen-and-a-half and finally moved out of the Carsons', his departure was no more than a formality—an uncomfortable one, though.

It was fall. Leaves were blowing around; the sky was steel gray, but it wasn't raining. They were all standing outside the house: Jess, Nate, Maria. Maria was crying silently. Jason had his duffel bag slung over one shoulder, trying not to look at her—or Nate.

Then Jess grabbed for his free hand and shook it. "Good luck, son. We enjoyed your time with us." His voice got uneven, and he worked to smooth it out again. "I'm sorry to see you go, but I understand. I reckon a young man needs to follow where opportunity lies."

Jason nodded. He kicked at a tuft of crabgrass sprouting from a crack in the drive. "Thanks for everything, Mr. Carson. You were ..." The sharp stone in his own throat stopped his own speech. He ventured a glance at Maria, who was wiping her eyes and putting on a brave face. "I mean—and thank you so much, Mrs. Carson. You were both like ..."

That was as far as he got, but they nodded back, as if he had been able to put it all into words.

"You always know where to find us," said Jess, half under his breath. Jason managed a half-nod and an *uh-huh* to that.

Nate couldn't come up with any words at all. It wasn't like they wouldn't still see each other all the time, at school, at basketball, but it wouldn't be the same as Jason living there. Jason knew it, and Nate knew it.

Later he thought that maybe Nate never quite forgave him for that first departure—that first desertion.

For his own part, Jason bounced back with all the elasticity of youth. He had free rein in Sam's big house on a farm, where the old guy was just starting to grow grapes. Sam let him do whatever the hell he wanted, and it turned out Jason wanted to do a hell of a lot.

On his sixteenth birthday, they hit the car dealerships. "George O'Brien called me," Sam said around his trademark Cohibas. "The 1982s are in. Let's take a quick look."

Jason raised an eyebrow and muttered something that sounded like "emissions bullshit," but Sam only grinned, pulling into the Chevy lot. A sparkling red Camaro Z28 held pride of place, and Jason forgot his razzing long enough to say, "Wow! Look at that beauty!"

"It sure is," Sam agreed. "Just think how many babes you could attract with that."

The salesman, who had been lurking in the shade, smoking a cigarette, ground it under his heel and strode over. "Quite a car, huh?" he asked Jason.

"I'll say."

"Too bad it's sold. God knows when we'll get another one in like this one."

Jason's shoulders slumped a little, even as he continued to admire it. "Yeah."

"Older gentleman bought it," said the salesman. He and Sam exchanged looks, and then the guy dug in his pocket. "Here are the keys, Sam."

"Lookie there." Sam took in Jason's perplexed face and then tossed him the keys. "Happy birthday, Jason. I hope that backseat gets plenty of action."

Jason only stared, openmouthed, first at the keys, then at the car.

"Boy may never shut his mouth again," the salesman said, chuckling.

For a while there, Jason was inclined to agree. How could it not turn his head, to go from a trailer park to the teenage top of the world in two years' time? It was whiplash-inducing. And if he neglected to look back at everything he had left in the rearview mirror—well, it wasn't that hard to understand.

The seasons turned.

In Jason's senior year, Sam Steele wasn't just the coach of the select team but Walla Walla High's varsity, as well. They almost won state behind him, Jason always in the spotlight, with numbers the district hadn't seen before or since. But by the time he turned eighteen, Jason's golf prowess eclipsed even his moves on the court. It got to be his favorite game, not least because Sam said that golf was about money. Rich people golfed; poor people hooped.

"Just another reason," Sam said, "that, when all is said and done, basketball is for kids. But golf—golf is for men."

And Jason was all about becoming a man, Sam Steele-style. For Jason's eighteenth birthday, Sam got him a fake ID, so his education might be complete—the court, the green, and good old Sin City.

Las Vegas was no family playground then, but it still had its thrill rides. Chief among them was the Monte Carlo Room at the Desert Inn and Country Club, where Frank Sinatra had revived his career in the early 1950s. In those days, during the early 1980s, the Monte Carlo had a dress code and gilt-and-red-velvet elegance. As they strolled through the lobby, past the lounge with its Sinatra impersonator crooning "Luck Be a Lady" and the banks of chiming slot machines, Jason thought it couldn't get any better. Sam had bought him a sportscoat and slacks to fit his tall frame, and Sam had bought him the lady on his arm as well. Brandy, she called herself. Or was that the other one, and this one was Nicole? Jason had been too distracted by the diving necklines that displayed their wares to pay proper attention.

"M'sieur Sam," purred the maître d', striding forward to greet them at the entrance to the Monte Carlo Room. "So good to see you again."

"Good to see you, Phillipe. You remember Jason, right?"

"Of course, of course! He is even taller and more handsome than the last time you were here."

Sam waved toward the woman clinging to his arm. "And this would be Brandy and her friend ..."

"Her friend Nicole," Jason said, grinning.

Phillipe did his French thing and kissed each woman's hand, and Brandy and Nicole giggled at each other. "*Enchanté, mesdemoiselles*! Now, your table is ready, but would you like to spend a little time with Danny, *comme toujours*?"

"You've got my routine down, Phillipe," said Sam.

Danny was the bartender, suave and tanned, his hair pomped up. With pleasure, Jason noticed he was finally as tall as the Frenchman—maybe even a shade taller.

"Such a pleasure, Sam," Danny called, his accent even more pronounced than the maître d's. He extended a ringed and manicured hand. "I hope the gods have given you good fortune so far."

"We're killing 'em, Danny. If we keep this up, Farkas might not invite us on his junkets anymore."

"No, no, never!" cried Danny, feigning horror. "That will never happen! You are one of the DI's best patrons of all time. And this young man"—he ran caressing eyes over Jason—"is always welcome. My, my. Jason is looking even more beautiful than the last time I saw him."

Danny always hung on a beat too long when he shook Jason's hand, and this time was no exception. That got the girls to giggling again, and Sam interrupted. "Okay, Danny. After you make us your usuals, plus two glasses of Dom for our lovely companions, let's see some magic. Ladies, you are in for a treat."

Jason had been watching Danny's magic shows since he was sixteen, but this time he got to sit back and let the girls do the work.

From his humidor-sized kit, the bartender set out coins, cigarettes, matches, and cards. He handed Nicole a tall, thin glass. "Please check this out, my gorgeous one. It is solid on the bottom, no?"

Her eyes sliding sideways at Jason, Nicole said, "No—I mean, yes—it's solid all right. And I love things that are really solid."

"I can only imagine. Now—wrap your hand around it and turn it upside down."

When she obeyed, Danny picked up several of the coins he had laid out on a silk handkerchief. Palming the coins, he tapped the solid bottom of the glass, sending each one tumbling, one by one, through to the bar below. Brandy and Nicole gasped and laughed, Brandy clapping her hands together.

"Now, Sam," Danny went on, "may I borrow one of your many hundred-dollar bills? I promise to give it back." His eyes widened when he saw the money clip Sam pulled out. "Ahh, I can see that you have been fortunate indeed!"

Taking two empty liquor bottles from under the bar, Danny set one upright and balanced the bill atop it. Then he turned the second bottle upside-down and placed it on top of the bill, so that the two mouths of the bottles were opposite each other. This time he turned to Brandy. "I beg your pardon, mademoiselle. What is your name?"

When she told him, he said, *"Formidable!* What a perfect name for someone attempting a bottle trick. Do you think you can pull the hundred dollars out, without toppling the bottles?"

She gave a lopsided grin. "Well, I might. I've always been good with tricks."

Winking at Nicole, Brandy reached for the bill and gave

it a quick tug. The bottles went tumbling into the bartender's waiting hands.

"*Tant pis*—too bad," said Danny consolingly as he set the trick up again. "A nice try. Let me show you how it is done."

Grasping the bill in his right hand, he raised his left and more quickly than their eyes could follow, it flashed down. The bill slid out, and the bottles didn't so much as tremble.

Brandy and Nicole broke out in whoops and applause, but Sam only rolled his eyes. "You need to get some new material, Danny. How many times have we seen that one?"

Giving a Gallic shrug, Danny sniffed. "Is that so? Well, I suppose I better just give you your money back and let you go to dinner." Tossing the bill back to Sam, he whisked the empty bottles away and began to wipe the bar, only looking up when Sam, the note halfway in his clip, gave a roar of surprise.

"Hold on a damned minute here, Danny." Ripping the money back out, Sam held it up. It was a two-dollar bill.

"Oh, Sam," Danny said, sighing, "you have always been an excellent tipper. And now here is Phillipe, to show you to your table."

"Gotta hand it to you, Danny," Sam said, chuckling. "No one does sleight-of-hand better than you do. It was worth the ninety-eight bucks to watch."

"*Merci bien.* And I must hand it to you, Sam. No one picks more attractive young people to dine with."

"That was fun," Brandy cooed when they were seated at their banquette table and her glass had been filled with Dom Perignon by the tuxedoed waiter.

Sam nodded, rotating his bucket glass of bourbon to admire it. "Danny's a fine bartender and a great magician, but I'll be damned if he isn't as queer as a three-dollar bill."

"I knew it!" squealed Nicole. She threw Jason another look. "I was, like, getting jealous!"

"Don't worry, darlin'," he said, grinning, "the only French thing I like is the kissing."

Squirming, she giggled again. "Ooh ... we're not supposed to kiss, but I think I'm going to make an exception for you, young man."

"Speaking of which," said Sam, lifting his glass, "I'd like to propose a toast. To Jason on his eighteenth birthday."

Nicole's lipstick-covered mouth dropped open. "He's only eighteen?" Her voice lost its throatiness and came out a skeptical squeak.

Brandy was frowning. "They let him drink and gamble?"

"He's got the best fake ID money can buy," Sam assured them. "He's been doing the Vegas scene with me for three years now ... but I didn't let him drink until he turned sixteen."

"Wow, how fatherly of you," muttered Brandy. But she raised her glass for the toast.

Nicole seemed to have recovered from the surprise because when she set her glass back down, she was watching Jason through lowered lids. "So, this will be, like, your first time with a woman tonight?" Ignoring Sam's bark of laughter, she scooted closer to her companion, tucking herself against his side. "I never would have guessed. You're, like, so big for eighteen. Look at your huge hands." She reached to stroke the one that held his cocktail.

"What size shoe do you wear, Jason?" asked Brandy.

"Sixteen."

The women's eyes met, and they broke out in raucous laughter.

Brandy raised an eyebrow at her companion. "Good for you, dear, that latex stretches so much. Come on—let's go powder our noses—and other body parts. I think this is going to be quite a night."

Rising languidly, they glided across the restaurant, all eyes on them, including Jason's. But when he finally tore his gaze away, he found Sam watching him.

"You know, Jason, I gotta say, I envy you."

Jason gave a bark of laughter. "What? Why would you envy

me? You're the guy with all the dough and all the women you want. You do what you want, when you want. Hell, Sam, you've got the perfect life, as far as I can see."

"As far as you can see," echoed Sam. "And that's how far, at eighteen?" He pushed his glass away from him and sat back. "Let's face it, Jason. My best years are behind me. I've worked hard and I've played hard, and I'm smart enough to know there will be a price to pay for that before long. If you learn just one thing from me, don't ever kid yourself. But *you* ... you've got it all—looks, size, athleticism, brains, charm, and—on top of all that—youth. You've got what every red-blooded American male would give his left nut for."

"Kinda defeat the purpose, wouldn't it?" cracked Jason.

But when Sam didn't answer, Jason ran a finger round the rim of his bourbon, seeing the liquor shiver and gleam in the dim light.

His brow furrowed in contemplation before the realization slowly hit home.

And then he smiled.

3

It seemed like mountains were only worth climbing so you could get a good look at the next one—the one that was just that little bit higher, that little bit more remote.

Sam always had that instinct, that premonition of the Next Big Thing. And the Next Big Thing in the Walla Walla Valley was wine. Sure, he'd always been one of the shrewdest land tycoons around, buying and selling larger and larger orchards and farms, but by the mid-'80s, Sam had lost interest in apples and cherries and wheat. With the valley's hot days and cool nights and latitudes that matched the best wine country in France—why, any fool could see this was some of the finest wine-growing acreage in the state. In the country, even! The trick was getting that land and transforming its potential into reality before the rest of the world caught on.

Coaching basketball was the first casualty of Sam's new obsession. Keeping an eye on Jason might have been the second, except, like all things where Sam was concerned, Jason caught the bug as bad as Sam ever did. They both smelled the lovely aroma of money mixed with wine and threw themselves into transforming cheap wheat land into some of the finest wine-growing acreage in the state. Golf stuck with them too—it was good for business.

After high school, Jason turned down the basketball scholarship offers and didn't even glance at the golf free rides because he spent his waking hours at Steele Cellars, putting the farm experience he had learned from the Carsons to work. It was Jason operating the heavy machinery in the vast building stacked with oak barrels and gleaming metal vats, Jason who convinced Nate to put off college as well. Instead of stuffing opponents on the court and feeding each other the ball, they shared the forklift duties and Sam's Midas-touch business tutelage.

Within a few years, Steele Cellars boasted some of the finest merlot and Cabs in the valley, right up there with Leonetti, and Sam's wines were stealing ribbons from all but the very best of Napa's offerings. Only then did restlessness seize Jason. He'd played Sherpa to Sam Steele's winemaking ascent, and now, up here where the air was thin and the view heady, it was time to see if he couldn't do it on his own.

Or almost on his own.

Nate went everywhere Jason went, and where Jason went next was UC Davis. Never mind the University of Washington; never mind the big LA schools. Davis offered degrees in viticulture, the study and science of winemaking—as far as Jason was concerned, the study and science of the universe.

UC Davis had something else as well: Sarah Nordquist.

The first time Jason saw her, the sun was shining, as it almost always does in the Sacramento Valley. She was walking off to the side of a campus street with the grace of a runway model. He came up from behind her, rolling along in his BMW convertible, going not much faster than all the students on bicycles. She was wearing tight little shorts that showed off her mile-long legs, and her lush blond hair swung almost to her waist. Jason slowed, checking the rearview mirror to make sure her front half lived up to what her backside promised. When it did—and then some—he pulled over, blocking the bike lane and lifting his sunglasses.

"Hey, can I give you a ride somewhere?"

Vivid blue eyes narrowed, and her mouth drew up in a smirk. "Are you crazy?"

"Absolutely. But don't worry—they locked up Ted Bundy years ago."

The girl didn't laugh. She only looked at him a beat longer, shook her head, and kept on walking.

The second time he saw her he was drunk, but not so blitzed he didn't remember her. It was December, the fraternity's annual pre-finals blowout, and Jason was plugged in—literally. He was wrapped in Christmas lights with branches stuck to him and a few ornaments dangling off, and he'd been sticking close to the outlet, cocktail in hand, ribbing the guys in Santa suits and letting the girls in elf shorts come to him. By his fifth drink, he was swaying gently, eyes bleary, crooning along almost in time and key with Bing Crosby, when a random parting in the crowded room revealed Nate to him, leaning against the massive fireplace yonder. He wore a large set of antlers and a Rudolph nose, and he was talking to an elf.

Not just any elf.

Jason recognized those long, long legs.

Jesus.

Nate was talking, and the girl was smiling. What could he be saying to get that out of her?

Jason took one step toward them and another. He wove his way through the revelers, fending off another elf or two, until the limits of his extension cord jerked him to a halt. Looking back, he saw it was fully taut. One of the elf girls tripped on it and fell shrieking against a Santa, who spilled his beer. Jason swung around again. Nate and the girl had noticed his predicament, and it was the amusement in the blonde's eyes that decided him. Jason shrugged, seized the cord wrapped around him, and gave an almighty tug, ripping the plug from the outlet. Suddenly liberated, he staggered the rest of the way to them.

"Well, Jason," Nate drawled, "I guess it's lights out for you now."

"Nate's what you think," Jason said, trying not to slur his words. "This lovely young lady is going to provide all the lumi—illuni—illumination me and my many limbs require."

Leaning in, he met those mocking eyes. "Speaking of limbs," he continued in a thick voice, his eyes running up and down her exquisite legs. "I recognize a couple of yours."

"Really?" Her eyebrows rose. "Since I don't know you, that seems unlikely."

Jason frowned, thinking. Then he snapped his fingers and emphatically tapped her in the shoulder. "Now I've got it! You're the walker."

"Cool, isn't it? I moved past the crawling stage several years ago." Taking his finger between her own pointer and thumb, she plucked it off as if it were a spider that had landed on her. But she was smiling.

Nate looked from one to the other and tried to sound casual. This wasn't the first time he had ceased to exist when Jason came around. "Judging by the way you're swaying in the non-breeze, Jason, I think you'll find yourself back at the crawling stage soon."

Jason ignored him. The girl had to recognize him. She had to. "Sure—don't you remember? You were walking down Campus Drive a couple months ago."

"That one time?" Her lip curled. "That narrows it down. Actually, I walk along there just about every day between classes."

"Wait, wait, wait." His hand was on her again, grabbing the fur cuff at her wrist. "This will help: I'm the one who tried to pick you up. I'm Ted Bundy."

"Jason, that's sick, even by your standards," said Nate.

But the girl's head went back. "Now I remember—you're the wacko who wanted me to get in his car. His convertible, wasn't it? A BMW."

"See!" Jason swung around to crow at Nate. "I told you. We know each other."

Something passed over Nate's face, but when he spoke, it was in the old razzing tone. "I don't know how to break this to you, Jayce, but going around telling women you meet that you're Ted Bundy isn't a great way to get to know them. You're definitely unique, though."

"Who you calling a eunuch?" demanded Jason. Without waiting for Nate's comeback, he returned his lurching focus to the girl. "Since you're obviously one of Santa's little helpers"—he held up an unsteady hand to measure the negligible height difference between her and Nate—"well, okay, maybe not that little ... but you certainly have the potential to be very helpful—how about if we talk about what presents you're going to put under my tree?"

Jason felt an elbow to the gut as Nate put some space between the girl and him. "Jason, let me properly introduce you two. This is Sarah Nordquist. She and I are, you know, seeing each other."

His mouth forming an O of mock surprise, Jason said, "So this is the reason I haven't seen much of you lately? Well, Nathan, I must commend your taste in elves. Tell me, Sarah, have you been naughty or nice this year?"

"I don't confess to Christmas trees," she answered wryly. "Now, if you had a Santa costume on, that would be a different story."

"And if I had a Santa suit on, that would be a story I'd love to hear, with you perched right on my lap. Nothing I want more for Christmas than a lap dance—"

Nate cut him off. "On that off-key and off-color note, we'll be on our way. Sarah and I are heading out."

"But thanks for your offer," Sarah called back over her shoulder. "Maybe you better go plug yourself back in and see who, or what, you attract."

"I'd say he's plenty lit as it is," muttered Nate, giving a tug on her arm. "Come on. Let's get out of here before this tree comes crashing down on us."

She gave Jason a look of mixed amusement and disdain as she went, which he would have loved to return, if his swaying attention wasn't already devoted to her long legs and perfectly shaped ass. Now that was a woman he could get into, so to speak. Even through his drunken haze the thought flitted through his mind: she might be the one—tall, thermonuclear hot, sassy. What kids they could have! They'd be basketball and volleyball stars, every last one of them. The fact that she was dating Nate didn't bother him much. Nate always had a thing for one girl or another, and no way could this girl be as perfect for Nate as she was for Jason.

He put the full-court press on her: money, flattery, persistence, presence. She didn't stand a chance, and Nate and his piddly few dates with her were pretty soon ancient history.

Those were good times. Sarah Nordquist was every bit as hot as advertised and the sex so mind-blowing that it took Jason some time to remember she had a *mind* to go with that body. But she did, and it was one worth knowing—not just for how smart she was (her organic chemistry and calculus grades were higher than his, and more than one all-nighter combined sex and studying), but for what she brought out in him. She would laugh at his bullshit, but she never let him get away with it. And for a short space there, he nearly gave it up.

"Check this out, babe. How beautiful is all of this?" From their vantage point on Howell Mountain, Jason made a sweeping gesture over the vineyards spread out below them, most with their charming Burgundy- or Tuscany-themed winery buildings. He and Sarah could see most of the Napa Valley from where they were perched on the hood of his Beemer, glasses of red wine in hand.

"It's incredible. I can't believe I've never come over here from Davis before. This is ... breathtaking."

He leaned in. "Like someone else I know—and love."

Sarah reared back with a grin. "Whoa, boy! Let's not be throwing the L-word around so loosely."

Reaching for her, he pulled her back toward him and stroked her hair. "Hey. I'm the guy. I'm supposed to say things like that. Besides, I'm not using it loosely. I want to share my life with you—and my dreams. Look at those wineries down there. Mine is going to be bigger and better than any of the ones you can see. You've never been to Walla Walla, but it's like Napa was in the seventies—ready to take off. And I'm going to be one of its first pilots. I'm going to do for Walla Walla what Robert Mondavi did for Napa. And I want you to be my copilot."

Instead of going dewy-eyed as he'd hoped, she laughed. "Well, that's not the most romantic proposal I've ever heard—I'm not even sure it was a proposal—but points for originality. Seriously, Jason, it's way, way too soon."

"There you go again, sounding like a guy." Though his words were reproving, the smile that went along with them was meant to melt her like butter. "You know, I've never minded you wanting to be on top, but let me play the male role once in a while."

"Right," she said with a shake of her head. "One thing I've never worried about is your masculinity, Jason. I'm guessing no one will ever dominate you. What worries me is, would I ever even be your equal?"

"Are you kidding?" He gave a playful yank on her hair. "It would be like when we go running together. I'm killing myself just so I'm not totally chicked."

"Chicked?"

"It's like, you know, when a girl beats you one-on-one at hoops, or she outdrives you on the golf course. That's being chicked."

"Uh-huh." She considered this. "So, Jason, have you ever

been chicked?" Then, smiling mischievously, "I mean, other than by me?"

He slid off the hood to laugh at her. "Hell, no! I've never even been guyed! Even when we lost the state basketball championship, I was the leading scorer."

Her eyes narrowed. "Oooh, how I love a man who just exudes humility."

"Just tellin' it like it is—or was. Those days are long gone. Now I've only got time for golf and wine—and you."

"Thanks for fitting me in there at the end," she cracked.

Grabbing her hand, he pulled her up to stand beside him. "That's what I'm talking about. I love to banter with you. I've never met a woman who could do that."

"Oh, yeah? Are the girls up in Walla Walla just seen and not heard?"

"Hey, lady. Do I detect a little SoCal attitude in your voice?"

Pulling away a little, she met his gaze head on. "No, not at all. I just couldn't be a passive, stay-at-home type, Jason. That's not me, and it never will be."

"Who said anything about staying at home?" he countered. "Fine, you don't like aprons and being barefoot and pregnant. That's one of the reasons I love you. Look—we both walk next month. Let's get married after that."

"No way. You know I'm planning to go to vet school. That's the whole reason I came to Davis. Being a vet has been my dream since I was little."

They stared out at the quilt of vineyards below them, blocks of green and gray. Sarah swirled her wineglass while Jason frowned in concentration. When she took another sip, he said, "You know, WSU has a fantastic vet program. Every bit as good as Davis. And it's only about a two-hour drive from Walla Walla. We could buy a place in between. I've got enough saved up for a down payment on a house."

Her laugh was silent this time. "WSU? That place I've only heard you call 'Wazzoo' and 'MooU—watch where you step'?"

"Well, hell, if you want to be a vet, you must like cows, and they've got plenty of those." Dropping to one knee, he made another snatch at her hand. "Sarah, will you be my wife? I promise to bust my ass and give you everything you could ever want. I'll make you the queen of the Walla Walla Valley."

"Queen of the cows and the state prison!" Sarah crowed. "Where do I sign up? You're certainly the reigning king of unusual proposals."

"Come on, be serious," he urged. "Make fun of everything else, but this isn't something to joke about. I need you, Sarah. I want you, Sarah. I love you, Sarah."

Her grin faded, but she only shook her head again.

"Let me think about it."

He won, of course. He always did.

They were married at First Presbyterian Church of Walla Walla, the Carson's church, tuxedo and white gown and the works. Sam Steele was there, and it was his wine served at the reception. Jess and Maria were there, Maria smiling and Jess throwing rice. And Nate was there with his celebration face pinned on, like the friend and brother he had always been.

It wasn't all celebration, however. Sam had a few words to the wise, shared at the bar while he and Jason watched Sarah dance with her father.

"You know, Jason, you're pretty young to give up your cocksman pursuits."

"Well, I started early, now didn't I?" Jason said, grinning.

Sam swirled the liquor around in his highball glass. "You're lucky to be living now," he said slowly. "Marriage these days doesn't have to be a prison."

"With a jailor like Sarah, I'm thinking they can throw away the key. And besides, I like it when she puts me in cuffs."

But Sam wasn't interested in smart-ass repartee. He downed

the last of his drink in one swig and set the glass down on the bar. "Does Sarah have an open mind?"

Jason stared at him. "You mean like an open mind about an open marriage? I seriously doubt it. Not to mention, it's way too early. I'm in love with her, Sam, swear to God."

"Sure you are. Sure." Sam's tone was soothing. "I remember right after the war when I married my first wife, Ann. Every day seemed to be sunny, even when it was raining like hell, as long as I was around her. It never lasts, though. Remember, women are great for sex and having kids, but don't let marriage suffocate you. You've got so much living ahead of you."

Not for the first time, Jason thought wryly that a lot of the living he had to do was on Sam's behalf. He tried to shift the subject. "Do you wish you were still married, Sam? How many wives did you have? Three?"

"Four, counting the annulment." Sam shook his head in amusement. "Do I wish I was still married? Now there's a tough question …"

"What about kids, then? Wish you had any?"

This was met with a shrug. "Jason, a man can always go back and wonder. But when I was in that foxhole at the Battle of the Bulge, freezing my ass off, ready for a German mortar shell to blow me to smithereens at any moment, I swore to myself that if I got out of there with my skin intact, I'd never deny myself any of life's pleasures. You've got to make your choices and not look back."

"Looks to me like you accomplished your mission then," Jason said. "That's the way you lived your life, Sam. It's why you're my idol and always will be."

Breaking into a smile finally, Sam stuck out his hand, and they shook on it. Then they toasted it with a few pours of Maker's Mark. By the fourth or fifth round, there was Nate tapping him on the shoulder. "You got a sec, Jason?"

Bolting the bourbon had done things to his head. Jason threw an arm around Nate and mumbled, "For my best bud, of course! Sam was just drinking to my happiness. Are you having a good time, Nathan, old pal?"

"Great time." Nate paused, waiting until Sam strolled out of earshot. He put up a hand to refuse the drink Jason offered. "Look, Jason—I've been thinking about this day ever since you and Sarah—ever since you two got engaged. I know you better than I know anyone—"

"Damned straight," slurred Jason.

"Maybe better than you know yourself. And I know how you've treated women over the years."

"Like princesses. Every last one of 'em."

"Jason, listen to me. Sarah's a great girl." Nate's gaze drifted to where she stood teasing her brother and the maid of honor. "She's—well, she's like no woman I've ever met."

Releasing him, Jason hammered him on the back. "Hell, I know that. Why do you think I'm marrying her, bud?"

"You tell me," Nate retorted, his jaw set. "I never figured you were the marrying kind. I always thought you'd wind up like Sam, playing the field until the last whistle blew."

"Ha! Sam. Hell, he's been married more times than one of those Hollywood types. A true romantic."

Grabbing Jason by the shoulder, Nate gave him a level look. "That's what I'm talking about. You're not going to break Sarah's heart, are you?"

"Jesus, relax. Of course, I'm not going to break her heart, old chum. She's the love of my life, right?" He threw a wave to the love of his life, which she received with a sardonic expression. "Uh-huh. Look at that. All mine. And she loves me. Hey, it looks like it's time to launch the garter. You better get out there, and I'll try to get it to you, just like you used to feed me on the basketball court."

Nate stayed where he was for another minute, studying the newlyweds. Jason happy and careless, dipping his bride back for a kiss while he slyly ran a hand under her skirt. When he let her back up, he gave a whoop and held the stolen garter aloft. Sarah laughed, blushing, and socked him in the arm.

Hell, thought Nate.

Maybe he was wrong. Maybe Jason would surprise him.

Sarah didn't seem worried. Quite the opposite, in fact.

"Leave it," he muttered to himself.

Pinning his smile back on, he went to join the scrum of single men.

4

Remarkably, the young lovers were able to sustain a vow of sexual abstinence for the month leading up to their nuptials. As a result, their honeymoon night spent at the Fairmont on San Francisco's Nob Hill was a rollicking affair.

They had a huge suite on the top-floor of the new tower. It faced due north and early the next morning, Sarah sensed Jason's absence in bed. She rose and threw on one of the hotel's ridiculously fluffy robes. She walked slowly through the multiple rooms calling his name, but Jason was nowhere to be found. After a few more loops around the fifteen-hundred or so square feet, she noticed he was sitting on the deck staring into the distance.

"Darling," she said gently, as she opened the sliding door to the balcony. "What are you doing out here?"

"Thinking about IT."

"Lover, you don't need to just think about it. Come back to bed and I'll give you everything you've ever dreamed about."

Jarred from his trance, he turned and looked at her. He smiled slightly. "Believe it or not, I wasn't thinking about that. I was thinking about Napa." He gestured toward the north. "It's just sixty miles up there. Only an hour's drive but a world away from this Babylon by the Bay. Where the finest winemakers outside of France are working right now to leave us even further in their dust."

Sarah sat down on the edge of a lounge chair and wrapped the robe tighter around her body. "But, Hon, isn't that why we are going to France—besides the fact that the Bordeaux is a gloriously romantic place to be on our honeymoon? So you can learn their secrets, right?"

Jason snorted softly. "Look, Princess, the French winemakers have been guarding their secrets for centuries. Besides, Robert Mondavi has been sucking up to Baron Rothschild for almost twenty years, ever since they met—supposedly by accident—over in Hawaii. He's already got a joint-venture with the Rothschild family. Have you heard of Opus One?" She shook her head, sheepishly.

"Well, it's a Bordeaux-style wine made from Napa cab grapes they have done together, and it's gotten rave reviews." Jason sighed deeply. "We are just so far behind."

Sarah smiled, rose, and pulled him to her. "If anyone knows how to play from behind, it's you. Now, how about coming back to bed so I can play with yours?"

"My what?"

"Your behind, silly." She took him by the hand and led him inside.

A few hours later, Jason and Sarah were seated next to each other in wide seats in the front row of a Boeing 777 with sparkling wine and appetizers in front of them. He reached over and topped of her glass with more champagne.

"Oh, Jason, I love this whole first-class thing. I've never even been upgraded on stupid old Alaska Airline much less flying in the front of the cabin on British Air."

"Get used to it, Darling. It's going to be your new mode of travel."

"But it's so much money. Shouldn't we be using it for a down payment on the house?"

"Not to worry. Sam paid for our tickets. He said it's the least he could do for interrupting our honeymoon."

Sarah's hand stopped with the champagne glass in mid-air. "What do you mean Sam interrupting?"

Jason swallowed and patted her hand. "Don't worry, sweet girl, I made him agree to wait until we'd been there a week before he comes over."

Sarah's face went dark. "A whole week, huh? Wow, how special! You never once brought this up, Jason. Sharing you with Sam Steele is *not* my idea of a honeymoon."

His rate of speech picked up noticeably. "Look, Darling, we are on the verge of signing a deal with the Richard family. This is huge for us. No other Walla Walla winery has been able to get a quality French label to JV with them, not even Leonetti."

She turned away from him and dabs her eyes. "Jason, our honeymoon. Our precious, once-in-a-lifetime honeymoon. How could you? How could he?"

"Come on now, Darling, I will make that week we have on our own seem like a month."

Sarah didn't answer but just stared out the window at the endless blue nothingness racing by.

The conditions could not have been more perfect. It was early July in Bordeaux. The weather was clear and the air was warm but fresh. The setting was just as idyllic—a Michelin 3-star restaurant inside of a grand Chateau set on one of the few promontories in the Bordeaux region. Sarah could not have asked for more, but she definitely would have preferred less—as in one less dinner companion.

Sam, Jason and Sarah were seated at the best table on the terrace overlooking the town of Bordeaux itself. The wine was flowing freely and so was the Maker's Mark. Plied with copious amounts of this "story juice", Sam was in unusually loquacious form.

"You know, Sweetie," he began with a slight slur and a less slight glance at her exceptional décolletage, a sight few of the male patrons had missed when walking to their seats. "Forty-six years ago, I was pinned down in the hedge row country up north of here with General George S. Patton's Third Army."

Sarah shot Jason a searing look. He cleared his throat and said gently, "Sam, Sarah doesn't like to be called Sweetie." In fact, she detested it and was growing to hate every moment she had to spend with Jason's mentor (who was quickly becoming her tormentor). The correction didn't cause Sam to miss a beat.

"See, the Krauts had us pinned down and were slaughtering us with their 88s and their new high-speed machine guns, the MG-42s. Those hedge-rows were so thick even our tanks couldn't get through them. But then my buddy and I came up with a shovel, like a cow-guard on an old locomotive, to slice through that shit. Once we did that, we made the big breakout at St. Lo and the Krauts were on the run—and they stayed that way 'til the Battle of the Bulge."

Jason again cleared his throat. "C'mon, Sam, you didn't come up with that thing."

Sam rose in his seat, a look of intoxicated indignation on his face. "The hell I didn't! I was building highways in Eastern Washington working for the WPA before the war. I knew construction equipment like you...like you, knew how to dunk a basketball." Sam took a long draw from his Maker's on the rocks. "You young people, you have no idea. You've never been to war. You don't know what it's like to be scared shitless every day."

Sarah looked at him with a steady gaze. "Actually, Sam, I do."

The old tycoon looked confused and turned to Jason. "Wuz she talkin' about?", he slurred.

Jason put his arm around Sarah. "Nothin', Sam. She's just kidding. Now, let's talk about tomorrow. We have a huge meeting coming up with the Richards. Let's think about how we seal the deal."

Jason and Sam would get their precious joint venture.

Unbeknownst to Sarah—at least consciously—the deal was sealed with a kiss, a long and passionate lip compression with the stunning oldest daughter of the Richard family patriarch. She was always her father's favorite and she had enormous influence over the old man. She also had a weakness for younger, handsome men and Jason qualified on both fronts. The kiss they shared on the veranda of her family's chateau, under a radiant moon after everyone else had retired for the evening, would be the first of many to follow in the years to come. It was the last, however, to occur when they were fully-clothed.

On the flight back to the US, Sarah wasn't able to shake a sense of foreboding that even being in the luxurious first-class cabin on a British Air 777 couldn't dispel.

Over the early years of their marriage, you could track the trajectory of Jason's life by the cars he drove.

The Beemer of the Davis era gave way to a Mercedes 450 SL convertible after Sam made him head of sales at Steele Cellars. Not that selling Sam's wine was tough. The awards they racked up made it child's play and the new deal with the Richards gave their label the prestige it needed to be considered among the Walla Walla valley's elite winemakers. Jason really earned his bonus that year.

The soaring revenues led to higher production and more money—lots more money. More than a renegade from the Whispering Breezes Trailer Park could ever have imagined. Hell, the whole Walla Walla Valley was going to the grapes in those days, but Sam was in the vanguard, and the flash of his sales director proved it.

Where Jason went, Nate Carson continued to follow, and Sam put Nate to work on the production side. It was Nate Carson in the fields, the vat rooms, and managing all the equipment, and Nate Carson making a lot less than Jason's two-hundred-grand a year. In those days in the valley, a salary like Jason's allowed him to live as large as the new class of techie *nouveau riche* in Seattle. Both Nate Carson and Jason Knightbridge might be men of emerging talent, but the flash was all Jason's.

Not that Nate cared much about money. He stuck with a pick-up truck like his dad, Jess, when he wasn't driving the tractor and pulling a trailer full of grapes. Sam and Jason figured Nate would shadow Jason for the rest of his days, hanging off his foster brother's success, but Nate had other ideas. Toward the end of Jason's Mercedes 450 SL era, Nate moved on, going to work for another winery as the assistant winemaker. He and Jason still saw each other—the valley was a small place, despite the money and big dreams pouring through it—but not nearly as often. And somewhere in there, Nate got married himself and Jason did the best man honors, and later, kids came along. The time ... it just kind of got away.

After Nate was gone and Sam's head winemaker retired, Jason moved on to the next stage—heading both production and sales for Sam—and the 450 SL yielded to a black 500SL sedan. Jason hardly remembered that car because he was working such long hours. Steele Cellars won still more awards on his watch, put still more acres into production, added employees, and minted money like a mini-Microsoft. The black sedan slid into the garage most nights after the house was already pitch black, just like Jason slid into bed beside his sleeping wife and—after those first heartbreaks—their baby boy.

He was a decent husband there for a while. Sarah had everything she wanted—or at least everything Jason thought a woman would want, when he spared a thought that direction: a house to decorate, a baby, the clothes, the help, the free time. If she wanted more—or something entirely different—he was too occupied, too driven to ask. The sex was still good, if infrequent, after J.J.—Jason Jr.—came along, but Jason Sr. wasn't the first man to discover that sex with a wife was more complicated. Not just sex—day-to-day life was more complicated. Her questions like, "What time will you be home?" and "What does Sam want now?" and, the dreaded, "Would you rather play golf or be with me?" became shots fired over the bow and she was becoming as tired of delivering them as he was of being the recipient.

The next few years roared by at an accelerating rate, as if a turbocharger had kicked in on the invisible engine that was propelling Jason and Sarah's life. The Walla Walla wine industry was doing a parallel surge as the 1990s began. National, even international, accolades were raining down on the valley's winemakers like the incessant precipitation on the west side of the Cascade mountains, where another boom—this one based on based on bits and bytes rather than sunshine and grapes—was in its infancy.

For a spell there, Sarah's fears from their honeymoon faded, despite his frequent trips to France that he seemed to look forward to with unusual enthusiasm. Like Jason, she thought she had won.

After taking two years to settle into her new life, she was accepted at WSU's vet school, just as Jason envisioned. In her first year, she had graduated toward the top of her class, a position with which she was both familiar and comfortable. But something odd happened in the second year. She was having trouble concentrating in class and couldn't shake a strange gnawing feeling in her gut.

Much of her time alone was spent attempting to figure out why she felt that way. Fortunately—or not--she had plenty of opportunities for uninterrupted self-analysis because Jason was almost never around. He was working sixty hours a week at Steele Cellars during slack times and eighty hours a week during the crush and other "all-hands-on-deck" periods.

It was at some point in that first semester of her second year of vet school that she began to inadvertently pick up on the rumblings. It was never anything overt—just a few odds looks and interrupted conversations when she would walk over to her friends at a party or come up to them at the grocery store.

At several of the Holiday parties over Christmas, 1990, this had happened a few times and it was making the pain in her stomach all the more intense. It got to the point that she went to Jason's M.D, now hers, a few days before Christmas to be checked out. She could count on one hand how many times she been to a doctor in her young life.

Since he was not only Jason's but also Sam's physician, naturally she couldn't talk about what was really eating at her insides. But she couldn't—or wouldn't—believe there was anything to it. If nothing else, when did he have time?

The day before New Year's, she got the results back. They weren't what she was hoping to hear.

A few days later, she got out of bed before 5:00. It was the first day of the new semester. Jason was still sleeping. She was out the door before he woke to make the long drive to Washington State University, what the locals called "Wazzu". Even though Jason had bought them a home about twenty-five miles north of Walla Walla, it was still nearly a ninety-mile trek each way. Fortunately, it was clear so she wouldn't have snow to contend with, but her car thermometer read fifteen degrees as she got on Highway 12 northbound.

For many miles it was pitch dark, with not even a hint of the sun's pending emergence to the east, on her right. The darkness mingled with her loneliness to create a searing pain that, combined with the relentless ache from her stomach, was so intense she pulled over several times. After the last stop, she decided to turn on the radio to break the solitude. The Eagles—she'd always loved the Eagles when she was a kid.

But this time the lyrics of one of her favorite songs of theirs was also what she least wanted to hear. "She wonders how it ever got this crazy, she thinks about a boy she knew in school."

Subconsciously, she mouths his name and then catches herself, drawing in a sharp, hurting breath. She hadn't realized that part until now. The sudden awareness only intensified her anguish.

"Did she get tired or did she just get lazy…?"

She reached for the knob and flicked off the radio.

It was almost 4:00 in the afternoon and the classroom was empty except for Sarah in her seat hunched over her notes. Without realizing it, she rubbed her stomach with her free left hand. In her right, she white-knuckled a pen as she repeatedly hit it against her forehead.

Her instructor walked in the large classroom from the hallway outside and stopped to watch her. Sarah was his star student last year and unquestionably his favorite. If he was honest with himself, he would admit it wasn't just her academic prowess but also her exceptional beauty that caused him to have such warm and protective feelings toward her.

He began to walk slowly and softly in her direction, a look of concern becoming more intense with each step. He stopped a few paces away; she was totally oblivious of his presence.

"Sarah," he barely whispered. When she didn't respond, he spoke louder. "Sarah."

She jumped in her seat and looked at him like he was an apparition.

"Dr. Wagner. What...what are you doing here?"

"Young lady, I think the question is, what are *you* still doing here?"

"I...I...I'm struggling with..."

His eyes narrowed. "Sarah, would you please come in my office for a bit."

She swallowed and nodded.

Dr. Wagner's office was a warm and comfortable place. In the past, she had always enjoyed being in there. It reminded her of her dad's study with rick wood-paneled walls. It even had a fireplace with a real wood fire going most of the time during the winter, including today. He motioned for her to sit in an overstuffed chair close to the hearth, as he began to stroke his neat salt and pepper beard.

He took a pipe out of the inside pocket of his obligatory tweed jacket, pulled a bag of tobacco from his desk drawer and began to tamp it down into the bowl. Her dad used to smoke pipes, too, until his doctor made him quit.

"Is it ok if I smoke?" he asked.

"Of course," she murmured.

"Sarah," he began haltingly. "Last semester I noticed something was amiss. Your focus, your grades, your attitude..." Before he went any further, she began to cry. He pulled a handkerchief out of his jacket.

"My dear, you don't look well. Are you sick? Have you seen a doctor?"

She nodded and began crying harder.

"Well, did he—or she—say? Are you ok?"

"No, I'm not ok," she blurted through her tears. "I'm pregnant."

Dr. Wagner leaned back in his chair and began to blink his eyes rapidly. "Well...well, that's wonderful news."

She gagged at those words. "Maybe for most women, but not for me, not now."

"But, Sarah, I don't understand, didn't you want this. I mean if you didn't, couldn't you have..."

"Prevented it?" she interjected with an intensity that surprised them both. Of course, she could have...if she had wanted. What did she want? Did she want to bind Jason tighter to her? Did she want to deny herself the career she'd always dreamed of? Was she punishing herself for the direction her marriage—her life—was heading?

"Yes, Doctor, I guess I could have. But now...now it's..."

"Now, now, my dear. You need to look at the bright side. You're going to have a beautiful baby and be a wonderful mother."

Sarah looked up at him, desperately wanting to believe the words he had just spoken.

Fortunately, a good-Samaritan trucker saw her car veer

suddenly off onto the shoulder just before 6:00 pm, about forty miles north of Walla Walla. He was on a tight schedule so he didn't pull over but he noted the next mileage marker and radioed it into the Washington State Patrol. By the time the trooper pulled up to Sarah's car, she was severely hemorrhaging. She was medevacked by chopper to Walla Walla General.

Jason rushed to the hospital and was there within minutes of her arrival, but by then she had been given two units of blood and was stabilizing. The baby, of course, was no more.

After that, Sarah quit vet school. To his credit—or perhaps to create cover for his own workaholic ways--Jason often urged her to re-enroll. But she adamantly refused. Then, there were two more miscarriages, each one later term than the last. Jason didn't bring up her returning to school again. Thankfully, J. J.—Jason, Jr.—came along a year after her last miscarriage, and by then they could have afforded an army of nannies to care for him.

For a while, J.J.'s arrival gave their marriage a welcome lift. Jason was more present and more attentive. Sarah blossomed as a mother, adoring the precious little creature who craved her time and comfort. She felt alive again. Maybe Dr. Wagner was right after all.

However, it wasn't long before Jason's time at home returned to what it had been prior to J.J.'s birth—minimal at best, non-existent at worst. If Jason chanced to say, "Hey, J.J., buddy, did you get a new tooth?" or "Why's he crying this time?" Sarah took these as proof positive that his son wasn't a priority with him, that nothing—not even J.J. and certainly not her--could compete with the work, the wine, the business golf, the money, the swelling fame.

The complications were increasing. Sex, marriage, kids, life. But simplicity was still out there for him. More and more.

"Thanks for watching J.J., Chris," Sarah said, her heels

clicking across the hardwood floors as she reached in her handbag. "Did he give you any trouble?"

The babysitter hopped up from the couch and smoothed her short-knit top. "None at all. He was a piece of cake." Accepting the cash, she worked it into the front pocket of her tight jeans. "Did you two have fun? You look amazing." Her eyes slid past Sarah in her evening gown to where Jason stood in his tux, tossing his keys and bill clip in a stone bowl in the entryway.

"Uh-huh, thanks," Sarah replied vaguely. "If you don't mind, I'm kind of beat. Jason will run you home."

Chris pressed her lips together so she wouldn't smile too broadly. "Awesome."

It wasn't like the college-age babysitter was the first comely woman to notice Jason in recent times, but he'd sure gotten better again at noticing them back.

Other women were simpler. They wanted one thing from him; he wanted one thing from them. Everybody was happy, right?

He opened the front passenger door of the 500SL for Chris. After giving him a slow smile, she climbed in, the tanned stripe of her exposed midriff twisting as she reached for the shoulder belt. Lips forming a silent whistle, Jason slipped around to his side.

"So ... Chris. I'm guessing you're going to be a sophomore at Whitman this year?"

"Nope," she said, glancing sidewise at him in the glow of the dashboard. "A junior."

Jason did whistle then. "Really? Wow! You must be almost old enough to drink—legally, that is."

She laughed.

Chris's parents' street had few lights on it. When Jason shut off the engine, neither one of them moved to get out. She ran one hand along the burled walnut of the dash.

"I love your car."

Tracing the shining wood, her hand drifted down to the gear-shift knob between them, stroking its smoothness. "Mr. Knightbridge …"

"Call me Jason."

"Jason." Her lips curled. "Do you know what DILF stands for?"

His lips parted in surprise. "Well—I've heard people throw the term MILF around at the club or J.J.'s games, when a hot mom shows up, but I've sure never heard of DILF." As Chris inclined toward him, his puzzlement gave way to a grin. "Lemme see … D. What could that D stand for?"

Her hand left the shift knob to bury itself in his hair, as she tugged him toward her.

"Use your imagination."

Yes, the 500SL years were good. That car took Jason up the mountain to the peak. He was behind the wheel of the black Mercedes when he pulled up to Steele Cellars for the last time as an employee.

Per usual, Sam was sitting at his desk—the massive kind that wouldn't budge if a tornado blew through or so much as rattle if the Wallula Fault Zone decided to rupture them into eternity. Behind him hung a giant portrait of General George Patton. The general was sporting his usual severe look while holding a small whip. He was clad in leather riding breeches, along with a holster containing two ivory-handled pistols. In contrast to this painted Western demigod and surrounded by racks and shelves of his own wines, Sam looked oddly diminished. Jason frowned, wondering when the guy had gone and got that old and shriveled.

Shaking the thought off, he dropped in a chair opposite and began without preamble. "So, Sam, you know that George Givan is losing his place to the bank. Most of it is shit, but some of his acreage is in the Red Mountain appellation, and you know how good that is. I want to buy that section from the bank. I'm ready to start my own operation, and I'd love to have you as a partner.

I figure I can still supervise your production and distribution. You know, like a joint venture. There'll be a lot of synergies."

Sam's smile was faint. "What do you think that land is gonna cost?"

"I think we can get it for three-hundred grand. I can find a hundred, if you can put up two. And I'll give you thirty-percent of the stock in Knightbridge Estates."

"Knightbridge Estates." Sam rolled it around in his mouth.

He said nothing more for a minute, and neither did Jason. They both knew it was a golden opportunity, even if it meant a partial parting of the ways.

Sam reached in his desk for the leather binder of his business checks. His hand was steady and quick, but Jason saw something in his mentor's eye when he tore the check off and handed it to him. "That's great dirt. It'll produce terrific fruit. Good luck, Jason."

They shook on it. At the door, Jason turned and said, "Thanks, Sam. I want to make this the best investment you've ever made—and I know how high that bar is. Hell—maybe you'll even make enough to buy yourself a new car."

"That'll be the day," Sam growled. "All that goddamned emiss—"

"I know, I know—all that goddamn emissions bullshit," Jason said, laughing. "But you know, even Cadillac is making some pretty good cars these days. Not as good as BMW and Mercedes, but I know you'd never buy one of those."

"Goddamn right! I fought those bastards at Bastogne."

But Jason had heard that one before too. He tipped the check at Sam as if it were the brim of a hat and shut the door behind him. For a long time after, Sam sat unmoving, his gaze fixed on the door but his eyes seeing instead the receding back of his protégé and the past they shared.

After starting out in a Quonset hut, it wasn't long before Jason built the Knightbridge Estates winery in a French Chateau style, and with all the press it got, you would think it the real deal and those stone heaps over in France the pretenders. It started small enough, with articles in the *Union-Bulletin*, but it wasn't long before Seattle's papers picked up on the Cabs coming out of Knightbridge. *Parade* took it national, followed by the glossies. When Jason made his first *Wine Spectator* cover, he'd already scored the club championship golf cup for his sixth straight year, and he celebrated by retiring the Mercedes 500SL. When you didn't know how many millions you were worth, who wanted a car that could be bought and driven off the local lot like a Ford Fiesta?

In those days, his ultimate salad days, Jason spun up to the Walla Walla Country Club in a Ferrari, like a king arriving in his royal coach. He'd waited almost a year to get his Italian stallion—even after bribing the sales manager at the Seattle dealership with two cases of his '02 reserve cab, just to get an order slot. While Jason's growing band of acolytes—his "wine groupies," as he called them behind their backs—fawned over his new ride, Sam wasn't pleased. After all, he'd fought the Italians, too, in North Africa with Patton's Seventh Army. The dividend checks to Sam Steele grew larger and larger, but the amount of time they spent together dwindled.

Some of his wine groupies threw waves at him as he strode through the clubhouse, slowing only to catch the bartender's eye and point outside. No matter how many guys were gathered on the patio, a vacant seat always opened for him, and Jason dropped into it as the waiter hurried up with a bucket glass of Maker's.

"Ahh, thanks, Jose. Some mother's milk, just in time. Guys, did I tell you what Bud here did last week?" Jason gestured with his drink at a husky older man beside him. "You know, he had a rough round last Sunday, and so he comes storming into his house, throws his golf bag in the front closet, and slams the door. His wife says to him, 'Looks like you had another big number on the course.' So, what does Bud here do? He walks up and bitch-slaps her across the face! 'What did you do that for?' she bawls. And Bud here doesn't miss a beat: 'I've been hitting everything fat today.'"

Amid the hooting and howling, Bud grumbled, "Now, wait a goddamn minute—that's all bullshit."

Jason pounded him on the back. "Come now, Bud. You're among friends. We won't judge you."

Shaking his head, Bud shrugged and tossed some peanuts in his mouth. "Well ... there've been times I've been tempted."

Another man raised his pint. "I'd like to propose a toast. To Jason Knightbridge, who just yesterday tied the course record of sixty-four, first set in 1959 by Rod Funseth."

"Good old Rod. Played with him in a tournament once. Too bad he's not on this side of the grass anymore—damned cancer." Jason grinned, holding up his own bucket glass like a trophy cup.

The applause died away, but the ribbing continued, Jason having a hell of a good time until the fun and games were interrupted. A woman's voice from the other end of the patio rose above the men's banter.

"No, no, *no!*" screamed the woman, her bracelets clinking as she made furious arm gestures at some of the club's service staff. "You've got it all wrong. The flowers are supposed to go on these tables over here and the balloons are for those over there, where the children are going to sit. Children. *Niños.* How many times do I have to tell you that? Jesus, I know you don't speak English, but are you people just born to be stupid?"

Taking a hefty pull from his bourbon, Jason held out his glass and took aim at the woman with his forefinger. "Look there, gentlemen," he said in a carrying voice, "you don't see that but every other day from her. THAT woman puts the 'cunt' in country club."

Stiffening in her St. John knit pantsuit, the accused whirled around and marched toward him, her face aflame with anger. "I heard that! I *heard* that!"

The men surrounding him parted as if swept apart by the force of her, but Jason only smiled and took another leisurely sip of his drink.

"I know you," she spat out, her voice trembling. She raised her arm to point at him. "You're that Knightbridge fellow. So the stories I've heard are true. You think you own the world." Narrowing her eyes, she shook her head. "But you really are the biggest prick of all time."

At that he was on his feet, pointing his own finger of doom right back at her. "Correction, madam! I *have* the biggest prick of all time." Reaching down, he put his hand on his crotch as if he were about to unzip. The woman's mouth fell open. Covering her face, she spun around to flee, knocking into tables and chairs as she went.

A swell of appreciative laughs rocked Jason's court, and a few of the beleaguered wait staff hid smiles. One of the younger ones gave Jason a thumbs-up, which he returned with a wave.

The king was ruling his country club, and all was right with the world.

The Ferrari told Jason how far he'd come from the trailer park, and it couldn't be trusted to any hands but his own. He kept it spotless, polished and buffed it himself, added a porte cochere to the garage to showcase it. Each glance at the prancing horse on the hood told him he had arrived (and he spared it many more glances than he did the ten thousand–square-foot dream home he and Sarah had built).

On one particularly postcard perfect Saturday morning in the Walla Walla Valley, Jason was caressing his pride and joy with his usual meticulousness and just one more coating of wax. He could not have known that, just a few miles away, an event was unfolding that would bring him even greater satisfaction than his beloved "Italian Stallion".

Despite the valley's prosperity—accentuated by the sudden wine riches—a seedy underbelly remained. Gritty trailer parks, not unlike the one Jason grew up in, continued to populate the backroads, just off the main highways. One of them housed a notorious puppy mill, and on this same idyllic day its proprietor, wearing a wife-beater T-shirt and stained jeans, charged up the steps, one of which was missing, and through a ripped screen door into his forlorn single-wide. He blew through the door, cursing like a Red Sox fan when the Yankees are in town.

"Goddamn you, woman!" he bellowed. "You are going to bankrupt me."

Inside the tiny hovel, a woman sat nursing a baby. There were two other little kids at the table which looked like it hadn't been cleaned in months. All had a look of terror on their faces as he entered.

"Goddam it, where's Rex?" he demanded, his neck cords bulging grotesquely.

"I...I don't know," the woman murmured tremulously. "The kennel, I guess. That's where I last saw him."

"The kennel you *guess*?" the man in the wife beater sneered. "Well, you better guess again because he's gone. The door was open."

"But I know I closed it," she stammered, tears beginning to flow. "I know I did."

"You may have closed it but you didn't' *latch it—again!*" He was now shouting inches from her face. Do you know how much a bull mastiff puppy is worth?"

Dropping her head and crying softly, "Yes, Eddie, I know they are valuable and I'm really, really sorry. I didn't mean to."

Eddie stood up straight, ebbing ever so slightly. "You're just damn lucky none of the others ran off with him. But Rex was the best of the litter. The strongest and the smartest. He would have brought top-dollar. Put the baby down."

Reluctantly, as if she knew what was coming, she carefully placed the baby into a carrier on the table. Eddie moved over to her and slapped her hard across the face. The baby and the other children began to sob. The mother didn't make a sound but just dropped her head to the table. Her tears quickly created a puddle on the grimy table top.

His face aflame, consumed by feral rage, Eddie vowed, "If you keep this up, someday, I swear, I'll kill you. I won't let you break me."

Meanwhile, Rex' sturdy body—already weighing in at forty pounds even though he was just four months old at the time of his Great Escape—was miles away. Eddie was right—he was strong and smart. Strong enough to pry the partially latched kennel door open and smart enough to realize that his former home was no place he wanted to hang around. If he'd been able to put it into words, he would have said the place had "bad ju-ju".

His powerful legs were taking him rapidly to the main highway, to his new life…and name.

By this time, Jason had fired up his Ferrari in the driveway. All the buffing and coddling was through; it was now show time. He sat there as he often did just taking in the thrilling sound of the engine's roar. Then, he slammed it into first gear and peeled out of the driveway at a speed that always upset Sarah—which is maybe one of the reasons he enjoyed doing it so much

It was the car, of course, that led him to Ringo—the two purest joys in his life, on a collision course. Jason was on a stretch of country road, flooring it just to hear the growl of acceleration, when something darted across the pavement. Curses erupting from him, Jason slammed the brakes, and the Ferrari fishtailed wildly. The creature, whatever it was, darted across the road, the front left tire just missing it, then vanished into a ditch, leaving the car spinning till its rear end slid forward, off the road. The same ditch that swallowed the animal yawned under the right rear wheel, and before Jason could do more than yell, the car thundered and crashed downward, shuddering to a stop as it met the ditch's far wall.

Jason vaulted out, hands flying to his hair in horror as he surveyed the damage to his precious ride. "Christ!" Spinning in place, he ran his eyes down the length of the ditch. "What the hell was that goddamned thing?"

It didn't take long to spot, the small, trembling heap cowering away from him in the belly of the ditch.

"I'll be damned."

Feeling his fury begin to leak away, he squatted down beside it, inspecting its sleek, tawny body and black muzzle. He put out a hand for it to sniff. After a moment, the dog crept forward and began to lick it. Jason picked him up, laughing when the puppy began to lick Jason's chin.

"That right? Is that how it is, little guy? Yeah—check out what you did to my three-hundred thousand–dollar ride, bud. You almost exited this vale of tears at a pretty tender age, not that I don't know what that's like." In response, the puppy only moved his eager licking to Jason's ear, making him laugh harder. "Guess this means you owe me one. Come on, then. You're coming with me." He cuddled the still trembling dog—soon to be called Ringo—in his left arm while he dialed AAA with his free hand. He laughed to himself, imagining what his friends would think if they could see the great Jason Knightbridge loving on a renegade mutt who nearly destroyed his most prized earthly possession.

Ringo the bullmastiff grew large enough that Jason took to calling him the "bull massive," and everywhere Jason went, the dog was sure to go. Once the Ferrari was repaired and good as new, Jason was back on top, now with a canine sidekick who, in dog terms, was as physically imposing as his master.

There weren't many flies in the ointment in those years, unless you counted the ointment itself going a little rancid.

"Come on, J.J.!" roared Jason from where he stood by Sarah on the sidelines, both of them watching their boy dribble the soccer ball downfield. "Kick it! Kick it!"

J.J., setting his small face, managed to evade one defender who was hot on his tail, but when he got within ten yards of the goal, he caught a cleat in a tuft of grass and went down.

Jason threw up his arms. "Goddamn it! At his age, I always scored when I was that close."

Sarah didn't look at him. "Wouldn't surprise me a bit. Scoring's always come easy to you."

Hearing the hard edge to her voice, he threw her a wary look. So, it was gonna be like that this morning, was it? But when he opened his mouth to dish it right back, a fit of coughs convulsed him.

"Hmm," she murmured. "Still got that cough, huh?"

He didn't bother answering. Turning away, he slid a metal flask from his pocket and took a draw, feeling the soothing heat in his throat.

Sarah inspected her manicure. "And still taking the same cough syrup, I see."

Jason slipped the flask back in his pocket and cleared his throat. "You know, it would have been nice if you had put in an appearance at the winemaker awards last night, Sarah."

Her head rocking back in a mirthless laugh, she said, "I didn't realize my absence would be noticed. Far be it from me to come between you and your adoring fans—especially the ones in dresses."

"Oddly enough, it wasn't all about me."

"Don't tell me it was about Nate, then," she said, a hopeful note inflecting her voice. "He won something? He told me he thought he'd come in second to you, as always."

"He did," Jason said shortly. Seeing the light fade from her eyes again, he added, "I didn't mean Nate. At the dinner they were honoring Bill and Sue Brojan—you know the big apple and cherry growers? They run that troubled-kids ranch thing—the one where Nate's always making me fork over donations. Anyhow, Nate said he wished you were there to hear about it and meet some of the boys."

They both watched as a scrum of kids raced their direction, chasing the ball.

Sarah shook her head. "I'm sorry I missed that part, then. Nate's always cared about the important things. He's always cared about people, even me. He's given me a lot of good advice over the years." Her blue eyes regarded him flatly. "Wish I'd listened to the half of it."

The ball got kicked out of bounds, flying their direction. Jason deflected it with his shin, and then, wrapping Ringo's leash around his hand, he followed the ball away from Sarah, toward the huddle of soccer moms. One of them broke apart and took a few steps to meet him.

"Congratulations, Jason," she said, her voice a purr. "Another big win last night." Retrieving the ball for him, she watched him kick it back onto the field, clearing the heads of the kids. "Nice footwork." Her eyes flicked Sarah's direction, but Sarah was watching J.J.

Moving a step closer, her hand dropped to his belt. "And speaking of big, when do we hook up next? I miss Big Jason and his Argonuts."

"No worries, my dear. Jumbo Jayce and his pals are always at your service."

Jason wasn't the only one getting ideas, however. Ringo chose that very moment to explode into a full sprint, ripping the leash from his grip.

"Ow! Oh, shit!"

Shit was right. In the blink of an eye, Ringo bounded thirty yards away and jumped onto a golden lab, mounting her in full view while the owner yelled hysterically and tried to break the dogs apart. The guy was too panicked and intent to hear Jason's shouted warnings as he rocketed toward them: "Don't! Stop—don't put your arm in there! God damn it—*stop!*"

With an all-out leap, like a linebacker tackling a ball carrier at the goal line, Jason hit his dog squarely in the side, sending both him and Ringo tumbling. Before Ringo could react, Jason had a hand over the bullmastiff's face, covering his eyes and nose.

"Ringo—*leave it!*"

Both of them were panting, but Jason could feel Ringo's rigid body relaxing under him as he took hold of the leash again and wrapped it around his forearm.

The lab owner was on them in no time, screaming, "How dare you bring a dog like that to a kids' soccer game?"

Sure enough, the game had halted, and all eyes were on them, one little girl on the sidelines even crying. Jason only growled, "How dare *you* bring a bitch in heat out where you know there are going to be other dogs? You never get in the middle of a bullmastiff fucking unless you want to lose your fucking arm!"

"I told you to leave her at home, Gary," said a woman who strolled over to them. She gave Jason a wry smile as he got back to his feet, brushing off his slacks.

"Next time, Gary, listen to your wife!"

The crying girl had gotten a hold of herself, and of the golden lab's leash. Unrepentant, the lab kept wagging her tail and trying to get back to Ringo, who only looked back, head tilted, his big tongue sweeping his lower face and chin, as if he'd enjoyed a particularly tasty treat.

When Jason rejoined Sarah, she gave another of those humorless laughs. "Wonder where he learned to behave like that? I can't take you two anywhere."

More often than not, though, it wasn't Sarah accompanying them. More and more, Jason and Ringo ventured out on their own.

5

One of the last normal days in Jason's life began in the usual fashion.

"Morning."

Striding through the enormous kitchen of his faux chateau, he grabbed the remote from the polished granite countertop and flipped from the Food Network to CNBC. Sarah threw him a dirty look from where she was making J.J.'s breakfast, but Jason ignored it.

"Goddamn that Ballmer! Until he leaves, Microsoft will never go up."

No one but Ringo on his dog bed had any response to this oracle, the bull mastiff lifting up one ear to listen and furrowing his brow.

Downing his coffee, Jason picked up his keys, his eyes still on Bill Griffeth. "Gotta run. Doing that waste-of-time tour of Jubilee this morning and their fundraiser golf thing at the Wine Country course. Nate wore me down. I'll grab something on the way. Don't wait up—there's dinner after the tournament." He walked over to Ringo's bed and leaned down to pet him. "Sorry, buddy. Can't take you with me today. You'd be sitting in the car for hours, and it's going to be a hot one."

He straightened and headed out of the kitchen, whistling.

His son and wife stared after him, a vague sadness in J.J.'s eyes and in Sarah's, blankness.

"Jesus. Who died? This looks like a funeral procession."

It did. The long line of black Tahoes, Escalades, and Navigators wound along the two-lane road connecting Walla Walla and Prescott. Nate and Jason were in the backseat of the second vehicle, Jason with his aviator glasses on and flask at the ready, Nate a mix of eager and hostile.

"If there's any corpse in here, it's you, Jayce. I think you've had enough Maker's Mark over the years to embalm you nicely." He drummed his fingers on the windowsill. "I can't believe I'm finally, finally getting the great Jason Knightbridge out to Jubilee."

"What do you have to bitch about? I've given money over the years."

"A few crumbs out of the millions you've made."

Jason mock sighed. "There you go again, Nathan, letting your jealousy get the upper hand. Dare I say that's not very Christian?"

But Nate wouldn't be baited. "This isn't about me. It's not even about you, as hard as that must be for you to believe. It's about what the Brojans are doing for all those boys out there."

"Fine, Gandhi. I'll write a bigger check today."

Throwing his hands up, Nate shook his head wryly. "It's always about the money with you, isn't it? No—wait. It's always about the money, unless it's about the sex, wine, Maker's Mark, or golf."

"God, you're fun to be with today. Look—you wanted me to play in this fundraiser and I'm doing it, even though it's Monday and I should be at the winery. And you should be too. Who schedules these things? It's almost crush."

"Right. Don't give me the martyr act, Jason. You know I've been asking you—begging you—to come out to Jubilee for years.

I know the only reason you finally said yes is because Johnny Miller is going to be there today."

Shrugging, Jason took a pull from his flask. "My martyrdom happened to coincide with a big star's visit. So sue me."

Nate reached for the flask, and Jason batted his hand away. "Get your own."

"What's on the side of that flask? That's not an American Express card logo, is it?"

"Damn right. Never leave home without it."

Nate did laugh then. "Wow. They've got their target demographic nailed, I guess. Come on, Jason—writing checks is easy for you. How about if, this time, you actually invest some of yourself out there?"

Screwing the cap back on the flask, Jason tucked it away. "Now don't start with that mentoring bullshit again! We're going slow enough—I might just jump out and make a run for it. Cut through some pig farmer's paddock. I've told you before, Nate. I don't have time."

"Good point. If you did give up a little time, your handicap might go up a couple of strokes. Or—God forbid—you might have to sleep with your own wife."

Jason's head jerked to look at him. Nate saw his own face reflected in the mirrored aviator lenses. Double trouble.

Then Jason turned pointedly away and stared out the tinted window.

"Fuck you."

The Jubilee Youth Ranch nestled in a valley surrounded by steep hills. Neat white buildings clustered in the center, outside of which radiated pastures with grazing cows and horses, a ropes course, and a driving range.

When the caravan pulled up at last in the parking area, it was met by a middle-aged couple Jason recognized from the winemakers' dinner as founders Bill and Sue Brojan. They were flanked by two black men in their late thirties or early forties, and with camera crews hovering nearby, the foursome was already chatting with the golf and television celebrity Johnny Miller, who had emerged from the lead Escalade.

"What an amazing place," said Miller. "I've been told how impressive it is, but seeing is believing."

Extending her hand, Sue Brojan introduced herself and Bill. "And we're so thrilled to have you here for our inaugural golf tournament! Let me introduce you to our executive director, Rich Williams, and our athletic director, Alvin Williams."

"Let me guess," Johnny said, grinning, "Rich and Alvin are brothers."

Jason lost the rest of the small talk in the buzz of the entourage, now fully emerged from the line of cars and a hundred strong. But when the tour began to head past the flag pole, across the vast lawn that fronted the admin building, he saw a group of teenage boys in blue and gray Jubilee uniforms approaching.

"Mr. Nate!" called one of them, a massively built young black man. "Whazzup? Who's this big boy with you?"

"Hey, Dez." They went into some elaborate handshake. "You're looking good today."

"Dressed up to hobnob with the visitors."

"This is my buddy Jason Knightbridge I've told you about. I've known him since I was way younger than you."

Dez ran appraising eyes over Jason. "So this is the dude who can do it all. Seems like Mr. Nate here spends most of his time braggin' on you. Says you can really hoop it."

Shooting Nate a startled glance, Jason said, "Well—not really. Not like I used to. Mostly I'm a golfer these days."

"Golf!" yelped a wiry Latino boy from behind Dez. "Mr. Alvin been tryin' to teach us that game, but I think somebody needs to teach him first."

Laughing, the kids nodded at Nate again as the group moved on.

The tour held little interest for Jason. And not being Johnny Miller, he felt no pressure to ooh and aah over the woodworking shop or the welding setup or the classrooms, the stables, or the cow barns. While Miller signed autographs for students, Jason fielded texts from his vineyard manager. While the entourage watched boys work with horses, Jason tweaked and then signed off on a label design. Only when the tour reached the gym did he put his phone down, and that was just to do a little showing off for a woman on the tour with the body of a yoga instructor. Motioning for her to follow him to the other end of the court, he grabbed a ball and went up for a hoop, slamming it through the net.

The rest of the group broke into applause and whistles when he landed, and Miller joked, "Maybe instead of me putting on a golf clinic, we should take a seat in the stands and watch that guy put on a basketball clinic."

Jason only sketched a bow, throwing a wink at the woman, who gave him a sidewise smile. Not bad—he made a note of her to be dealt with after the tournament. Or sooner. With any luck, she would be part of his scramble.

Instead he got stuck with Nate and the big black Jubilee guy Alvin, while Jess caddied for them.

The little thugs at the ranch were right—Alvin's game could use some pointers. But it was Nate Jason picked on. He was still pissed about the guilt trip on the ride up.

"Well, Nathan, that's quite an enfuckment you've got yourself in," he said from high up on the green, grinning down at Nate, who glumly surveyed the side of huge pot bunker where his ball was buried.

"Don't let him get to you, son," came Jess's voice over Jason's shoulder. "Just play the safe shot and get it on some grass."

"You mean play it like I always do, right?" Nate snorted below them, shaking his head. "Play it safe and smart and let Jason get all the glory."

Giving a bark of a laugh, Jason turned to nudge Jess. "Why don't you hit that one for him, old man? You've always been good at digging."

Jess shrugged, but Nate took a big swing at his buried ball. It flew upward in a spray of sand, catching the top lip of the bunker and rolling back down. Jason's laugh boomed out then, and Nate took an angry swat at the sand with his club. "Let's face it, Dad—Jason knows how to get his digs in on both of us."

Beside the elevated tee box of a par three, they found Johnny Miller standing under a small tent. There was a Mustang convertible gleaming in the sunlight nearby, ornamented by an attractive young woman. "Buy a ticket and get a hole-in-one to win," she called to their group.

Jason took in her snug-fitting golf shirt and short shorts as he pulled out his money clip. "What's your name, darling, and how much are the tickets?"

"That would be Brittany, and forty dollars each." Her eyes widened as he peeled off two hundred-dollar bills.

"I need another car like I need a tax audit, but you're an offer I can't refuse. Gimme five tickets. With that many chances, I've got a decent shot."

"Been playing well?" Johnny Miller asked.

"Tough to tell in a scramble format, Johnny, but I think I'd probably be a few under."

Taking out an iron, he began to hit shots at the green in rapid-fire succession. On his final attempt, the ball hit the flagstick and bounced a few feet away, to the chorus of yells and groans from the onlookers. Brittany was leaping up and down like a cheerleader whose team just pulled off a pick-six, and Jason favored her with an admiring look.

"That ball should've gone in," said Johnny Miller, shaking his head. "You've got almost a reverse pivot, but you still hit down and through it. Who taught you that move?"

"That would be Sam Steele, from Steele Cellars. Same guy who taught me how to make wine. You ever tasted my juice? My winery is Knightbridge Estates."

The golf legend chuckled. "You know, Jason, I live in the Napa Valley, and I can tell you it's no fun being a Mormon boy surrounded by all that great wine. But I think I've heard of your winery and Steele too. Let me see that club you just hit." Taking it, he flipped it upside down. "Wow—a nine-iron for a hundred sixty-seven yards! You are long, my man."

"I've always been known for my length." Jason delivered this with a wink at Brittany.

She responded with an appreciative giggle, but Miller was already grabbing a club from his bag. Walking back to the markers, he teed up a ball. He set aside his iron and picked up Jason's.

"First I'm going to try to get there with your nine-iron. Wow—this thing has a grip the size of a tennis racket! I'm going to try to hit this using your stack-and-tilt technique, and I'm going to have to hit it hard and pure to get it there."

"Hell, Johnny, you were one of the best iron players on the tour. This should be a Laker lay-up for you."

"Uh-huh. And that was about nineteen grandkids ago," Miller replied, standing over the ball and doing his signature waggle. He swung smoothly, with unforced acceleration, but he finished slightly off balance. His ball hit the front of the green, coming in hot, and wound up slightly short and some yards left of the pin.

"Shoot. Yanked it, just like I always do when I try the stack and tilt. That's why I never liked it. Okay, now I'm going to hit my eight-iron and make my usual short-iron swing." Miller treated them to another graceful swing and perfect follow-through, this time with his hands high at the finish and on-balance. His ball ended up inside of Jason's flag-stick shot, drawing enthusiastic applause from the small group on the tee.

After he shook hands with Jason and let their group move on, Miller turned to Brittany. "That guy's an animal."

"I know!" she squeaked. "While you were hitting, he asked me out. He drives a Ferrari."

"I wouldn't let you near that guy if you were my daughter. He looks like trouble."

The warning was wasted on her, however. Brittany only gave a mischievous smile. "Yeah, he sure does."

Jason found her again at the close of the tournament, outside the clubhouse where the scoreboard was set up among tables, chairs, and barbecues. Passing the small stage with its podium and speakers, he strode over to the golf cart where she sat alone, counting money.

"The only thing more alluring than a beautiful woman," Jason drawled, "is a beautiful woman surrounded by money."

"Oh, hi, Mr. Knightbridge." She gave a little pout. "I'm not that good at counting—maybe you could help me?"

"Darling, I'd love to help you any way I can," he answered, climbing in beside her. "When it comes to adding up money, I'm even better than at golf. Here, let's organize these by the size of the bills."

He wasn't as helpful as he might have been—Brittany's form-fitting top was too distracting at close range, and her ingénue appreciation of whatever bullshit he threw at her made him pull out all the stops. It wasn't until the Brojans were announcing the winners of the golf tournament and Jason heard his name called that he sprung up again. He tossed the wad of bills in Brittany's lap and took the stairs to the stage two at a time to accept his trophy and an envelope from Rich Williams while the cameras rolled. Bouncing up and down in the crowd, applauding, Brittany blew him a kiss. Jason waved to her. It looked like another bonus was coming his way later.

It did, in the parking lot after dark, when everyone else had left. With his seat fully reclined in the Ferrari.

Just another day in the life of Jason Knightbridge, when it felt like every day was better than the one before.

He had no way of knowing that was the last of them.

6

The first thread of his life unraveled imperceptibly.

"Whew, we're finally done!" Nate said to Sarah. He slid a pile of dishes onto the counter beside where she stood rinsing. "Another successful Knightbridge Labor Day Bash. Where's Jason? I wanted to say goodbye. Mary's got the kids at home, so I should be getting back."

"Do I look like Jason's keeper? Your guess is as good as mine." Sarah handed the clean plate to him to replace in the cabinet. "Why didn't Mary come anyway, and bring the kids?"

Nate's hand slipped, and the dish rattled into place. "Oh, you know, the last time she was around Jason ..."

Smiling, Sarah flipped the faucet on again. "Yeah, I do know, and I loved it. She called him a conceited asshole. You married up, Nate. You married up."

"Right." He shut the cabinet softly. "So, I thought your party would be a little less stressful if Mary didn't give a repeat performance."

She gave the scrubbing sponge another squirt of detergent. "Aww, too bad. It would have made busting my butt for all his ass-kissing friends bearable."

The hardness of her voice made him wince, and he went to slip an arm around her shoulders. "Hey there. Jason is Jason. He'll never change. We love him despite his flaws, right?"

"Absolutely. I'm head over heels," she answered, not raising her eyes from the sink. "Such an honor for me to be head whore in the harem."

He hated to hear her talk like this, but to argue was impossible. Nate released her slowly. "See ya, Sarah. Thanks for everything. Say bye to him for me." He kissed the cheek she offered him, wishing she would look at him.

She didn't.

Leaving the unhappy wife, Nate only made it as far as the entranceway before Jason, Jr. came barreling into him, face red and eyes streaming. "I hate him, Uncle Nate! I hate him!"

Nate bent down to take the sobbing boy in his arms, just as he had the boy's dry-eyed mother a minute earlier. "Who, J.J.? What's wrong? What happened—are you okay?"

Burying his face in Nate's chest, J.J. choked out something inarticulate before crying again, and Nate stroked his hair, muttering soothing sounds until J.J. paused for breath. Then Nate took him firmly by the arms and held him a little away, ducking his head to meet the boy's swollen gaze. "You're scaring me, little guy. Did somebody hurt you?"

"In—in my room, Uncle Nate," J.J. said, hiccupping. "They were—they were naked in my room. Daddy—" His face went scarlet again. "I *hate* him!"

Footsteps in the hall.

Jason emerged, tucking in his shirt and running fingers through his disheveled hair. Without glancing their way, he crossed the tiled floor and slipped into the kitchen to rejoin his wife.

The Blue Mountain Bar and Grill was old school. Low lighting, peanut shells on the floor, barstools and booth benches worn smooth by decades of Walla Walla hindquarters. Nate Carson occupied the seat around the L of the bar with a view of the door, so that Jason would have time to do no more than throw a smile at the young women on the end before he joined him.

"To what do I owe the privilege of your invite, Nathan?" Jason drawled, signaling the bartender for his usual. Rob set a bucket glass with ice in front of him and poured him a triple Maker's Mark. "No Danielle tonight, Rob? I thought she worked Thursdays."

"On break. She'll be back in a bit."

"Good. 'Cause I sure as hell don't come here for your watered-down drinks."

"I've only been trying to get together with you for two weeks," Nate broke in, while Jason raised his glass at the young women and took a long pull.

"With the crush under way, I'm surprised I'm such a high priority. But you're on my list, clearly, because I got away, even though my prima donna winemaker didn't drag herself in today and wasn't even answering voicemail."

"Kim is AWOL? That's weird."

"Not just weird—immoral, considering what I pay her." Jason thumped his glass down to shake up the ice. "How's your harvest looking? I think we're going to have one of our best ever."

"Fine. It's fine." Nate shrugged this off. "Anyway, the reason I've been hounding you ..."

But Jason had his eye on the women again.

"Do you mind if we move to a table, Jayce?"

"What? I guess not. But there are two of them and two of us, Nathan. Could be a fun night." He picked up his glass, despite the allure, and followed Nate to the back of the lounge. "What's so damned important? You haven't invited me for a drink in years. You'll kidnap me in an Escalade to milk me for money, but when's the last time you just wanted the pleasure of my company?"

This time it was Nate hesitating and taking a slow sip. "Well ... this'll sound weird, but so be it: I wanted to talk to you because I've been dreaming about you lately."

"Didn't know you liked guys that way," Jason wisecracked. "Though it explains a lot."

Nate ignored his baiting. "I'm serious. I've never had dreams like this. They're different, and lately they've almost all been about you ... and Sarah and Jason, Jr." He waited for Jason to prod him on, but when he didn't, Nate sighed and went on anyhow. "They—the dreams—they've made me realize ... I wouldn't be your friend if I didn't tell you that—that your life has a huge hole in it."

"That so?" Jason feigned horror. "Huge hole like what, dream weaver?"

"Like ... like love."

Jason nearly coughed up his drink. This time he gave Nate the hell-raising grin of their boyhood. "Are you kidding me? If I had any more love in my life, I'd have to grow a second dick!"

"I don't mean sex. Everyone knows you get plenty of that, Jason. Much too plenty, as a matter of fact. I don't know why Sarah puts up with it."

"Easy—she doesn't know."

"Now who's not being serious?"

Jason slid his now-empty glass away. "Or maybe she doesn't care."

"She cares," Nate said simply. "Who knows why?"

"Because I'm the man of her dreams," Jason snapped.

"More like nightmares," muttered his friend.

"Jesus. Was this all you wanted to say to me? Let's talk about something else. Like the article coming out on me in *Wine Spectator*. I've heard they're going to rate my '04 Cab in the top ten in the whole goddamned *world*. You've got to admit that's impressive."

"Yep, I admit it, Jason. But what do you admit?"

Jason's eyes rolled with impatience. His gaze wandered past Nate. "I admit I'd like to do Danielle tonight. It's been way too long."

Nate didn't have to look over his shoulder to picture the barmaid in her usual short dress and minimal neckline. "Haven't you had that pleasure, off and on since high school?"

"True, but lately it's been too much off and not enough on ... top of her."

"Witty too, huh?" Nate jeered. "You never let your marriage get in the way of your fun, do you?"

"Shit—this is what you wanted to have a drink for? Why the hell should I let my marriage get in the way? I work hard, and Sarah's got everything. I deserve a little play. Sam taught me that. I'm damned good at what I do, and I'm gonna reap the benefits."

"And what about J.J.?" his friend persisted.

"What *about* him?"

"He's old enough now to know his dad is a world-class cheater."

"Oh, yeah? But does he know 'Uncle' Nate is a world-class blowhard? What are you bitching about, Nathan? Rest easy—J.J. doesn't know about my private life."

"The hell he doesn't."

Jason's chin jerked up. "What do *you* know?"

"I know that J.J. saw you screwing someone who didn't look like his mom, in his own bedroom, at your Labor Day party."

"Who the hell told you that?"

Nate didn't back down when Jason leaned forward, jaw clenched. "No one told me. I was there."

"What do you mean you were there? Are you some kind of peeping Nate, looking in the windows?"

"I was leaving your damned suck-up fest, and J.J. came running out of the bedroom wing, bawling his eyes out. When I finally got him to say what was wrong, he told me what he saw. Then you go tearing past, zipping your goddamned pants back up, so intent on feeding Sarah another load of bullshit that you didn't even see us by the front door."

Even in the low lighting Nate could see Jason had gone ashen, his mouth hanging open. So, the man still did have chinks in the armor, then.

Danielle bustled up, clearing their empty glasses and

congratulating Jason on his Winemaker's Award, and Jason's eyes followed her as she swayed back to fetch another round, but his look was absent, glum.

"Look, Jason," Nate tried again, "I know your childhood sucked. Your mom—your mom—well ..."

"My mom was a fucking bitch!" snarled Jason.

Grimacing, Nate said, "I've always hated that word."

Jason's scowl cleared, his face brightening at Nate's discomfort. There was a hint of teasing in his voice again. "Which word? 'Fucking' or 'bitch'?"

"It hit me a few years ago how bizarre it is, that something describing the most beautiful act between two people has become the ultimate cuss word."

"'Fucking,' then," Jason said, grinning. "Hell, Mr. Sanctimonious, I heard you use that handy word a couple of times at the Jubilee golf tournament."

"Yeah, yeah. It's hard-wired into me from all those years playing sports, not to mention hanging around you since we were kids. I try to catch myself, but it does tend to slip out from time to time."

"Times like when I whip your ass on the golf course," Jason taunted, "even with strokes, as I almost—"

"As you almost always do," finished Nate. "Let's face it, Jason: as far back as either of us can remember, you've been better than me at everything. It used to piss me off, but then I realized you're better at everything than almost everyone. It was nothing to do with me. It's like God gave you every natural ability a man could want. You've been phenomenally blessed."

Jason leaned back and folded his huge hands behind his head. "That so? Guess I should be counting my blessings." He flicked his chin Danielle's direction, where she was bent over, wiping down a table. "Speaking of, that'll be one more blessing for me when I get a little of that tonight. And have no doubt I will." Giving a short whistle, he called, "Hey, Danielle, quit your housekeeping and bring our drinks."

"Rob got slammed with a bunch of orders from the restaurant," she explained with a little flutter, hurrying to deliver their glasses. "You're such a beast." She gave Jason a playful push before turning to go.

"She loves my wine, by the way," said Jason. "I give her a case once in a while, and she gives me everything I want."

"You should engrave that on a plaque and hang it in your house, Jason," Nate mused. He held up his hands like he was placing the plaque on an invisible wall. "'Everything I want.' It's your life motto. And you're right—I used to envy you, but now that feeling's been replaced by a different one—"

"Let me guess. Self-righteousness? Holier-than-thou smugness?"

"Sadness."

Jason threw up his hands and then slid Nate's drink away from him. "That's it. What the fuck are you babbling about? I'm cutting you off because this has got to be the liquor talking. This *better* be the liquor talking. I'm at the top of my game, you moron, and I don't mean golf. Knightbridge's case volume has doubled in the last three years since we landed Costco. I'm probably making more money than anyone in the valley, except maybe Bill Brojan. Hell, I could probably sell to Constellation Brands if I wanted for forty or fifty million."

"Uh-huh. And you did it all on your own, right?" countered Nate.

"Now you sound like that fucking Obama. Hell yes, I did it on my own. No one sure as hell did it for me."

"Really?" Nate's eyes narrowed. "What about Sam showing you the ropes? And what about my mom and dad taking you in, when you had nowhere to go? And—hell—what about my dad pulling you out of the river and saving your damned life?"

"Shit—that was decades ago." Jason waved a dismissive hand. "We all need a little help when we're young."

"But not everybody gets it. Sam taught you everything about

making money and the wine business. You were incredibly lucky, Jason."

"There's that jealousy again. Thought you'd given that up." The corner of his mouth turning down, Jason took a pull at his drink.

"No, you're wrong," Nate retorted. "You just don't get it—you're not hearing me. I'm not jealous of what you've done—I'm proud of it. I'm proud of what you've *done*. I'm just not proud of what you've *become*."

With that, Jason slammed his glass down so hard it shattered, sending whisky, ice, and broken glass flying. Heads turned and Nate threw up an arm to shield himself, but Jason paid no attention. He seized the edge of the table like he wanted to overturn it. "I am sick of listening to this! You are making me feel shittier than shit."

"Maybe that's how you should feel," Nate blurted, shaking the drops of Maker's from himself. "You've certainly been good at making everyone who cares about you feel that way." Glancing over, he saw Danielle trying to distract the bar's other startled occupants, even as she reached for the little whisk broom and a rag. "Not to mention those who don't care about you," he added. "Barroom outbursts might scare off the wine tourists, Jayce." Danielle hurried over to a table where a middle-aged couple sat. The man looked particularly ruffled.

"Don't worry," she whispered to them, "those two have been the best of friends since they were kids."

"They have a most interesting way of showing their mutual affection." replied the man in a professorial tone.

Blood dripped from Jason's hand onto the table. Cursing, he began to wrap it in a napkin, warning Danielle away with a glare. "Nathan, you are really starting to piss me off. I don't need to take this from anyone—not even you. I listened to you this long because growing up together gives you some capital in the bank, but you, my friend, are now way overdrawn. Mind your own fucking business."

Nate was breathing fast, but he didn't look away. "Somebody's got to say these things to you. You've got nobody to answer to."

"And that's just the way I like it."

"Everybody needs someone to answer to," Nate insisted. "Otherwise, anything goes."

"Exactly. *Danielle*, we've had a little mishap here!" he hollered, "Get me another Maker's, and make sure it's a heavy pour."

"You think it's good—having no one to answer to?"

"Damned right I do. No one to control me and no one to stop me. Not you, and no woman, that's for goddamned sure."

"Don't you see what's going on here? Jason, you're so damned talented that you think you don't need anyone. All these natural blessings have turned into a curse! And for some reason—God knows it's not because I feel close to you anymore—I feel like I need to warn you before it's too late. These dreams I'm having about you—they've been getting worse. I woke up drenched in sweat the other night."

"Dr. Nate, barstool psychiatrist. Specializing in head cases. Well, I didn't make an appointment with you, so why the fuck do you feel like you need to worry your pretty little head about me?"

Nate slid away the napkin he'd been using to sop up Jason's mess and waited for Danielle to sweep the glass away and deposit the replacement drink on the table. When she was out of earshot again, he said in a low voice, "Because, honestly, I think I'm only friend you have left."

"Bull*shit!*"

"None of those parasites you've gathered around you care what happens to you."

Sliding out of the booth, Jason dug for his wallet and threw a fifty-dollar bill on the table. "We're done here. You're jealous, and you're wrong, and I hope to shit you're drunk—"

But Nate grabbed his wrist and pinned it. "You're even more deluded than I thought, if you think I'm jealous of that collection of ass-kissing, money-sucking, amoral, *worthless—*"

At the word *worthless*, Jason tore his arm away. With a roar, he lifted the table by the corners, upending it and sending the new drinks crashing to the floor. Before Nate could navigate the mess and get to his feet, Jason's napkin-wrapped fist slammed into his jaw, sending him flipping back against the next table. Cries and protests from the other bar patrons erupted around them, but Nate only rolled and leaped back up, rubbing his jaw.

"Well. I was wondering when I'd finally get through to you."

"You got through to me, all right." Jason was shaking with rage, ignoring the professor and his companion scrambling to escape behind him. "And now *we're* through. No one, and I mean no one, ever calls me, my friends, or anything I care about *worthless*!"

"Must have hit a nerve. Oh, yeah—now I remember. If your mama was still alive, she'd know exactly what to call those sewer rats you call friends."

Jason gave another wild cry and charged him, right arm cocked to nail Nate again. But when he threw his fist, Nate ducked, coming up under Jason and punching him hard in the stomach. Jason doubled over, winded. Nate was surging with adrenaline himself, but when he saw his friend rocking in place, helpless, he held back from hitting him again. Jason showed no such mercy, however, only waiting to see Nate hesitate before he lunged for him, tackling him and sending them both barreling into another table. The group seated at it screamed, scrambling away from the falling dishes and furniture and the flying limbs.

"Jesus!"

"Somebody call the cops!"

Clambering to his feet, Jason flew at Nate again, faking with his right and catching Nate with his left as Nate dodged. Nate reeled from the blow, but when Jason tried to follow up, Nate spun around, using Jason's momentum to launch him onto a busing tray loaded with empty glasses and wine bottles. The whole thing collapsed in a thunderous crash, the sound of splintering glass and falling tableware muted by another wave of screams from the onlookers.

"Do you realize this is the first time we've ever fought each other?" Nate panted, looming over Jason where he lay amidst the wreckage. "We didn't do this, even when we were kids."

Pressing at the gash below his eye to staunch the blood, Jason snapped, "That's because you weren't an arrogant motherfucker back then, but you've sure as hell become one."

"Well, you would know," Nate replied with maddening calm. "If there's a club for arrogant motherfuckers, you would be the founding member."

Jason let fly another expletive and heaved himself up to go for Nate again, but Nate aimed a kick to his side almost casually, dropping Jason to his knees. Over the piped-in music and the buzz of the fellow patrons, the whine of a siren grew louder.

Jason's head dropped. Among the debris covering the floor lay a broken wine bottle. With a last effort, Jason snatched it by its neck and swung around to spear Nate, but as soon as he whipped his arm up, he gave a sharp grunt and crumpled, clutching his side. The bottle rolled away to stop at Nate's feet.

"Lookie there," Nate chuckled, reaching for it and pretending to admire the label. "Leonetti. Didn't you swear, Jason, that you'd never touch another bottle of Leonetti as long as you lived? I guess you must be a dead man."

Making no answer, Jason only kicked at the glass around him in frustration as two cops burst into the lounge.

It was late when Jess Carson got the call from Sergeant Gay Goodrich, but he headed for the jailhouse straight away. He arrived to find his son and Jason locked in separate cells, both passed out, and the sergeant talking in muted voice to a woman in the short, tight outfit of a barmaid. He hadn't seen her in years, but he still recognized Danielle Stevens as one of the cutest cheerleaders who ever bounced the sidelines of Walla Walla High stadium.

"Carson!" Goodrich nodded at Jess. "Glad you could swing by. Look at our two Fight Club boys. You would've been proud of Nate, Jess—he whipped Jason good. I don't remember Jason ever losing at anything."

"Me neither. But that's not the only thing I can't believe—these two boys have been like brothers for the past thirty years. Jason even lived with us for a couple of them, if you remember, Gaylord. He's like another son to me. I can't imagine these two fighting."

"That's what I thought," put in Danielle.

Jess eyed her. "You were there, young lady? What set off this melee?"

"They were arguing," she said, "but I wasn't paying much attention because we were busy. But then Jason—flipped out! He threw his drink and knocked over the table and yelled something about 'don't be calling him or his friends worthless.' Next thing I knew, people were screaming and they were knocking the bar to hell and going for each other."

"Mm." Jess nodded at this, his eyes narrowing. "'Worthless,' huh?"

Nodding, Danielle leaned to look around Jess. "Didn't *she* come with you, Mr. Carson?"

"Who?"

"Jason's ... wife. Gay said he called her."

There was a pause, and then Jess answered heavily, "I think that after I bail him out, Jason will likely have to find his own ride home. I don't think Sarah was any too pleased."

"Oh ..." Danielle made a sympathetic face. "Poor Jason. He's still bleeding and everything! Look—you get Nate, Mr. Carson, and I'll worry about Jason."

Startled, Jess gave a shake of his head. "That won't be necessary, Miss. I can get them both."

But Goodrich only laughed. "I don't think either one of them would be thrilled with that idea. Especially Jason. When Gay here told them, 'Jason, you and your best friend here will have to pay for damages at the bar,' Jason was like, 'Make that my best *ex*-friend. And everyone in the house gets a case of Knightbridge's finest because his juice is shit.'"

Jess made a weak effort to smile at her account, but he had a feeling more things had been damaged than just the Blue Mountain barroom.

7

From there, the downhill slide of Jason's life picked up speed.

He pulled up to the house as the sun was setting, to find Sarah's Porsche Cayenne parked before the open door. Easing the Ferrari in behind it, Jason watched his wife march out and down the two steps to the open hatch of her SUV, her arms heaped with clothing still on the hangers. Without glancing at him, she tossed them in.

"What the—!" His shout was muted by the three-hundred-grand's worth of glass and metal separating them.

Cursing Nate Carson, Jason twisted gingerly to open his driver's side door with his right hand. With teeth gritted, he maneuvered his way out, cradling his left side. He peered over the bundle of clothing in the back of the Cayenne and saw the trembling face of his son, J.J., in the front seat. The boy had one hand reached back to touch Ringo, who gave a low whine when he saw his master.

"No fucking way," grunted Jason.

He turned just as Sarah emerged with another armload, and with a hiss of pain through his lips, Jason moved to block her path.

"Just what the hell do you think you're doing?"

"Just exactly what the hell it looks like," she threw back. "I'm leaving you."

"You can't do that. No one leaves me."

"Really."

She made to go around him, but he took another step in front of her. Sarah's eyes flashed. "No one leaves the great Jason Knightbridge, huh? Well, I guess there's a first time for everything. And judging by your face and the way you're babying your side, it looks like you've been enjoying a lot of new experiences lately. Got your ass whipped, did you? Ha. Who said God never answers prayer?"

This time when she tried to dart past him, he grabbed her arm, gasping at the stab of pain this caused.

"Let go of me, Jason. It's over. It should have been over a long time ago. I can't believe it took me this long to figure out that no one can love you as much as you love yourself."

"I will *not* let you go!" He was amazed to find himself shouting. "You belong to me."

Her gaze met his then, with a directness he hadn't seen in years, and he almost retreated before it.

"You're drowning, Jason," she said, her voice low and steady. "Drowning in your own self-worship. And I'm not going down with you."

Yanking her arm free, she elbowed past him, throwing the last load in and slamming the hatch. He saw J.J. was crying now, Ringo eagerly licking tears off the boy's face.

As the tires spun on the gravel, Jason pounded on the back window and roared, "Stop! Stop, goddammit! You will *not* leave me!"

But she did.

They did.

The doctor's waiting room smelled like orange air freshener. As Jason approached the reception desk, the young woman seated there sat up straighter and smiled, her eyes flicking uncertainly to the steri-strips that still covered his fading bruises.

"Jason Knightbridge. Here to see Dr. Carlson. You should have all my information from yesterday."

"I do," she twinkled at him, "and I can see why the gal who worked yesterday said I wouldn't mind taking her shift today."

He tried and failed to produce an answering smile. "I'm not sure why the doctor wanted to see me again so soon."

In the face of his disinterest, the receptionist's enthusiasm faded. She shrugged. "I'm sure he'll tell you. Like I said, I was off yesterday. I'll let the doctor know you're here."

Jason had only flipped halfway through *Golf Digest* before Dr. Carlson came into the exam room. He was an athletic man with receding brown hair and a good-natured expression, and he gave Jason a firm handshake.

"First off, Jason, I forgot to thank you yesterday for that fabulous case of your Cab you got me for Karen's fortieth. She almost took my head off last night when she found out you'd been in and I didn't tell you that."

"No worries," he said, brushing this off. "But, Curt, why the hell did you want to see me again? I'm doing fine. I mean, my ribs still hurt like hell, and whenever I cough I feel like that son of a bitch is kicking me again, but other than that …"

"Speaking of coughing, I heard you yesterday." The doctor dropped onto his leather stool and rolled closer. "How long have you had that?"

"I dunno. A while."

"Days? Weeks? Months?"

Jason shifted in his chair. "Months, I guess."

"Did you ever smoke?"

"No … but my goddamned mother smoked like a Weber barbecue on the Fourth of July."

Dr. Carlson chuckled, shaking his head. "That's funny, in a sad way. Did you just think of that?"

"Not I. My pussy-whipped father used to say that, until one day she slugged him and knocked him out."

"You're kidding. Your mother knocked out your dad?"

"No joke. She could hit like a fucking Chicago Bears linebacker. She didn't even have to take the cigarette out of her mouth while she beat the shit out of him." Jason grimaced, one knee jogging up and down. "But what's the deal? Why all the questions?"

"Not so fast there," Dr. Carlson said. "I know you're used to running the show, but this is my gig. Tell me some more family history—any siblings?"

"Nope."

"Okay—are either or both of your parents still alive?"

"Strike two."

"Both gone?" The doctor raised his eyebrows.

"If you mean dead, yes. They managed to slowly but successfully poison themselves. My pathetic excuse for a father did us all a favor by drinking himself to death—cirrhosis."

"And your mother, the Weber?"

Jason let out a short breath. "The cigarettes got her."

The stool rolled back a foot and squeaked as the doctor leaned forward with his hands on his knees. He cleared his throat. "Look, Jason, when we x-rayed your ribs yesterday, we found something else: a spot on your left lung."

"What kind of spot?"

"I don't know. That's why I wanted you to come in right away. We need to biopsy it."

The next thing Jason knew, he was crossing the parking lot to the Ferrari, his breath coming tight, as if whatever was blooming inside him had already wound itself around his chest.

His cell rang.

"Hey, Marcie," Jason said flatly. "What's up?"

He couldn't understand his assistant's reply at first, her voice was so choked.

"What? For Christ sake—"

"I said," she sniffed, taking a shaky breath, "'Boss, have you heard the news?'"

"News. What news?"

"Okay. You haven't." There was another pause, and he could picture her gathering herself. "Boss—it's about Nate."

Going very still, Jason waited. Where he stood, the sunlight blazed off the side mirror of the car, but he stood in its beam, feeling the sweat break out on his forearms.

"What about Nate?"

She swallowed hard. "He was—he was killed last night. Around eight. The other driver was drunk."

Jason said nothing.

A crow swooped down to light on a trash can nearby, regarding him with cocked head.

"And there's more," Marcie said slowly.

"How the *hell* can there be more?" he bit off. He watched the crow. It shook its feathers and began strutting along the perimeter of the can.

"The guy who hit him," she began again, "he'd been tasting all day, throughout the valley. It's just that—Knightbridge was his last stop, right before we closed."

Jason's arm dropped nervelessly to his side, the cell phone falling to the asphalt. As he swayed, stumbling against his car, Marcie's concern squeaked from the tiny speaker: "Boss? *Jason*? Are you still there? We cut him off, but he bought a case, and, apparently, he had a full bottle beforehand. It wasn't just us. Jason, are you still there? *Boss*?"

There were more gathered than he would have imagined. Fifty boys from the Jubilee Ranch alone, some doing the tough-guy thing and some openly weeping. Near them stood Rich Williams, Alvin Williams, and the Brojans, all somber. On the other side of the minister he saw Mary, veiled in black, her two kids gathered close. Jess was behind her in dark glasses.

Jason pushed up the bridge of his own sunglasses. It was an overcast day, but the glasses were his shield against the eyes of others. Against everything.

The minister was saying something, and then Rich stepped up next to the guy and cleared his throat.

"It just doesn't seem right, when death comes to someone so young." His throat tightened on the last words, and his mouth worked a moment. Then he went on. "Especially when they have a lovely, loving wife like Mary and two beautiful little ones."

The crowd shifted, murmured. Mary put an arm around her boy and a hand on the girl's head.

"I know there are a lot of us—a lot of us mad at God for letting this happen," Rich said, "but if we truly are believers, we know in our hearts that Nate has never been happier than right now. He's in a beautiful place—beyond description. Our ... sadness is for our own loss, for the hole we now have in our lives. And it's a big one because Nate Carson was a big man who touched so many of us here. I look around and see the faces of the young men he helped and bonded with from Jubilee. Those faces are all any of us need to know that Nate's was a life well-lived. We—I—all of us were so lucky to have known him." Turning, he rested his knuckles on the casket, giving a gentle rap. "Until we meet again, Nate. I'll do my best to carry on with these young men you loved so deeply and who loved you in return."

The mourners closed in as the casket was lowered and the minister led them in a hymn, but Jason found himself backing away, stumbling. He got back to his car he didn't know how, but before he could climb in and get the hell away, he heard someone call him.

Jess.

Shoulders slumping, Jason shut the door again and waited.

"Jason." Jess's voice was hoarse. "I want to thank you for being here today. I know how you feel about funerals."

For a minute, Jason couldn't get his voice to work.

"Wouldn't—couldn't miss it." He swallowed. "He was the closest thing I had to ..."

"To a brother."

Jason gave one nod.

"Yeah," said Jess. He scraped the gravel underfoot with the toe of his uncomfortable-looking black dress shoe. "He thought of you that way too. And you know, my beloved Maria and I looked at you almost as a second son. Even after Sam came along."

This drew only a grunt from Jason. The lenses of his sunglasses revealed nothing, but from the angle of his head, he must have been watching Jess's shoe trace its arc in the dust.

"And I know you well enough, Jason, to know you aren't wearing those dark glasses to hide any tears—more likely to hide the black eye Nate gave you." Jess let out a slow breath. "'Cause I never saw you cry once, not even when you broke your arm falling out of that tree, remember? Or after I pulled you out of the—" Here he broke off, but Jason didn't look up. Not even when other mourners passed by, patting Jess's shoulder and murmuring Jason's name in greeting.

Car doors opened and shut. Engines started. Still Jason stood there, as if turned to stone.

"Still favoring your left side, I see," Jess muttered, when silence fell around them again. "Don't recall hearing that you ever lost a fight before, but you know, Nathan dabbled in the martial arts in high school and then got his black belt after he came back up here from Davis. He felt bad about breaking your ribs the other night, though. He was going to tell you he was ..." The older man's throat closed, and he shook his head, pounding his fist into his thigh.

Jess took another ragged breath. "I still can't believe he's gone. Jason, he was going to apologize to you. But Nate also wanted you to know that the reason for your fracas is—was— that he was worried about you ... and the direction your life is headed."

Finally, Jason stirred. Grunted, "Yeah, so I heard. He made that quite clear."

Jess laid a hand on Jason's shoulder. "If he spoke too bluntly, it was because of how much he cares—how much he cared about you, Jason." His grip tightened. "You know, I've been going through some of Nate's things that I still have at the house. Wanted to see if there was anything to offer Mary or the kids, in—in memory of their father. I found this box—actually more than one box—that had 'Jason' written on it."

"My stuff?" asked Jason, perplexed.

"Nah. Not your stuff. Nate's stuff. Stuff he collected about you." Jess gave him a little shove. "He was your biggest fan, you know. There were pictures he'd taken of you shooting the winning basket, or holding a golf trophy. Dozens of newspaper articles about your sports triumphs, and later ones about your winemaking awards. I even found an album of your wedding pictures, when he was your best man."

"I didn't know," said Jason inadequately. "He ... never said anything. I had no idea."

"You had no call to." Jess gave a long sigh. "You know, it's not just Mary and my grandkids I'm worried about. I mean, they're fine, money-wise, because of Nate's life insurance policy and the investment portfolio he built up, but they won't have him. He was always thinking about the people he loved and how he could protect them. Losing a young husband and a father—especially such a good one—well, that's almost more than the human soul can stand. Lord knows it's tough on me, losing him just a few years after my precious Maria—"

He trailed off, fighting once more for control. Jason waited, even though he didn't want to talk about this or think about this. Didn't want to think about Maria, or Mary and the kids, or Jess's pain, and, most of all, he didn't want to think about Nate.

But Jess kept on. "Most of all, Jason, I'm worried about you."

This wasn't what he expected to hear, and his head jerked back. "Me? Why? I'm fine."

"For one reason, Nate was worried about you." Jess removed his sunglasses, revealing his red, swollen eyes. "For another, I think you've lost your lucky charm."

"What do you mean?"

"He was your wing man, even when you didn't know it. You know why he learned martial arts? Because he got tired of getting beat up, sticking up for you in high school. All the boys knew he was your best friend, and you did stir up some jealousy back in those days." A soft chuckle broke from him. "Some things never change."

Jason shook his head, refusing this burden. "He should have just told me. I'd have kicked their asses."

Shrugging, Jess said, "Maybe he just had something to prove to himself. Even later, when you were both in the wine business, he was still looking out for you. Remember the year your vines got that phlox-thing disease, and you lost most of your crop?"

"Harvest. Phylloxera," Jason corrected automatically. "I forgot about that. Yeah. But I helped him out at times too."

"I'm sure you did, Jason. I'm sure you did. But my point is, you've lost someone who was always in your corner, always looking out for you, even when you didn't know it or you forgot about it. And we both know you wouldn't be standing here today if Nate hadn't raced up the hill to our house on the morning you nearly drowned."

Jason's fists clenched as he fought an urge to writhe under Jess's words. He couldn't hear this. Not now.

"Don't you have to be going, Jess?" he said roughly. "All those folks will be waiting at Nate's—at Mary's to pay their respects to her and you."

"Yeah." Jess put his sunglasses back on and retreated a few steps, leaving Jason to sag with relief. But then the old guy turned back to him one last time.

"Jason, I fear you're going to have to live without your guardian angel. And at a time when you might need him the most."

It was bullshit, of course. The guardian-angel business. Because there was no one, absolutely no one, with Jason hours later, when he was parked at the edge of the bluff, several hundred feet above the Columbia.

There was no one to see him with the driver door open, sitting on the hood of the Ferrari, drinking straight from the bottle as the empties lay scattered on the ground and the sun set, blood-red.

"God damn it!" Jason roared, sliding off the hood to a shaky stand. "God damn *you*, Nate!"

He grabbed the last bottle by the neck and hurled it into the gorge, doubling over the next instant to clutch his ribs, his breath heaving.

"And God damn me."

8

"She's coming after you hard, Jason," said the lawyer, looking at him over his reading glasses. He slid the document in his hand across the desk. "Everything you've got is community property. Quite frankly, she wants half, and I don't see how we're going to stop her."

"That's your fucking job, Frank," Jason snapped, shoving the papers away without glancing at them. "That's why I pay you five-hundred goddamned dollars an hour."

Frank's leather chair creaked as he sat back and tented his fingers, the gold of his Rolex gleaming as his cuffs fell back. "You can rant all you want, but either you give her half of everything, including the winery, or you come up with twenty million, maybe more, to buy her out. The reality is, Jason, that almost all of your net worth was built up after you married Sarah."

Already on his feet, Jason's brow was thunderous. "I did all the work, and she gets half? Nice system you represent, Frank." His lip curled in a sneer. "Thanks for nothing. But I'll find a way to buy the bitch out."

Before he could do more than indulge in a revenge fantasy or two, however, he had one more appointment with Dr. Carlson. It didn't take more than a glance at the doctor's face when he entered the exam room, x-ray in hand, to know the shit storm engulfing his life was gathering force.

"Let's hear it," said Jason, throwing aside the *Sports Illustrated* he'd been paging through blindly.

"We got the results back, Jason. It's not good news."

"What the hell do you mean?"

Carlson took off his glasses and rubbed his temples. "I mean it's not good. It's cancer. Of the lung."

The doctor braced himself unconsciously, expecting swearing—maybe even violence. But Jason only sat back hard in the chair, face gray and mouth dropping open. Carlson waited. He didn't even mutter the customary, "I'm sorry," because Jason wouldn't have heard it.

Slowly, very slowly, the shock faded from his face, to be replaced by an expression the doctor hadn't seen before on him. He looked as if he were miles away, his thoughts withdrawing to distant places.

Well, sure.

No one could follow Jason Knightbridge now.

"Boss, you really are back!" His assistant Marcie hurried to greet him as he stalked through the winery office, ignoring the dozens of people racing around and talking on cell phones in Spanish and English. He paused outside a door with the nameplate "Master of the Universe," a coughing fit convulsing him.

"Are you okay?"

"I'm fine, fine. Just a bug. How's the crush going? I've been so focused on goddamned bankers and attorneys—I feel like I'm out of touch. Gus from Sterling Bank hasn't called, has he? When he does, put him through right away."

She nodded, making a note. "Crush is going well, boss. Have you seen the prices, though? I haven't seen them drop like this before."

His face darkened. "I know they suck. It's that friggin' Wall Street. Those dickheads are taking us all down with them. Hold the other calls, okay? Just give me Gus."

Before he could enter his office, Marcie threw a hand across the door. "You should know, Jason—Kim's in there. She heard you were coming in today and really wants to talk to you."

"You're kidding, right? For weeks, she's been avoiding me like I've got some terminal disease." The aptness of the comparison struck him, and he gave a humorless snort. "What the hell does she want to talk to me now for? I'm the one that should be doing the talking—or shouting."

Marcie made a little face, stepping aside to let him pass.

"Well, look who's here—if it isn't my head winemaker." Jason greeted the forty-something, smartly dressed woman who stood before his trophy case. "If I didn't know better, I'd say you've been dogging me these past few weeks. And during crush, when we should be in constant contact."

Kim hastily replaced the gold cup she had been straightening. "Actually, that's why I'm here." She swallowed hard. "I'm not going to finish the crush."

Jason kicked the office door shut behind him, shaking the framed certificates on the wall. "What the fu—?"

"Leonetti has made me an offer I couldn't refuse."

"*Leonetti*? Those bastards!"

The corner of her mouth went down. "Funny, Jason. That's exactly the word they used to describe you."

"I'll match whatever they're offering," he said quickly. "Plus ten-percent."

Kim sighed, some of the defiance draining from her. "It's not the money, Jason, although it's a whole lot for a farm girl from the Palouse. Thanks for the vote of confidence, though. Thanks, but no thanks. It's just that, here, it's always about you. I want it to be about me for a change."

"Uh huh." He shook his head, favoring her with a sardonic grin. "'It's not about the money'? One of the things I learned from Sam a long time ago is that, when somebody says it's not about the money, it's about the money."

His cynicism was the last straw. Crossing her arms over her

chest, she came a step nearer, her chin lifting. "So that's what Sam taught you, huh? You know, it's amazing."

"What's amazing?"

"That, for two smart guys, neither one of you knows jack*shit* about people. You have no clue what makes them tick. What they care about. What motivates them."

Ignoring the dangerous narrowing of his eyes, she only shrugged. "How could you, when all you really care about is you?"

With that, she pushed past him and was gone.

Jason thought, as he sat in the Knightbridge Cellars conference room, heading the rough-hewn table at which his board sat, that Kim might have had a point after all. Sam Steele sat to his right, tubes coming out of his nose and an oxygen tank beside him. He looked frail, shrunken. Like the air from the tank was failing to keep him fully inflated.

What the hell *had* they learned?

Nothing about normal people, it looked like. After all, Sam had always taught him they were smarter and tougher than everyone else. He never said so, exactly, but he didn't need to—Jason had picked up on that at a tender age.

The four other men gathered were turned to Jason, attentive. Gripping the table by the corners, he took a deep breath. "Well, gentlemen—and you too, Sam" —he waited for their chuckle to pass— "as my board, you should know that I've been able to secure financing to buy out my soon-to-be ex. I've had to put up everything, both personally and from the winery, but Gus over at Sterling says he can get me the money."

There was a low whistle and some raised eyebrows, and Sam croaked, "Even with Washington Mutual filing for Chapter 11 this morning, and the market in free fall?"

"*Despite* the bullshit on Wall Street," Jason agreed, his teeth gritted. "I've deposited the funds, and my attorney will soon be cutting her a check—assuming she signs the final release papers. Knightbridge will continue to be run by me, with your able counsel, and majority owned by me. Your equity interests will, of course, be unaffected."

Not a bad speech, and the board members had even begun to applaud, when a coughing fit took him, one so violent that their excitement petered out awkwardly.

Marcie came to the rescue, popping her head around the door. "Oh—great—you're wrapping up. Let me get you some water, boss. There's someone named Diamond, or something like that, trying to reach you from New York. His assistant has been holding for at least fifteen minutes. She says it's very important."

When the other board members had filed out, she muttered, "You all right? You look pale."

He waved this off. "Just transfer the call in here."

When the button flashed, he punched it. "Jason Knightbridge."

"Would you please hold, Mr. Knightbridge, for Jamie Dimon?"

Straightening sharply, he was about to ask if she was kidding, when a familiar, clipped voice came on. "Hello, Jason. This is Jamie Dimon. Thanks for taking my call."

"I—uh—recognize your voice from CNBC. This is the real Jamie Dimon, isn't it? How do you have time to talk to me when Wall Street is going down in flames?"

"That's why I need to keep this short and to the point," the CEO of JP Morgan Chase rapped back. "I'm calling about my wife."

"Your wife. I ... I don't understand."

Jason's mind started racing back over all the women he'd bedded in recent months but he couldn't think of any from the East Coast.

"Yeah, she's turning fifty next week, and she loves your 2002 Cab reserve. My assistant has been trying to find it all over New York. In fact, all over the country, and she can't locate any. So, I thought I'd go to the source. Can you help?"

Jason's shoulders sagged, and he leaned back in his leather chair. "Of course. Will a case be enough?"

"Perfect. My assistant will fax over the credit card information. Thanks very much. And by the way, Wall Street will survive this, and JP Morgan will come out stronger than ever."

That's one of us, Jason thought. Aloud he said, "That's good to know. Maybe I should buy more of your stock. I think I have some already. But—but Mr. Dimon … are things really as bad as they're saying on TV and in the papers?"

"Call me Jamie. Look—all I can tell you is to make sure you're not overleveraged. This is no time to be in debt. We're looking at what is essentially a global margin call. Sorry, I've got to hop. Bye—and thanks very much."

When the line went dead, Jason actually laughed. His face was bloodless.

He tossed the handset back on its cradle.

Would Jamie Dimon consider $20 million "overleveraged"? Because that was the size of the check cut to Sarah.

The size of the grave Jason Knightbridge had dug himself.

He used to thrive on the chaos of the crush, but this year he couldn't take it. With no head winemaker and his body turning against him—the country club was the one place he could imagine his life was still normal. Besides, it was time for him to do what he did so often: win the club championship. Take refuge in competition and give the old ego a needed boost.

But the running joke at Walla Walla Country Club—that they should just put quote marks under his name for every year on the damned championship trophy—fell flat that autumn. He got the tournament committee to postpone the match all the way into mid-October so he could heal up, and with the typical Indian Summer they were enjoying, you would never know how late it was in the year. So, there was the usual glorious fall weather; there was the usual big gallery, standing on the high bank behind the ninth green, with the stately clubhouse in the background; and there was Jason, as always, in the final twosome. What was throwing everyone—not least of all Jason Knightbridge—was that he was losing.

He was two down after eight holes and on nine, a long par-four, his wayward second shot buried itself in the wall of a bunker to the left of the green. Jason's twenty-year-old opponent, Billy Wood, had hit his approach shot stiff and was lining up a short birdie putt. Grimacing, Jason surveyed his ball that was so plugged only the very top was visible. Hooding his sand wedge, he gave the ball a mighty whack, causing him to clutch his left side, but it barely budged, before slowly trickling to the bottom of the bunker.

The onlookers gave a dismayed murmur, from which he could pick out damned Bud Atkins, standing close to the green, muttering, "He better get his ass in gear soon. He's going to be three down going into the back nine." And some other member chimed in, "You sure Jason's ribs aren't still bothering him?" There was more to the interchange, but Jason turned away with determination, putting distance between him and them, the better to ignore their nattering.

On the back nine, with the holes running out and Jason still three down, he and his caddy were standing in the deep grass to the right of the fourteenth fairway, shaking their heads. Once again, the ball was barely visible, but the hush of the spectators by now owed more to embarrassment for Jason than reverence. Jason himself was so absorbed in his disgust that it took him a moment to register the agitated sounds that broke the silence.

Voices, yelling.

Jason glanced over to one of the houses lining the course. A middle-aged man in a bathing suit stood on his patio, laying into a Hispanic woman in a maid's uniform. Though they were a good forty yards away, Jason could catch every syllable of invective, and the man's gestures and the woman's shaking shoulders needed no words.

Before he knew it, he was in motion, hijacking a cart from a man watching the match and slamming the accelerator to the floorboard. Jolting through the rough, the cart passed the white out-of-bound stakes, hitting a large grass mogul and going airborne.

The man in the bathing suit and the weeping maid watched dumbstruck as Jason leaped from the vehicle, rolling away on the lawn, just before momentum carried the cart straight into the pool. It skimmed for a split-second across the water and then began to sink.

Before the homeowner could even form a protest, Jason was on him, running up and punching him square in the jaw. The man stumbled backward over a lounge chair, and the maid began to cry again. Instead of looking grateful for Jason's interference, she started to shriek at him in Spanish, pummeling him with both her fists. The sliding glass door to the patio winged open, and another woman burst out, lean and bikini-clad and wielding an aerosol can, which she sprayed directly in Jason's face.

Jason roared, throwing up an arm to block her and fleeing toward the fairway, his other hand rubbing furiously at his face. "Goddammit! What the fuck was that shit?"

"Get the hell away from us!" the woman shrilled, still waving the can and spraying the empty air. "I'm calling the cops on you, you crazy bastard!" Her chest still heaving with excitement, she murmured, "I've always wanted to do that. It felt good, *real* good."

Which is how he found himself in a jail cell, for the second time in four weeks. This time he lay on the bench with a wet rag over his face.

"This is becoming your home away from home," jeered his old classmate Gay, the sergeant outside the bars. "Maybe we should set up a little putting green in here, so you don't lose your stroke."

Without uncovering his face, Jason flipped him the finger.

"Yeah, I love you, too. Somebody's here to see you—as hard as that is to believe."

Jason heard the cell door opening and footsteps—a tread he recognized.

"Well, Jason," said Jess Carson, not without humor, "it appears that you've got yourself in a real enfuckment this time."

"My face feels like it's on fire," Jason grumbled through the rag. "What the hell happened?"

"According to Bud at the club, after you knocked that guy out, his trophy wife gave you a whole snootful of pepper spray. What set you off this time?"

"I didn't like the way that prick was screaming at his maid. I thought he was going to hit her. I thought she was just this helpless little Hispanic woman—although the bitch started slugging me when I was just trying to stick up for her. Some gratitude for you."

"Turned superhero, did you? Whatever for?"

"Hell if I know. I don't know—before all that craziness—when the guy was yelling at her, she reminded me of someone."

"Uh-huh." Jess nudged Jason over and sat down next to him. "Bud said this wasn't the first time you stuck your neck out defending the Mexicans at the club."

"Whatever. If this is what it gets me, they're going to have to fend for themselves from now on."

Jess's voice was soft. "My Maria always did say you had a gallant streak you worked real hard to hide."

Jason shifted uncomfortably and blew out a breath that made the rag flutter. "She said that, huh?" he muttered. The cot squeaked beneath him. "How come you're here, Jess?"

"Oh, I guess mostly because I know Nathan would be here, if he was still—" Jess's throat caught, but before he could clear it, Jason was sitting up, letting the washcloth fall from his red, swollen face.

"Thanks, Jess," he said shortly. "I appreciate it. I really do. Now if you can get Gestapo Boy to give me back my cell phone, I'll call Marcie, and she'll get me out of this shit hole."

"Jason, look—I know you don't want to talk about Nate, but—"

"But nothing," snapped Jason, on his feet. "You're damned right. I don't want to talk brother figures, especially with Gaylord the Gay Coppallero listening in. And I've about had it with father figures too. I just want to get the hell out of here. Thanks for your concern, but no thanks."

The universe must have taken him at his word, about not wanting father figures, because Sam Steele was the next pillar of Jason's life to collapse. There was no miraculous rebound from the frailty Jason noted at the board meeting. Instead Sam fell into a coma. The portable oxygen tank gave way to a battery of machines and monitors, tubes and wires.

Sam's room was empty of visitors when Jason got there.

Careful not to disturb the humming and blinking medical equipment, he dragged the vinyl-upholstered chair closer to the bed and threw himself in it. Waiting, he thought the old man might sense his presence even now and open his eyes, but he didn't.

Jason swallowed hard and then cleared his throat. Awkwardly, he leaned toward his unconscious mentor. "Well, Sam—they tell me people in a coma can't hear anything."

Outside in the hall, a nurse walked by the open door, and Jason straightened up, drumming his fingers on the chair's wooden armrest. He waited for her steps to die away and then began again. "But I've read that sometimes people who come out of these things remember everything that was said to them when they were unconscious. So that's what I'm counting on.

Because you're gonna come through this, and I've got a lot to get off my chest."

Again, he waited. One of the machines clicked and began to whir. Sam gave no sign of any change.

"You were like a real dad to me," said Jason, fighting the tightness in his voice. He rubbed his palms down his jeans. "Not like Leon, my pathetic pussy of a father. You—you taught me so much about business. Winemaking, money, women—about getting what you want out of life. You always made me feel like I could be something—some*one*—someone big and important."

His knee was jogging like a jackhammer, and with an effort, he made it stop. "You made me feel like I was worthwhile. And hell, if you hadn't put up that two-hundred grand, I never would've been able to buy Givan's acreage. There never would have been a Knightbridge Estates."

There was no response, of course. Jason might have been confessing to the wall.

"I was going through your papers—they made me. And I found this letter from some army buddy of yours. How come you never mentioned what you went through at Bastogne? I mean, you might have mentioned it once or twice—you told me it was hell, but I was too young to ask the right questions. And then you didn't anymore, and I ... forgot all about it. God—I get it now. No wonder you lived like you did. When you saw kids right and left being blown up by eighty-eights, tree tops raining down on you like shells 'cause the SS was targeting them—I get it, Sam. I get it. You came away thinking you had to grab whatever you could out of life."

Hesitating, Jason rested his hand on his old mentor's, as it lay lifeless atop the sheets. The feel of Sam's papery skin sent a shudder through him, but he left his hand where it was.

"And you did it, Sam," he said slowly. "Lived like there was no tomorrow. Taught me to do the same."

If Sam had any response to Jason's epiphany, he kept it to himself. The dying man just lay there. The machines hummed and ticked and beeped. And suddenly Jason wanted to grab him by the shoulders and shake him.

Shake him awake.

Shake him *alive.*

His grasp on Sam's hand tightened, and he winced to feel the bones so light beneath their thin layer of skin. Then the words came tumbling from him, and the begging note he heard in his own voice added to his swelling panic. "Don't die, Sam. Please don't die. I need you like I haven't needed you since I was a kid. I gotta tell you—I'm scared. You know I've lost Nate, I've lost Sarah, I'll probably lose J.J. She took me for twenty million, Sam, and everything I put up to raise that money—it's all going to hell. The stocks have tanked. I might lose the winery. Jesus, between Sarah and the economy ... She even took the dog."

His knee was going again. Or maybe that was his whole body shaking. Jason shut his eyes for a moment, trying to slow his breathing and recover himself.

"That two-faced bastard Gus at Sterling Bank—the one who used to kiss my ass whenever I came in the branch—now he looks at me like I'm something he stepped in and can't scrape off his shoe. The son-of-a-whoring bitch had the nerve to say I'm screwed. He even tried to get out of me if I could expect something from you to bail me out, when you—if you—"

He exhaled in a gust. "I damn near took his head off."

Sam's hand lay unresponsive in his, indifferent to Jason's anguished clutch. Heart-to-hearts, panic, bravado, humor. It was all past him now.

Carefully, Jason replaced it on the blanket. "The thing is, Sam ..." His voice dropped, so low that even if Sam had been conscious, he might not have heard him over the hospital machinery.

"The thing is ... you're not the only one. I'm sick, too. *Real* sick."

The cemetery was getting all too familiar, the manicured lawn like a mockery of the golf courses Jason loved. The surrounding trees were denuded of foliage. Dry leaves were tossed by invisible gusts under a leaden sky. This time, a few isolated snowflakes drifted down.

The group of mourners was smaller than at Nate's funeral, but there was some overlap. Jason was there, of course, but so was Jess, the two of them wrapped in jackets and overcoats like everyone else, collars hiked up against the wind.

One man in a suit stepped forward, his face red in the cold. "As you all know, Sam Steele wasn't a religious man, so I'm just here representing Mountain View Cemetery. But before his casket is lowered into the ground, would anyone like to say a few words?"

There was a short silence, and then the man motioned for the workers to approach. But before they could take hold of the straps, Jason gestured for them to stop.

"Look—" He cleared his throat. "Look, it's true that Sam wasn't the spiritual type. Hell—I mean, heck—I never heard him talk about God, though he did use his name in many colorful ways and phrases." He waited for the soft scattering of laughter to fade. "But he was a damn good man, regardless. He helped a lot of people, especially kids, and I appreciate the fact that some of those he coached in years past are here today. I wish there were even more, considering how many he helped. Sam was a good soul, even though he had no use for churches. And—and—I can't believe his soul is gone for good."

No one spoke, although there was some uncomfortable shifting from foot to foot among his listeners. Sam's crowd wasn't really one for metaphysics.

Jason raised his eyes to the threatening sky and threw up a defiant fist.

"Sam, you don't need to apologize for anything. You just … you just bust your way into heaven like you did every place down here. And I'll—see you again. Someday."

Silence fell again, and this time there was nothing to stop the workers from putting Sam in the ground. The Mountain View official made quick work of shaking the mourners' hands and beating a retreat to his climate-controlled office. Only Jason and Jess remained, both staring into the hole where the coffin lay.

Jess put an arm around him, nodding to the worker in the backhoe, who plainly wanted to get on with the job.

"Come on, Jason. I'll buy you a drink."

More familiar territory: a booth at the Blue Mountain Bar and Grill, an arm's reach from where Jason sat with Nate only a few months before.

"Wish you hadn't picked this place," muttered Jason. He didn't even glance at Danielle when she set down the drinks.

"Well, I have my reasons," answered Jess. "Besides, I'm buying. It's been a damn tough year for both of us, and I hear you've got some money trouble, on top of it all."

"Not unless you call being flat-ass broke money trouble."

Jess took a deep draw of beer. "Don't take this the wrong way, but didn't Sam have more millions than Carter has pills? You were the closest thing he had to a son. Aren't you getting everything?"

Jason gave a silent laugh. "That's what my worthle...piece of shit banker thought, too. Or hoped, at least. Sure—Sam was rich all right. Big time rich. But he left everything to the Boys and Girls Club. Sam being Sam, though, he put in a restriction that the money can only be used for the boys' programs."

"He gave 'em everything?" Jess choked. "Even his Knightbridge Estates stock?"

Jason sighed. "Even that. Shit. You know when he drew up his will, he thought I had more money than God. And you know how much he loved to help kids."

"I know that for sure," Jess said dryly. "Because I saw what he did for you. I remember he bought you that Camaro, as soon as you turned sixteen. I could never have done that for you. Not back then. And even if I could have, I don't think I would have."

He paused to take another sip. "Truth be told, I was a bit jealous of Sam."

That startled Jason out of his gloom. "You're kidding. You? Why? You had Nate—and Maria, the most loving woman I ever knew."

"That's right, I did. And a man had no right to expect a finer son or wife," Jess agreed. "But, remember, in those early years, after you ran off from your mama, I was like your second dad ..."

"And Maria was like my mom. We covered this."

Jess smiled then. "Yes. She was like your mama—for prett' near two years. And Nathan was the closest thing you ever had to a brother—until Sam drove up in that big white El Dorado convertible of his. Then you just kind of drifted away from us."

Giving a grunt, Jason said nothing. His shoulders slouched again.

"But Nate never let go," Jess added lightly.

Jason rapped his glass down. "That's right. You told me. He rooted for me from the sidelines and collected my memorabilia." He couldn't have this conversation again. He *wouldn't*.

"Maybe, Jess, we both just need to try to let go ... of everything. Damn," he chuckled ruefully, "in my case, I don't even need to try. The bank is going to take it all—my home, my place in Hawaii, my winery, my car, my future, my life. All gone. All over. It's time to totally let go."

"That bad, is it?"

"Uh-huh. It's sayonara time." He took another long pull on his Maker's. "Or make that more like hari kari time."

Jess shook his head. "There's always hope, Jason. You gotta keep going, keep trying. You gotta try to maintain a positive mental attitude."

"Oh, I've got a positive mental attitude. I'm positive that I'm totally fucked."

"Yeah—not exactly what I had in mind." Jess saw Danielle

look over to assess the state of their drinks, but he gave a small shake of his head to keep her away. "Did you know, Jason, that Bill Brojan went broke in the early eighties? Lost everything."

That got through. Jason looked up, curious. "You're shitting me, right? Brojan went TU? I don't believe it."

"Yessir. Lost everything, back when the interest rates were over twenty-percent. But then he played a bad hand like a riverboat gambler down to his last nickel. He outfoxed the bank because he figured out they needed him more than he needed them. You know, he's been a good friend of mine for years. I'm going to set up a powwow between you two."

Jason snorted. "Yeah. Maybe. Right now, I'm not sure I'm even sticking around here. Danielle!" he hollered for the barmaid, "More mother's milk. Wiki, wiki!"

But he thought of Jess's offer again some hours later, when he stood before his empty refrigerator in his empty kitchen, where even the echoes were gathering cobwebs and dust.

And he thought of it again when he pulled up at the winery and tore the auction notice from the doors, where Gus, the parasite, called for all interested bidders.

9

The squeal of tires tore the silence where the boy waited, kicking at the tufts of frost-glazed crabgrass bordering the highway. The rim of the sun just cleared the horizon, lighting a farm tractor as it lumbered toward him. But it wasn't any farm tractor making that sound, the sound of corners being taken at top speed and rubber fighting to grip the road.

From the rise where he stood, he saw a sports car swing into view. Rather than slow to take the curves, the driver hugged the outside of the lanes, accelerating out of the apex without regard for the dividing line. It almost looked like he was trying to slingshot off the guard rails, the right-side tires shooting up sprays of gravel from the shoulder.

"Shit," muttered the boy. Tightening his hood, he threw a glance at the tractor approaching and knew the sports car, closing rapidly, wouldn't see it until he crested the rise. He wasn't even sure the Ferrari driver would care if he did, the way he was coming. The boy backpedaled, anticipating the crunch of metal on metal and projectiles hurtling at him. He threw an arm up and leaped for the ditch, just as the sports car caromed around the last bend and rocketed toward its fate. There came another screech of rubber—through narrowed eyes, the boy saw the Ferrari swerve to miss the tractor and veer into the oncoming lane which was, thankfully, empty.

"Whoo-ee, that was close," breathed the boy again, pulling himself back up by the post of the guardrail.

The tractor driver was more eloquent in his relief, and when the sports car slowed up ahead and traced a deliberate U-turn, the farmer leaned out to meet it with a one-finger salute. "You stupid shit!" he roared. "Go back to Seattle with the rest of the rich pricks!"

Lowering his window, Jason Knightbridge returned the gesture.

He ground to a halt across the road and looked at the boy. "Get in."

The boy's head reared back. "Are you crazy? After what I just seen? You wanting some company for your suicide?"

"Hell. I drive like this all the time." He waved him over.

"That supposed to make me feel better?"

"You from around here?" Jason asked.

The teenager held up his arms in an all-encompassing gesture that took in his dark skin, his baggy clothes, and his smart-ass attitude. "Do I *look* like I'm from around here?"

Jason shrugged. "Well, you look like you're trying to get somewhere, so it's me or the next tractor. Get in. I'll keep it under a hundred."

The boy hesitated and then gave an answering shrug. "You do have a point. Guess I don't have much to lose." Crossing the two lanes that separated them, he gave Jason an appraising look before circling to the passenger side. He threw his backpack into the rear seat and climbed in, acting nonchalant but running his eyes over the leather interior. His covert inspection done, he thrust his chin at Jason. "You got a name, 'sides Stupid Shit?"

"You got any manners, besides those ones?" retorted Jason. He grinned and held out a hand. "Name's Jason. What's yours?"

"Daman." The boy pronounced it like *d'MAN*. "Any chance you can get me to the Tri-Cities without turning me into road kill on the way?"

In answer, Jason floored it, snapping them back against the head-rests.

"Guess not," said Daman.

"D'Man, huh? How do you spell that?"

"Just like it sounds: D-a-m-a-n. Daman."

"Shouldn't it just be pronounced Day-mon?"

Daman favored Jason with a supercilious look. "Not if you realize to whom you are speaking."

Jason's mouth twisted. Without a word, he hit the gas hard again, and Daman's hands instinctively clutched for the sides of his seat. Giving a silent chuckle, Jason headed for the Tri-Cities.

The kid ate like he hadn't been fed for weeks, his knife and fork almost a blur as he attacked the stack of pancakes. Jason shook his head, remembering the age. Like his legs were hollow, and all the food in the world couldn't fill him up. Maria had loved it, watching Jason and Nate scrape their plates clean and go back for more. Jess mock-complained that the boys' appetites would land them in the poorhouse, but Maria only laughed and made more.

"Obviously, wherever you've been must have been a diet clinic," Jason said, when Daman paused to deluge his plate with another wave of syrup.

"Yeah, something like that," he answered with his mouth full. "But more like a steady diet of bullshit."

"What were you doing anyhow, out in the middle of shit-kicker country? I'm not trying to be racist or anything, but you don't look like the poster farm boy."

Daman carefully swabbed up the last syrup and butter with his final bit of pancake. "Damn, you're quick."

"And you're a damned smart-ass."

"Thank."

"What do you mean, 'thank'? The word is thanks."

"Not where I'm from."

"And where's that?"

"Cabrini Green."

"Is that a golf course?"

The boy choked on his orange juice. "Shit, no! It's a project in Chicago, otherwise known as a ghetto."

"*Chicago!*" Jason echoed.

"Don't sound so surprised. You never heard of Chicago, neither? You ain't much good at geography, are you?"

"What the fu—what the hell are you doing way out here, where the men are men and the sheep are nervous?"

"Better not use the F word around me," Daman said mockingly, "it might offend my tender ears. Shit—where I'm from, you can't say 'mother' without it."

"You really are a smart ass."

"Smart, yes. Ass, no." His eyes fell to where Jason was tearing apart a sugar packet, and he whistled. "Look at the paws on you." Knocking away the packet, Daman flipped Jason's left hand palm-side up. "And lookie here, at them four finger joints. Only known one or two brothers with hands like that. You sure you ain't got no nigga blood in you?"

Jason yanked his hand away, from the contact more than the commentary, and nodded at the waitress. "Check!"

It was sunny outside, but cold enough to see their breath. They were walking the paved path along the Columbia, Jason wondering what he was going to do next with the kid or if he should just leave him here and get on with what was left of his life. As if reading his thoughts, Daman took off suddenly in a sprint across the grass.

"Hey, kid—where're you going?"

The boy kept running until he reached some shrubs. Bending down, he picked up a football half-hidden in the greenery. Striking a quarterback pose, he hollered, "Hope you can catch."

The pass caught Jason off guard, scything through the air to slip between his thrown-up hands and hit him hard in the chest before bouncing away.

"Guess not," was Daman's estimation.

"Shit, that hurt," griped Jason, rubbing the point of impact. "Where'd you learn to throw a football like that? I thought all you ghetto kids only played basketball."

"Nice to know you're not into stereotypes." Daman retrieved the football and passed it hand to hand, giving it a spin. "I can hoop it too. In fact, you might say I'm a natural-born athlete."

"Naturally modest too."

"Naturally. Hey, I saw a rock in the back seat of your car. How 'bout some one-on-one at that court over there? Cuz football, I'm guessing, 'tain't your sport."

Jason got some respect back on the court. He was taller than Daman, and the hands the boy remarked on could palm the rock like it was a softball. Faking left, Jason whirled and went up for a resounding, one-handed dunk.

"Shit! You white boys ain't supposed to be able to jump, especially at your advanced age. Now I knows you got black blood in those veins."

"I was All-State before you were born," responded Jason, trying not to breathe too hard.

Daman took the ball beyond the top of the key and started to dribble. "No shit? Well, that was a long time ago, Gramps. Try stoppin' this."

With a cross-over dribble, Daman blew by Jason for an easy lay-up. Grabbing the ball again, he gave it a spin on his finger before flipping it in the air and kicking it off the side of his foot at Jason. "*That's* what I'm talking 'bout!"

Not to be outdone, Jason seized the ball, backpedaling beyond the key, and then furiously charging the right side of the lane. He and Daman bumped each other, but Jason faded back and then went up effortlessly for a ten-foot jump shot that he swished.

"Shi-i-i-it," drawled Daman "I thought you said you played before I was born."

"That's right. And I was the leading scorer in the Walla Walla open league two years ago. We've got a few ex-Sonics that play in it."

"Sonics? Who they?" mocked Daman. "Ohhhh—you mean the Oklahoma City Sonics." He gave a derisive snort. "How the fuck did you lose an NBA team to Oklahoma?"

"It was that goddamned wuss Howard Schultz," snapped Jason. "He betrayed the whole state of Washington. Now shut up and play, so I can whip your ass."

"You goin' all the way to Seattle?" Daman asked, sometime later, when they were collapsed on a bench, sweating and steaming in the cold air.

Jason was especially wiped out, and it took him a moment to gather enough breath to answer. "What makes you think I'm from Seattle?"

"Well, you're obviously touchy about the Sonics, and you drive a car that costs more than most houses 'round here."

"How do you know how much a car like that costs?"

"I know a lot about Ferraris," said Daman, unfazed. "Your Ferrari is sweet, but I prefer the F430 body style. It was designed by Frank Stephenson, who also did the Ferrari 612 Scaglietti. And he redesigned both the Mini Cooper and the Maserati Quattroporte. Oh, and he did the BMW X5 too."

"Where did you learn all that shit?" said Jason, shaking his head.

"I read constantly, 'specially 'bout things I want. And I plan to buy a F430 when I sign my NBA contract."

Jason scoffed. "You've got as much chance of that as Seattle does of getting the Sonics back from those Okie sod-busters. But you dream big. Anyway, I'm not from Seattle. I live just outside of Walla Walla."

The boy didn't answer right away, his eyes fixed on the slow gray waters of the river slipping past. "Figures. No one that lives around here knows how to recognize someone with real athletic ability."

The memory of Sam Steele flicked through his mind, but Jason stuffed it back down. "You mean like you?" he said.

"Exactly." Daman gave the basketball another spin on his finger. "So if you're headed back to the twin Ws, you can just leave me right here. Never did like a town with a stutter for a name."

Jason hauled himself back to a sitting position. "I can't figure you out. Sometimes you talk ghetto, and sometimes you talk like you actually have a brain."

"You do know how to sweet talk, old man."

"So, how old are you?" Jason demanded.

"Fifteen. Almost sixteen."

"God! You're just a friggin' punk!"

"Who just schooled yo' ass," added Daman smugly.

"Don't give yourself too much credit," Jason rapped back. "I'm not in shape yet this season."

"Got that right. Noticed you coughin'. You do a lot of weed, or were you just stallin'?"

When Jason didn't rise to the taunting, Daman shot him a sidewise glance.

"You don't look too good, man. You pastier even than usual for white people. You okay?"

"Yeah," Jason managed, after another minute. "I'm okay. Just really tired, all of a sudden. I think I need a shower and a nap."

"A *nap*?" yelped Daman. "You still in kindiegarten? 'Sides, where you gonna do that? Walla Walla's at least forty-five minutes from here—though maybe with the way you drive it's more like half an hour—if you don't kill yourself."

Jason punched him lightly in the arm. "Haven't you ever heard of a hotel, genius boy?"

Daman sat up straighter. "Heard of 'em. Just ain't never stayed in 'em."

It was Jason's turn to stare. "You're almost sixteen and you've never stayed in a hotel?"

"You might say it's on my personal bucket list."

"Well, Da*man*, go out and buy yourself a lottery ticket because today's your lucky day. You get to experience Richland's answer to the Four Seasons."

"Dead Seasons, more like," muttered the boy, when they pulled into the parking lot of the Red Lion and he caught sight of the hotel's withered landscaping and misspelled reader board.

"What are you bitching about?" Jason razzed him. "This is a helluva lot better than sleeping in some cow shed, like you'd be doing if I didn't pick you up."

Unembarrassed, Daman shrugged. "Not bitchin', just sayin'."

"Reservations?" asked the woman at the front desk, without looking up.

"Hell, I always have reservations about staying at this dump."

With a sour smile, the clerk took his card and began to type in his information. "I can see you've stayed with us before, several times—always for one night."

"That's all I can take of this place. When was the last time you replaced the mattresses? When Jimmy Carter was president?"

She made a sound between a polite laugh and a growl and swiped Jason's card through the slot on her keyboard. "Oh, dear. It looks like there's a problem with your card. Let me try again." After the second swipe, her smile became genuine. "No, sorry ... your card is definitely being declined. Do you have another you'd like me to try?"

Jason glared at her. "That's impossible. That card's tied to my brokerage account at Merrill Lynch." The words were hardly out of his mouth before realization dawned on him, leaving him gray-faced. He slid another card from his wallet. "Here. Try this one. Two rooms. And this kid would like the presidential suite."

"You mean the one Jimmy Carter stayed in when he was here?" the clerk muttered, clicking away at her keyboard.

Jason was rallying. "If it was good enough for our first female president, it's good enough for him."

"Damn, checking in was a pleasant experience," drawled Daman. "I think I'll wait another sixteen years before I try it again."

Glancing at the room numbers on the doors they passed, Jason handed him a key card. "They have a strict rule at this place—they only hire people with shitty attitudes. It prepares the customers for their rooms." Stopping at a door halfway down the brown-carpeted hallway, Jason gestured at the room facing it. "Look—after I crash a while, we'll go to dinner." His eyes ran up and down Daman's bagging and sagging hoodwear, and he added, "Well, maybe after I crash a while and after we find you something else to wear, we'll go to dinner. Let me guess, you've never been out for fine dining, either?"

Daman shrugged, overlooking the comment on his clothes. "Plenty of times. I've washed dishes in some of Chicago's best establishments."

"Right." With a swipe of his key card, Jason opened the door to his room and disappeared inside.

For a moment Daman stood there. Throwing a glance up and down the hall, he swiped his own card and pushed on the door. It didn't budge. He tried again. And a third time, shooting a nervous look over his shoulder at Jason's door.

As if in response, Jason's door swung open. "Do I take it 'da man' can't open 'da door'?"

"I'll get it," grunted Daman. "You get on with your beauty sleep."

"And if you don't get it, were you planning on visiting our friend at the desk again?"

"Shit. I'll sleep outside before I ask that bitch for help."

"Uh-huh." Jason plucked the key from Daman's hand and ran it through the reader. Turning the handle, he pushed the door open and bowed to let the boy enter.

"Uh-huh," said Daman, pushing past. "If you're expecting a tip, forget about it."

There wasn't much selection in Daman's usual style at the mall, but after a series of wisecracks the boy seemed to resign himself. When they emerged, bags in hand, he looked almost preppy in his khakis and polo shirt.

Jason waited till he was behind the wheel of the Ferrari before regarding his passenger with raised eyebrows. "So, are you going to say anything, now that you've got a new wardrobe?"

Another comeback rose to the boy's lips, but he paused and left it unsaid.

"Thank."

"There you go again, with that 'thank' shit. Can't you say 'thanks,' even if you don't mean it?"

"Can. Just don't."

"And now we're back to hood speak. Great. Well, at least I guess you're bilingual, in a manner of speaking."

As if to prove Jason's point, Daman replied in clipped, buttery tones, "Actually, I'm fluent in Spanish. I learned it out here. Languages come naturally to me, as do most things."

Jason gave a snort. "Modesty sure as hell doesn't."

The boy abandoned his plummy voice. "Like Ali said, braggin' ain't braggin' if it's true."

"You know Ali, do you? Let me guess … you can float like a butterfly and sting like a bee."

"Got that right. But more like a scorpion."

Jason donned his sunglasses and fired up the engine. "Lovely."

The restaurant was one of several new ones that had sprung

up along the riverfront, and the table they were given commanded views of the city lights, such as they were, reflected on the dark water.

"Can I ask you a question?"

Daman didn't look up from his menu. "Guess."

"When I picked you up this morning in the middle of nowhere, and all you had was your backpack—you didn't even have a bike—how did you get there? Where were you going, and how did you expect to get there?"

Daman turned a page of the menu and scanned the new selections. "That's three questions."

"Okay, wise guy, answer one."

"Kindness of strangers. Like you." Daman's mouth twisted. "But you're one strange stranger."

"That's funny, coming from you. I've known a lot of kids your age in my life, but never one like you."

"Thank."

Jason shook his head but sat back to let the server deposit their beverages on the table.

"That's what you call a double?" he demanded, pointing at his cocktail. "Hell, it looks like scotch, not Maker's Mark."

Slipping her tray under her arm, the server made an apologetic grimace. "I'm sorry, Mr. Knightbridge. I told Tommy it was for you. He knows you like them strong."

Jason grunted and waved her away. "Never mind. Just don't charge me for a double."

"I'll be right back for your orders," she mumbled, making her escape.

Daman watched Jason take a swallow. "That ain't enough booze for you in one glass? You should meet my auntie." He pronounced it in his *Masterpiece Theatre* voice: ahhn-tie. "The two of you would hit it off great. 'Cept she hates white folks."

Jason made a face. "She probably lives off my tax dollars!"

Daman shrugged this off. "Doubt they're yours, but she does collect her checks."

"I'll bet!" He took another long pull and squinted at his companion. "You ever had a real job?"

It was Daman's turn to make a face. "I didn't wash no dishes as a volunteer. Yeah, I've had real jobs. Real bad jobs. That is, if you call bein' a slave a job."

"Come on," said Jason, "Where do you get that slave shit?"

"Shit is exactly what I done. Every shit job you can think of. In fact, I shoveled more shit than the mayor of Chicago does during one of his speeches."

"Where?" Jason pressed.

Daman didn't reply, and then the waitress rejoined them.

"I'll have a New York steak and a Caesar salad," said Jason.

"That any good?" asked Daman.

"No. I ordered it because it makes me puke," retorted Jason. "Of course it's good. Haven't you ever had a New York steak or a Caesar salad?"

"Where I come from," Daman pronounced, "you might say they were not part of the chef's repertoire."

"Make it two," Jason told the waitress. "I'll have mine medium, and he'll have his ..." Daman shrugged, "...the same."

When she was gone, silence fell. Jason took another hefty draw on his drink and stared at the boy. It was only when he lifted his glass again that he suddenly slammed it back down on the table, rattling the silverware and causing the diners at neighboring tables to start and look over.

"It just hit me," said Jason, ignoring them. "You ran away from Jubilee, didn't you?"

"Damn," breathed Daman in mock-wonderment, "you really are quick—for someone with senility."

"We've got to get you back."

"*We* ain't goin' back," Daman declared. "Course, you have my permission to go if you want to. But I'm done with all that Jesus shit."

Jason scowled at him. "Hey. The Brojans are great people,

and so are the Williams brothers. Didn't they save your ass from the streets? Where's your gratitude?"

"Yeah. The 'attitude of gratitude,' as they call it." Daman said mockingly, as he stirred the ice in his Coke. "Never did work for me. They were lucky to have *me*—won 'em a state championship in eight-man football."

Swallowing his retort, Jason took another gulp of his drink. Unappreciative little bastard. With his oversized ego. Couldn't see when good people were trying to dig him out of his shithole of a life.

The boy was picking through the bread basket and eyeing the little dish of olive oil with suspicion.

Jason turned his gaze out the window. It didn't matter, right? Whatever, man.

Not his problem.

Curiosity pricked at him, however. "Well, fine," he said. "I'm not going to force you." He grabbed a slice of the bread and squashed it in the olive oil. "But where are you planning on going?"

"Home."

"Home, as in Chicago?"

"There's that quickness of yours again," said Daman dryly. With a show of nonchalance, he dipped his own bread in the olive oil.

"Home and do what?" pressed Jason.

"Just live."

"Just live, huh?"

Jason let out a skeptical breath, his gaze flat.

"More like, just die."

10

It was roasting in his hotel room. The air was used and thick. He'd forgotten he cranked the heater to 80 before dinner. It didn't matter.

There were two queen beds in 212, covered in revolting quilted maroon bedspreads. On the one closer to the door sat Sam's old doctor's bag. Jason gave it a wide berth as he walked a bit unsteadily toward the window. En route, the second bed caught his knees, and he sat down hard on it. His reluctant gaze returned to Sam's bag.

The initials stenciled below the handles were faded but distinct: "SAS." After staring at them some moments, Jason leaned forward to trace them with his fingers. Then he unzipped the bag and opened it.

He remembered the ritual. He could see it play in his head: Sam at the Desert Inn, decades ago. The man knew his business. First Jason brought out the bottle of Maker's Mark, this one about a third full. Then came the Cohibas. A carton of Camel cigarettes. Sam's 101st Airborne lighter.

And the German Luger.

Jason studied them all, laid out on the coverlet, but it was the Luger which finally held his gaze.

Sam never thought he'd go out the way he did. Not with a bang, but a whimper. But how many people got to choose how they went out?

Only those who made their decision before the decisions were made for them.

Sam had kept his Luger clean and polished, and the dull metal still gleamed along the narrow barrel, the curling trigger. Jason had never seen him fire it.

There was a vibration in his pocket and a sound growing audible. Fishing his phone out, Jason saw Jess Carson's name on the display.

Not a chance.

But he held on to the phone while the call went to voicemail, his gaze distracted from the gloss of the Luger.

Jess Carson. It was like the man had telepathy.

With a grimace, Jason punched some buttons on the phone to replay the message.

"Ah—uh—Jason," came Jess haltingly over the speaker. "Damn, I hate these things … always feel awkward. Anyway, Jason, I'm worried about you, especially after what you said at the bar last night. Been trying to reach you all day. Nobody seems to know where you are … not even Marcie. Call me, okay? I mean, call me before you do anything—anything, you know, stupid."

The older man's voice cracked. "I don't want to lose another son."

Jason stiffened sharply, the phone falling through his startled fingers. Before it hit the carpet, it began to ring again. "Jess," he growled, bending to retrieve it, "you are one persistent son of a bitch."

He took the call.

"Hello, Mother. Have I missed curfew?"

"Thank God! Jason—where the hell have you been? I was at my wits' end trying to reach you."

"No kidding. You left more messages than a drug dealer looking for a score. Well, you found me, Jess. And I'm fine. Was that what you wanted to know?"

"Eh … just wanted to hear your voice," answered Jess.

"That's what I thought." Jason stood and flipped the bedspread over Sam's bag and its contents, as if to hide them from Jess's inspection. "Anyway, look, old man—I want to reach one of the Williams brothers out at Jubilee. I picked up a runaway kid from there this morning."

He hadn't known—until he heard himself saying the words to Jess—that he intended to do anything with Daman. If someone had pressed him, Jason would have said he changed the subject just to throw old Jess off the scent. Which he had, but there was more to it. A curiosity about the bragging tough guy he'd picked up. An awareness that Daman's disaster of a life had the power to distract him, if only momentarily, from the disaster of his own.

"Where'd you get that ugly thing?" the boy heckled him as Jason placed Sam's bag in the trunk of the Ferrari the next morning. It was cold, almost below-zero cold, and the sports car was glazed with frost like a sleek, oversized ice cube.

"That bag so old and ugly, no wonder you didn't walk in with it," Daman cracked. "Think a man like you could afford a new one."

Jason grinned. "Spent every last penny on the car. Come on—or is your backpack too good to be seen with my bag?"

"That's right. You got a bag that ugly, I be sure to keep my own stuff close," said Daman, opening the right side door and throwing his backpack on the floorboard in front of his seat. Then he ducked down to squeeze inside the low-slung car.

Jason hit the button on the key fob and watched the trunk lid lower. When it was closed, he pressed a hand on it, his smile fading. As if the thoughts closed in the black bag might spring out again. But the trunk was shut, the bag put away, the thoughts put away.

"Where we off to, today?" asked Daman, settling back in

his seat. "How 'bout heading east in the direction of the Windy City?"

"I wasn't planning on going quite that far," said Jason. "How about east on George Washington Way, for starters? We might get as far as Spokane. At least that's on I-90, and from there it's a straight shot to your beloved promised land of pimps and pushers."

Daman gave a shrug. "Spokane. Man, you sure you don't want to take a few days and go see one of America's most beautiful cities? Course, I could never guarantee your safety, if you drove into my 'hood in this ride."

Jason took the 182 ramp east and flipped his visor down against the glare. "Chicago in winter ... a blizzard slamming in from the lake ... the wind gently rustling, at about forty miles per hour, through the canyons of the ghettos. Yeah—that sounds irresistible, all right. Like I said, Spokane. You can use your innate sense of direction, not to mention bullshit, to get back to your war zone from there."

But at the junction of 395, Jason ignored the road sign reading, "Spokane, one hundred twenty-eight miles." Instead he took the right branch: Walla Walla, fifty-seven miles. The boy was dozing, so no explanations were needed.

It wasn't until they slowed and bumped off the highway onto a gravel road that Daman woke up, popping up in his seat and nearly smacking his head on the roof. He took a swift look right and left, and his face darkened in anger. They passed under the arch that read, "Welcome to the Jubilee Youth Ranch!"

"Goddamn you, Jason!"

"Don't you worry," Jason soothed. "He's working on it."

The boy's teeth were clenched. "You son of a bitch."

At this Jason laughed. "You didn't tell me you knew my mom!"

By the time the Ferrari pulled up outside the administration building, Rich and Alvin Williams, the Brojans, Jess, and an older black couple were already gathered outside.

"Quite the welcome committee for a spoiled punk like you," commented Jason. But Daman didn't respond, sinking lower in the seat and glowering.

The black woman, dabbing away her tears, started toward the car before they had even stopped, but Alvin got there first and flung open the passenger door. "Nice of you to return, young man."

"'Tweren't my idea," muttered Daman, with none of his usual mouthiness. From the perspective of the low-slung seat, Alvin Williams looked like a giant sequoia.

"No doubt," answered Alvin.

Rich Williams extended a hand to Jason as he climbed out. "Jason, we're all extremely grateful to you for bringing Daman back." (There was no "d'MAN" pronunciation for him, Jason noted with amusement.) "We were very worried about him. No boy has ever been gone for even one night, much less two. They try to leave, but they always come back in a few hours."

"Okay, then." Jason shrugged off the thanks uncomfortably. "Damn, it's cold! Mind if we go inside?"

Next thing he knew, Jess had an arm around him and they were walking with the Brojans toward the building. The older woman managed to get her tearful hug in before Alvin took Daman by the arm to walk him back to the dorm. They couldn't catch the words from where they stood, but the wagging finger and bursts of steamy breath issuing dragon-like from the Jubilee athletic director said enough.

"He's not going to kill him or anything, is he?" Jason wondered aloud.

Rich laughed and held the door open. "No, no. And I should know—Alvin's always been twice my size and threw his weight around plenty, growing up. He won't hurt him. But Daman's in for a few interesting weeks."

Compared to the frigid temperatures outside, the spartan Jubilee conference room with its Styrofoam cups of coffee felt balmy.

"I gotta be honest with you," Jason was saying, "when I pulled up with that kid, and all of you were standing there, and Alvin was acting like a marine drill sergeant getting an AWOL grunt back, I felt like a snitch."

Rich smiled into his coffee. "I understand. Totally. But Jason, if you hadn't intercepted him, there's a good chance he'd be on a bus right now, heading back to Chicago. When that young man sets his mind on something, the odds are he's going to attain his goal."

"Well, his family is in Chicago, right? Isn't it natural that he would want to go back? It sounds like he's been out here a while."

"Natural, yes, but also exceedingly dangerous." Jubilee's executive director emptied another packet of creamer into his cup. "Have you ever heard of Cabrini Green?"

"Only from him. It sounds tough."

"It's way beyond tough. The reality is, his odds of survival would be better if he was over in Iraq. We've actually had a number of former students sent to the Middle East, and praise God, we haven't lost one yet. Tragically, though, we've lost several young men who have gone back to Cabrini. In fact, the reason Daman felt so compelled to return right now is that one of his best friends, who was a student here last year, was just gunned down back there. The reality is, if they go home, especially to Cabrini, without finishing our program, we almost never see them again."

"So, you see, Jason," put in Jess, "you did a fine thing."

"Yes, Jason, you really did," added Bill Brojan in his soft voice. "Daman is a special young man, and we care about him very much."

Jason coughed on his swallow of bitter coffee. "That right? What's so special about him, other than that he's got an ego the size of Obama's?" He made an apologetic grimace at Rich. "I mean ... well, I didn't mean any offense."

"Jason, you know a thing or two about big egos, don't you?" Jess said, chuckling.

Jason only spared him a disapproving glance before turning to Rich again. "I noticed you guys call him Day-mon. He calls himself 'D'Man.'"

"That's our young man—or should I say, that's D'Man?" joked Rich. "He tried to use that for the first few days he was here, but between the other boys and Alvin, he got over that pretense in a hurry."

Jubilee's executive director leaned forward with sudden intensity. "Jason, we've had hundreds of at-risk young men through here over the last twelve years since Bill and Sue started Jubilee, but I can honestly say that we've never had one quite like Daman. As large as his ego is, or at least as large as he pretends it is, it's still not equal to his God-given athletic and academic abilities. His last name is Jordan, and apparently he's related to another Jordan, first name Michael. Daman can truly do it all, both physically and mentally—when he wants to."

"Reminds me of a young man I knew some thirty years ago," said Jess with a grin, getting up to refill his cup.

Rich nudged Jason. "Care to take a walk?"

The sun was breaking through at last, but it hadn't had a chance yet to warm the hills. Rich and Jason crunched through the thin crust of ice and snow, heading toward a small ridge, just as rays of light turned the slopes around them a radiant white.

"Shit!" yelled Jason, stopping and raising his right foot to inspect the underside in disgust.

"Yes, I'd say that's an accurate description," Rich answered, smothering a laugh. "Sorry. As you know, we have a number of farm animals around here, and they do wander."

Scraping his shoe against some frozen sagebrush, Jason only growled, "Lately it seems like shit is the story of my life."

His companion nodded, squinting in the morning light. "Well, you know what Martin Luther said," Rich replied. "That we were all just snow-covered dung."

Jason paused in his scraping. "You mean Martin Luther King?"

Then Rich did laugh. "No. I mean Martin Luther. As in Lutherans."

"Oh. *That* Martin Luther."

They moved on, arriving at the top of the ridge, where Rich brushed snow off a sign: "The Dick and Melissa Ray Driving Range."

"This is the reason I brought you up here," said Rich, "braving all those cow pies. To show you this range."

"Uh-huh. I remember it from when we did the tour last summer. When Johnny Miller was here."

Rich nodded. "One of our supporters donated money to build this driving range, but what we don't have is someone to teach our young men golf. As you may remember, that swale there is a bunker, and the range itself runs all the way up to that far hill over there. My dad Alvin Sr. mows and fertilizes it regularly. And Alvin Jr. tries to teach the boys. He loves the game, but—well—you've seen him play."

Jason squinted out over the range. "Yeah, that can't be a pretty sight—despite his best intentions."

"So, knowing that you're one of the best golfers in the valley," Rich said slowly, "would you be willing to work with the boys? Nate always thought you'd be great at it."

Wincing as he always did when he heard Nate's name, Jason turned away. He ran unseeing eyes over the glittering grounds while Rich waited him out.

"Let me think about it."

He cleared his throat and started back the way they came. "Right now, I'm not sure if I'm even staying around here."

The sunbreak was brief, and the snow came hard that evening. It was falling nearly sideways by the time the gates to Jason's home swung open, leading to the unplowed driveway and the darkened house. Backing the car up, he gunned it, trying to gain enough momentum to take the long incline, but he only got about halfway before the Ferrari veered off the drive into a snowbank. From there the wheels spun furiously, and there was no going forward. Putting it in reverse again only sent him fishtailing down the hill until he finally slid off the pavement into the bushes lining the driveway.

Clutching the garage-door opener, Jason clambered out the passenger side, slammed the door, and tried to vault over the hedges, only to slip as he landed, falling on his butt. The remote flew out of his hand and disappeared God-knew-where in the darkness.

"Another fucking day in paradise!" he roared.

Slogging his way to the front step proved futile because he couldn't find his house key. Maybe he'd left the back patio doors unlocked? The Ferrari headlights provided the only illumination on the property as Jason made his fumbling way around the back, stumbling over hidden steps and a hose.

The water in the undrained pool had frozen and lay blanketed in snow, but the deck was completely barren of furniture or ornament.

The French patio doors were locked. Cursing again, he groped in one of the planter boxes for a rock and then hurled it, shattering one of the panes so he could reach inside for the handle. Heedless of the mess he'd created, he flipped on the kitchen lights and punched in the code to shut down the alarm. His eyes blinked to adjust, not just to the light but also to the realization that the place was empty as a tomb. No people of course, but now no furniture. Just him.

The doorbell rang.

Jason whirled around, his heart lurching. "Shit! It's probably that prick Gaylord," he hissed, sardonically drawing out the sergeant's name. "Now he wants to bust me for breaking into my own house."

Peering surreptitiously through one of the sidelights that flanked the grand front door, he heaved a sigh of relief. Standing on the step was Jess Carson.

"Jesus," groaned Jason, throwing the door open.

"Saw your car stuck and thought you might need some help." He wiped his feet carefully on the mat before entering.

"Right," said Jason. "You just happened by, I suppose, even though this is about five miles out of your way."

Unruffled, Jess peeled off his coat. There was nothing to hang it on and no sofa to drape it over. He hooked it on the door handle. "Yeah. Sometimes I take this route, especially when it's snowing. Less hilly."

"That so." Jason headed back for the kitchen. "Look, Jess—I might be broke, but I'm not helpless."

"Lordie me," breathed Jess, taking in the vacant rooms and the echo of their voices. "Your friendly banker sure didn't waste any time taking his pound of flesh, did he? Does the whole place look like this?"

"Guess so. I haven't been here in a few days."

Jess shook his head. "It's about as comfortable as a cave in here. You know, you can stay with me."

"Thanks, but—"

"Where you gonna sleep?" Jess interrupted. "On the dog bed?"

Jason gave a short laugh. "Hell, Sarah took that when she left with J.J. and Ringo."

"Then that settles it. Mi casa is now su casa. At least until you get back on your feet. I'll call my buddy and get your car towed to my house."

For a moment, it looked like Jason might argue, but then his shoulders slumped. "Thanks. I sure as hell don't want that goddamned Gus to get my last remaining asset. No matter what, my Italian stallion isn't falling into his clutches."

Several hours later, he lay in the same twin bed that was his when he lived with the Carsons thirty years earlier. The same twin bed, separated by a nightstand from the other twin bed in the room.

Nate's old bed. With Sam's black doctor's bag sitting atop it.

The ancient clock radio on the nightstand had the flip numbers: 3:09. Jason stared up at the popcorn ceiling. He'd given up waiting for the sleep that wasn't going to come.

Sitting up, he threw back the covers and flipped on the light.

God, had this place always been such a *shrine*? Pictures of Nate crowded the dresser, from his babyhood through his grade school years. Jason recognized Maria's looping handwriting on one, where a chubby-cheeked Nate grinned like a fool: "First day of kindergarten!" Then came the wall gallery. With a start, Jason noted his own appearance in a photograph of a pre-adolescent Nate with braces. Eighth-grade Jason's arm was in a cast and Nate was signing it. Matter of fact, they were together in all the sports pictures, from that point on. Baseball, basketball, baseball, basketball. One on the golf course. And then standing in their high school graduation gowns, holding up their diplomas, with Jess and Maria beside them, beaming.

Zombie-like, Jason followed the storyline around the walls of the room, his chest feeling tight. He and Nate working at Sam's winery. Tractors and cherry-pickers and Jason pointing where to go. College graduation. Jason's wedding, with Nate at his shoulder, his smile fixed. Nate's own wedding to Mary. Nate and Mary's kids. Nate's *Wine Spectator* cover, the one he never thought he would get.

With blurring vision, Jason sat heavily on Nate's bed, his heel thumping against something underneath as he leaned to shove Sam's bag away. When he flipped up the bedding, he found several cardboard boxes labeled "Jason."

Not his stuff. These must contain Nate's rumored memorabilia collection.

Jason took a few ragged breaths. He wasn't going to look in them—what was the point? To be reminded that the closest thing he'd had to a brother, the guy who always had his back, was a great guy? The hell with that.

But after another minute, he reached down and dragged out the first box.

Sure enough—photos and newspaper articles recording Jason's sporting triumphs, some with Nate beside him, some not. Jason only made it through the top layer before he hurled the contents back in and kicked the box back under the bed.

His throat closed, robbing the dry sobs that racked him of sound. Everywhere he turned he saw the Carsons: Jess, Maria, Nate. The ones who saved his life. The ones who took him in. The ones who gave him the only real home and family he had ever had.

The ones he turned his back on and forgot about, when Sam Steele came calling.

Jesus. Look where it all got Sam.

Look where it all got *him*.

Why hadn't he stayed in touch more, after he took off with Sam? Why had he never realized he let them down? Why had he never noticed that, though he abandoned them, they always kept an eye on him?

The Carsons.

Well. Maria was gone, years ago. And now Nate. Only Jess was left.

Once again, he unzipped Sam's bag and laid out the items in their ritual sequence and placement, though his hands shook and the Luger clattered to the floor before Jason replaced it.

He, Jason Knightbridge, ex-millionaire, ex-award-winning winemaker, ex-husband and father—ex-everything. He was a fucking failure. Forty-four years old and nothing to show for his life but wreckage. God, it wasn't just his abandonment of the Carsons! His blindness to their love. Look at all the pain he caused Sarah. Look what a terrible dad he was to J.J. Look at all the jobs lost at the winery. Everything, every*one* in his life broken, lost, destroyed by his own hands. Suddenly, the worst thought he could imagine hit him: His mother was right, after all; that was the clincher.

"Well, Sam," said Jason quietly to the listening silence, "you used your cigs, ceegars, and Maker's Mark to kill yourself. You just did it slowly, I guess. But you always said I was the fastest learner you ever met. Guess that applies to what I'm going to do next too. What'd Daman say? 'Braggin' ain't braggin' if it's true.'"

Digging in the bag, he pulled out the pistol's ammo clip and slid it into the gun. Yes, Sam took good care of the Luger. Slide and click, as if it had just been loaded and fired the day before.

He took another rough breath. Slow and deep, to settle himself.

Then he put the barrel to his temple, shutting his eyes. He felt the sweat bead on his forehead. His shaking finger began to tighten.

An eternity later, his arm sagged. He lowered the gun. All he could see was Jess storming into the room after the Luger went off, to find Jason's brains and blood splattered all over the walls and bed, like a scene in a Tarantino movie.

He couldn't do that to him. Add that final trauma and mess, after all he had already done to him and all Jess had already been through.

He just couldn't.

Gently, he unloaded the weapon and replaced it in the bag.

Then he took up his car keys from the nightstand and headed out.

The snow had stopped, but there were several inches on the ground. Jason had to ease the Ferrari down the driveway. It slipped more than once, but by the time he reached the highway and the tires could grip older tracks, he gunned it. The car fishtailed, but Jason regained control, coaxing it under his breath. Then, his lips pressed together in a humorless smile, he opened it up.

Jess Carson's eyes snapped open when he heard the creak and click of the front door. Bolting up, he threw on his jeans and jacket and reached for his hat. He barely glanced in Nate's old room, knowing it would be empty, before grabbing his ancient cell phone from the kitchen counter and making for the garage.

His GMC King Cab roared to life and barreled down the driveway onto the road. Uttering a prayer, he slammed the pedal to the floor, sending a burst of snow up from the rear tires.

He'd had smoother rides, Jason thought as he glanced at the speedometer. Eighty. The car bounced and jolted and slid over the rutted snow of the highway.

Eighty-five.

Ninety.

A curve lay ahead. His mouth tightened. He smashed the accelerator as hard as he could.

He took his hands off the wheel.

Squinting, Jess approached the bend in the highway. It hadn't been hard to pick out the Ferrari's tracks—the newest on the road. No one else was out on a night like this. But at the curve he saw the tracks heading straight, straight off the road. Jess hit the brakes, the GMC slipping sideways as he did so, almost going off the edge into the ditch. When he got it stopped, he backed up, angling the headlights to shine onto Jason's tracks. About a hundred yards further ahead he could just make out Jason's car, its lights still on.

It was upside down.

Jess began to run, stumbling and skidding in the snow while he scrabbled in his jacket for his phone.

"Hello? Hello! There's been a terrible accident just off Highway One Twenty-Five by milepost twenty-eight. Send help right away!"

The Ferrari's airbags were deployed, the doors thrown open.

Bracing himself, Jess bent down to peer inside. No one.

Spinning in a frantic circle, Jess could see nothing outside the beams of the headlights, and he was forced to blunder back to the truck for his flashlight. He tried to be systematic, swinging the beam right and left, but in his unsteady hand the light swooped and zigzagged, and more than once he dropped it.

Finally, after what seemed like hours, the beam caught the foot and leg of a man off to the left. With numb fingers, Jess turned the full ray upon a crumpled body in the snow. Jason lay facedown in a bank.

"No," said Jess. "No, no, no. Come on, buddy." Gingerly, gingerly Jess turned him over.

Jason's face was covered in blood.

"Oh, no you don't," muttered Jess, putting his ear to Jason's chest.

Nothing.

He put his fingers against his throat.

Still nothing.

With hot tears streaking down his face, Jess began CPR.

"Damn you, Jason!" he shouted, counting the pumps to his chest. "How many times are you going to make me do this?"

11

It was like someone hit the play button on a DVD after a long delay.

Jason found himself right back where he had been thirty years earlier. He stood, if it could be called that, *somewhere*. A spinning light filled his vision, enveloped him as it rotated. How long this went on, he didn't know. Then it began to recede. Darkness appeared, first at the edges of the no-place place, then rushing in to fill the void left by the departing light. And Jason found himself in motion—withdrawing—without moving a muscle. But he was going the wrong direction—retreating from the light, even as it retreated from him.

Then the darkness was everywhere.

It was everything.

He stopped.

Fear prickled. And then, overwhelming the fear, came a sense of loss. The spinning radiance had not only kept darkness at bay; it had comforted him. And now it was gone.

Before he could grapple with this, he was in motion again. He felt himself falling, *hurtling*, as if he had been shoved from a fighter plane into a vortex. Wind tore at him. Black winds sucked him down, and the earth sped to meet him. There was no more time to ponder loss, not when awareness washed over him. He was being separated—forever—from the place he wanted to be. And the place he was spiraling toward—

The blackness gave way to a low, lurid, reddish glow. There was something below him. A swamp of brown muck, touched by the red, seething and swelling in response to unseen forces. As he fell headlong, ever closer, he heard indescribable noises emanate from its depths, pitched so low the sounds hit him like blows to the chest. From the rolling murk, horrible things—could they be appendages? grasping tree limbs?—stabbed upward, reaching for him.

Panic reigned. He opened his mouth to scream, but no sound could be heard above the pounding, wordless writhing of what lay below. He could do nothing. Nothing to slow his descent, nothing to cry for help. He would be swallowed by the limitless pit of swelling horror and never struggle back to the surface, never emerge again.

He was utterly—totally—helpless.

A brush of something.

Something flew past him in the storm. He forced his burning eyes after it, but he could discern nothing in the gloom.

Then he was caught. Lifted up. Streaking skyward twice as fast as he had been falling. A faint tear appeared in the utter blackness. He was breathing so rapidly he thought his heart would explode. The tear widened, widened, like a seam ripping open. Before it the darkness fled, withdrawing again to the margins.

In flowed life. Richness. Beauty.

Still panting for breath, he looked below him at the tapestry unfolding. In the grasp of his fingers he felt warmth and solid, rippling strength—a wing. He was not afraid to run his hand up and over and around the creature because fear no longer held sway here. When he realized it was a head he caressed, he lowered himself against it like a jockey gathering close to the neck of his horse.

He was not alone.

He had a rescuer. A companion.
But who was it?

"Well, hello there. Nice to have you back among the living."

A doctor stood over Jason, pulling up his right eyelid and shining his exam light into it.

Jason's first attempt to speak emerged as a groan. He tried to raise his head and found it was heavy with bandages.

"Wh—where am I?" he croaked.

"You're in the ICU at Walla Walla General, where you've been for the last ten days—ever since your car accident. I'm Dr. Wright."

Jason swallowed with effort. "Accident?"

"Yes. You don't remember what happened?"

When Jason went to gesture with his arm, he found it was in a cast. As was the other arm. And one of his legs. Jesus.

Sensation rushed in, and he realized every part of him ached. Even his mouth felt dry and heavy and his throat sore. But he would worry about this later. The pain, his condition, what the hell was happening—this didn't matter. Not right now. He had to tell someone—this Dr. Wright—

"I remember a lot of things," said Jason. His voice was thick but very deliberate. "But nothing about an accident."

"Really?" asked the doctor. "What kinds of things do you remember? Whoa," he added, seeing Jason wince as he tried to clear his throat and cough. "You'd better not try to say too much. You've had tubes down your trachea until this morning."

That would explain it. Shaking his bandaged head, Jason persisted. "But I want to tell you where I've been and what I've seen. This is the second time I've been there."

The doctor looked faintly amused. "And where is that? To death's door?"

Jason's mouth tightened at the man's skeptical tone. He studied the doctor's face for a minute and then slumped back against his pillow, letting his hand fall to his side. The heart monitor, which had been beeping more rapidly with his excitement, subsided into a sullen rhythm. This Dr. Wright was not a man you imparted mysteries to.

"Like you said, Doc—maybe I better not talk too much."

"Right, then." The doctor was all business now. "There's something I need to tell you, Mr. Knightbridge. Among your many injuries was a collapsed left lung. When we x-rayed that area, we saw a large mass."

"I know about it," Jason interrupted absently.

Dr. Wright didn't appear to notice his patient's lack of interest. "I thought you might. I bet you've been having some symptoms from that for some time. I wanted to let you know that, even though I wasn't planning on it, while we were in there, we removed it. You're lucky I'm a thoracic surgeon."

That reclaimed Jason's attention. "Really? So—do you mean I don't have lung cancer anymore?"

"It's not quite that simple. Based on how highly developed the tumor was, there's a good chance—in fact, I'd say a probability—that it has already metastasized. You need to see an oncologist right away."

This guy might be a skilled thoracic surgeon, but he wasn't winning any awards for bedside manner, Jason thought. Aloud he only said, "Okay."

"You really have been here before." remarked the doctor, brows raised. "You don't seem too concerned by the news."

Jason gave a humorless laugh, which broke off when another stab of pain went through him. "Look, Doc, if I tried to tell you why, you wouldn't believe me."

The nurse at the desk glanced up, checked her watch, and smiled. "Welcome back, Mr. Carson. You're like Old Faithful. And you're in luck this time—he's awake."

"Good morning to you, Nora," answered Jess. He pointed to his companion. "Got a friend with me this morning."

"Nice to meet you, Mr. Carson's friend. You two go right in."

Jason was sitting up in bed, reading. He must have been at a good part because it took him a second to insert his finger in the book and look up. The bandages had been removed from his head by this time, and his whole face lit in a smile. "J.J.! It's great to see you, son!"

The boy stayed by Jess's side, looking down. "Hi, Dad. How are you feeling?"

"Better. Loads better. I mean, I'm still in some pain, and if it weren't for my meds I'd be in deep sh—I'd be in misery. But every day is better."

Nodding, J.J. kept his eyes on the floor.

Jess squeezed the boy's shoulders. "Well, Jason, the doc told me they're getting ready to release you. Got my house all spiffied up in welcome. You're coming home."

It was Jason's turn to look away. "Yeah, I'm not sure that's such a good idea. It brings back too many memories."

"I know what you mean, Jason," said Jess, flapping his cowboy hat against his thigh. "I know what you mean. Every time I walk through those hallways, I hear Nate laughing or Maria singing. She used to sing every time she cooked a meal."

"Uh-huh. I know." He set his book on the side table. "How do you live there ... without going crazy?"

Jess sighed. "I focus on the good memories. Plenty of 'em, that's for sure." Releasing J.J., he dug in his pocket for some change. "Here, J.J. Why'n't you go get some of those chips you like out of the vending machine?"

When the boy dashed off, too glad to escape, Jess drew closer to the bed. "And when we've got you home and all set up, there's a—a story I've been meaning to tell you."

Jason thought about protesting some more, but he didn't have the energy. There was always going to be his history with the Carsons—his mishandled, unappreciated history—but he couldn't change it, and Jess didn't seem to be asking him to.

Nope. Jess was just being Jess. Solid, hopeful, persistent.

"A story, huh?" Jason answered at last.

Jess broke into a grin, knowing he'd gotten his way. "That's right. A story."

"Well," said Jason, "as a matter of fact, there's a story I need to tell you, too."

It was when Jason had been "home" for a couple days that Jess took up the thread again. Jason was propped up on the couch with pillows behind him and blankets over him, reading the same book he had in the hospital while Jess cooked dinner.

"Looks like you're almost done with that thing," remarked Jess, pointing with the wooden spoon he held. "When I gave it to you, I didn't know you'd like it that much."

"It's actually my second time through. I like it all right." Shutting the book, he frowned at the author's picture on the back cover. "What I can't figure out is why you gave it to me."

Sighing, Jess lay the spoon on a dish and turned down the burner. He gave the fire a few pokes and then took the armchair closest to Jason, drawing it closer.

"Well, to answer that, I have to tell you the story I mentioned to you, just before they released you from the hospital. In fact, it's really two stories." Seeing he had Jason's attention, Jess gave his chin a thoughtful rub and went on. "Where do I start? I guess it's best to go back to the very beginning ..."

He blew out a breath while Jason waited, watching him quizzically. Then he cleared his throat. Rubbed his hands on his jeans.

"Come on, old man," prodded Jason, only half-teasing. "Out with it. 'Back to the beginning ...'"

Jess grunted. "By that I mean, back to the first time you almost died—at the river. You remember that, of course."

"Of course. Not the kind of thing a guy forgets," answered Jason.

He didn't look nearly surprised as Jess thought he would,

considering neither one of them had mentioned what happened at the river in decades.

"Not that I thought about that day a lot at the time," Jason qualified, "but I sure have lately. More times lately than in the past thirty years." He sat up straighter against his cushions, as if preparing himself. "Go on."

"Well ... you and I never talked about that incident after it happened," said Jess.

"Ungrateful little bastard that I was," put in Jason. "Save my life and you don't even get a thank-you note."

But Jess shook his head. That wasn't what he meant. "No—you were a kid. No point in making you think about an experience like that more than you had to. I never forgot any of it, naturally—traumatic experiences are like that—but there was something that stood out in particular."

Jason waited as long as he could and then prompted, "Really? What?"

Turning a level gaze on him, Jess said, "It was the tune you were humming right after I revived you."

Disappointed, Jason made a face. "That's it? A tune? I don't get it."

"Now, hold on a sec—it wasn't just any tune. It was one so lovely, so beyond anything words can do justice to—" Shutting his eyes for a moment, Jess seemed to be searching for the notes in his head. "I'd never heard it before or since. Couldn't hum it to you—nothing. But even after all that time, I knew it the second I heard it again. That first day I saw you in the hospital after the car wreck, when you were waking up."

"You heard the tune again at the hospital?"

"You could say that." The leather armchair creaked as Jess leaned forward. "You could say I heard the tune again. Because you were humming it."

With a *hunh*, Jason sank back, his face getting a faraway look as he stared over Jess's shoulder. Odd how he didn't look surprised at this revelation either.

"You know," he said slowly, "funny you should mention it. There *was* something where I was. I mean, I've tried to come up with that ever since I came to. I can hear this melody in my head, but I can't sound it out."

"You sure were sounding it out the other day," said Jess. "And I don't know how I recognized it, but I did. That wasn't all to my story, though. Way back when, that day at the river after you almost drowned and we got you out of there—once you got done choking, you were all excited. Coughing and babbling. You started telling me about a place you had seen when you were in the water passed out. A place that was so warm and wonderful that you didn't want to leave."

Jason's intake of breath was sharp, and he clutched at Jess's wrist. The book slid unheeded to the floor. "That's—Jess—that's where I just was—again. That place. But something was different this time."

"I thought maybe." He covered Jason's hand with his own rough one. "What was different this time, son?"

"I thought—I knew I wasn't going to be allowed to stay there. I met someone who explained everything to me. She was beautiful and ... familiar. I was sure I knew her even though I couldn't remember how I knew her. She told me I needed to go back. That I had things I needed to do." Frowning, he lay his head back against the pillows and stared up at the ceiling. "I've been racking my brain trying to figure out who she was."

For a few minutes, they both were silent, and only the crackling of the fire could be heard. But then, on pretense of adjusting his position on the couch again, Jason pulled his hand away and gave one of the pillows a few punches before tucking it behind him.

"You said you had two stories to tell me?"

Jess nodded. "Uh-huh. I do." He drummed his fingers on his knee. "The other one has to do with Nathan. Now, hang on and listen to me," he ordered, when Jason grimaced. "After he passed, it took me weeks before I could muster up the strength to go back to work. But as you know, he crossed over right before harvest, so I had no choice. I couldn't let all that wheat just rot in the fields. And the first day I was back on my combine, it happened."

"*What* happened?" Jason's voice was low. He didn't take his eyes off Jess.

"Well, with no warning whatsoever, a feeling came over me—a feeling that was more powerful than anything I've ever experienced in my long life. It was like Nathan was right next to me in the cab. I mean, I couldn't see him, but there's not a shred of doubt in my mind that he was beside me. It wasn't some kind of ghost or apparition. It was *him*. He told me how happy he was and not to worry. He'd see me again soon. I couldn't even tell you if his voice was audible. I just know he was talking to me, and I was listening. And he told me—to take care of you."

One of the logs in the fireplace gave a loud crack, throwing a glowing ember onto the carpet. Jess popped up to sweep it back onto the brick, and he tugged the mesh curtain closed. Resting an arm on the mantel, he watched the flames thoughtfully. "Since that day, I've done a lot of studying of near-death experiences. Even though I've been a believer since I was a little tyke, I have to say, the stories I've read have eliminated any doubts I had about the hereafter. That's why I gave you that book. And there's no doubt in my mind that you've seen what they talk about in those stories I've read."

"Saw it," murmured Jason. "Saw it, heard it—even smelled it. The smells were almost the best—and worst—part."

"What do you mean, worst?"

Jason sighed, his eyes narrowing. "This second time, I saw both sides of the other side, you could say. Most of it was incredibly beautiful. Like you said, words can't do it justice. But some of it was dark and terrifying. There was this awful sound that pressed on you and kept getting louder. And the smells ... they were so bad you wanted to vomit, but you couldn't." His legs moved restlessly, and he threw the blanket off. "Without saying anything to me, the woman—my angel, I guess—she made it clear to me that trying to kill myself was a terrible mistake. I felt what it was like to be part of the light, and then I felt what it was like to be separated from the light. It was unbearable."

Tucking his hands behind his head, Jess sat back in the armchair to ponder this. And Jason could only think what a relief it was to tell someone finally, someone who came from a place of understanding, rather than skepticism. Who knew it was a crazy thing for him to be saying, and therefore only listened all the harder. How had he never noticed this tendency of Jess Carson's? The man took whatever life threw at him and incorporated it into his understanding. The exact opposite of most people. Most people were like that Dr. Wright, refusing to see or even be curious about what they couldn't make sense of. Jess was amazing.

After some time, Jess cleared his throat and rose, going to give the pot of sauce a stir. He ran a finger along the spoon and took a taste. Nodded. "Well, Jason, in the meantime, we've got to think about the here and now, not just the hereafter. We've both got work to do."

Jason gave a rueful chuckle. "Work? You mean like picking grapes? I don't know about you, Jess, but let's face it—my career is toast."

"That's where you're wrong." Reaching up, Jess took some plates down from the cabinet shelf. "Bill Brojan has agreed to meet with us. He has a plan. Once you've got your strength back, we're going to have a palaver with him."

"Aw, Jess—I don't know ..."

"From what I've read in that book you're holding, everyone who's been across to the other side says they found out how important it is to finish whatever task they were put on this earth to do."

The old Jason would have rolled his eyes and made some wisecrack about he'd done more than ten men in his lifetime and had the war wounds and belt notches to prove it. But this

Jason said nothing. He leaned down to retrieve the book from where it had fallen. Flipping the pages through his fingers, he easily found where he had left off this time.

Taking a deep breath, he dived back in.

12

Propping his crutches against the wall, Jason eased himself into the chair Jess pulled out. Jubilee Ranch's founder Bill Brojan must have been prepped because he didn't blink an eye at Jason's condition—the bandages on his face, the wrapped ribs, the arm in a sling, the walking cast with a boot strapped over it.

"Thanks for meeting with us, Bill," Jess was saying. "I know how precious your time is."

Bill ducked his head. "It's no more precious than yours, but you're welcome. Coffee?" He waved the pot around. "And I'm glad to see you're doing so well, Jason. That was quite a crack-up you had."

"You should see the other guy," muttered Jason with a half-grin.

"It sure was quite a crack-up," Jess put in, clearing his throat, "and as you know, Bill, Jason here has had some financial crack-ups too. In fact, you could call it the perfect storm. But I've told him about what you went through yourself in the early eighties."

"Oh, yeah." Bill gave a sheepish smile. "That was quite an experience. We owed Sea-First around three-million, and the prime rate went over twenty-percent. We lost it all."

Jason set down the coffee cup he had been raising. With a wince, he straightened. "You lost everything?"

"Everything. Except for Sue and the kids, of course."

The corner of Jason's mouth turned down, and Bill seemed

to realize he touched a sore spot. He hurried along. "As Jess knows, 'failure' isn't in Sue's vocabulary. She never gave up. I was fortunate."

"How did you turn things around so fast?" asked Jason quietly.

"Oh, well, it wasn't fast. It took years. But the bank had no way to run the orchards they took from us. So, we negotiated a deal to manage them on an incentive basis. You've heard of REO? Real estate-owned," supplied Bill. "That's how banks are required to classify what they've foreclosed on. They hate it because the regulators hate it. Banks want it off their balance sheet as quickly as possible."

Jason rotated his coffee cup thoughtfully on the table. "So, you mean my winery is REO for Sterling Bank?"

"That's right. And they're losing money on it every day."

"And they've also lost almost all the good people," Jason reflected. "Plus Kim, the head winemaker. She left before all the shi—I mean, before all the crap hit the fan."

Nodding, Bill leaned forward and tented his fingertips. "They want out, for sure. And they've got tons of foreclosed homes and building lots to deal with. This housing bust is getting to be almost like the 1930s. I've heard the FDIC might take Sterling over, which wouldn't be good for you."

"What do you mean?"

"Once the fed's get control, everything freezes. Your winery could be tied up for years and, you know, the customer perception ..."

Jason sighed. "Yeah. My label turns to shit—sorry."

"Couldn't have put it better myself," said Bill. "You're right. A winery isn't like an office building or a wheat farm"—with a nod at Jess—"or an apple orchard. It's not a commodity. It's a brand—at least the way you've built it up."

Jess rose to pour another round from the coffee pot. "I've heard rumblings Leonetti might try to buy Knightbridge from the bank."

This time Jason slammed his cup down so suddenly it sloshed over. "What?!"

"Yeah," said Bill, "that seems like a logical move on their part." He fixed a keen gaze on Jason. "I've heard there was some bad blood between you and them."

"Not only that, but Kim works there now." Jason swallowed the epithet he wanted to attach to that traitor's name. "She'd like nothing better than to take over Knightbridge."

Reaching for the napkin Jason used to sop up the spilled coffee, Jess tossed it in the trash. "Sounds like time is of the essence."

"Yup." Bill rocked back in his chair, nodding to himself. He didn't look too rushed, however. "The good news is that money's tight all over. Even Leonetti has been forced to make a big draw on their credit line, from what I hear."

Jason scowled impersonally at the pictures of the Jubilee sports teams on the wall. He knew he'd lost the winery, but having it go to Leonetti was yet another twist of the knife. God—anyone but them.

"So, what do you think we should do, Bill?" Jess prodded, interrupting Jason's unpleasant train of thought.

"Let's be honest, Jess," Jason snapped. "There's nothing to be done. I don't have a wine bottle to piss in. I can't *do* anything."

"Well, the wheat business has been good lately," said Jess, unperturbed. "I've got some money saved up."

"How 'bout that?" said Bill. "Turns out we've had a real good run ourselves, the last couple years. China's been buying all the cherries Costco and Safeway don't, and paying even higher prices. We don't keep much of what we make—give most of it away, as Jess has probably told you. But Sue didn't like the look of things back in 2007, so we sold most of our stocks, thank the Lord."

Jason stared first at one, then the other.

"I think I could come up with five-hundred grand," Jess surmised.

"You've got five-hundred grand—in *cash*?" gasped Jason.

"More than that, actually," Jess continued calmly. "You know, I don't exactly drive a Ferrari or live in one of them McMansions. And I haven't had anything to spend money on lately, save a new John Deere here and there."

"That helps." Bill inspected the ceiling while he made calculations, his mouth moving silently. "I don't think Sue would go for putting up enough to buy the whole place, though." He gave Jason an apologetic glance. "Your winery buildings and tasting room alone are worth over five-million, I'd guess. You did everything first cabin. But, of course, the real value is in the land. Always is."

Jason made a few sputtering sounds. To give him time to recover, Jess began topping everyone up, but when he reached Jason, Jason put a hand over his cup.

When he spoke, his voice was changed. Humbled. "I know Jess is crazy, but—Bill, you would do all that for me?"

Bill gave another one of his sheepish smiles. "Aw, well, I wouldn't say it was just for you. You see, Jess here is about as good a friend as I've ever had. Remember what all you did for us, Jess, back in eighty-two?"

If he did, he wasn't about to admit it. Face coloring, Jess gave a shrug. "'T'weren't much."

"At the time, it was more than you can imagine. That thirty-thousand you lent us was a big step in getting our orchards back." Brojan cleared his throat and looked away from Jess to save him embarrassment. "Also, I think we can make good money on this deal. Lord knows, we don't need another charity to support." With a chuckle, he gestured at the Jubilee conference room.

Jess gave Bill a thump on the back. "You've always had a knack for taking advantage of tough times."

"We've learned the hard way to get liquid during the booms and be a buyer during the busts—that's when you make the big money. Most folks do the opposite. And this is one doozy of a bust."

There was a new light dawning in Jason's face. "So, if I'm hearing you right, there's not enough to buy the whole thing back from Sterling. Which means we need to prioritize."

"I think that's best. That's what Sue and I did twenty-five years ago. We started buying back the best parcels. We knew what those were, just like you do. The bank doesn't."

"Yeah, but I'm not sure the bank will break it up."

Bill shrugged. "They may not have any better offers, at least not yet, with everyone still in shock over the crash. We want to move before things stabilize. Like Jess said, time is of the essence."

Some of the students were shoveling snow from the parking lot sidewalks. As Jason limped by on his crutches, one teenager with a hoodie pulled tight over his head turned to glower at him.

Noting Jason's raised eyebrows, Bill murmured, "Don't let Daman get to you. He'll get over it." They stopped on the passenger side of Jess's pick-up, and Bill leaned against the door. "But that reminds me—Rich wanted me to ask you again if you'd had a chance to think about coaching the golf team. It would mean a lot to the boys."

Jason smiled wryly. "Strangely, I've been focused on healing up. But you've kind of got me over a barrel now." Shaking his head, he cut off Brojan's demurral. "No—it's fine. It's not exactly like my schedule is overbooked right now." He exhaled in a puff of steam. "Sure. Count me in. Maybe I can even straighten out that prodigious slice of Alvin's."

Clapping his hands, Bill gave a hearty laugh and pulled open the pick-up door for Jason. "Let's take it one miracle at a time. Just helping the boys will be enough of a blessing."

"Hell, we'd have shut our doors months ago without the FDIC," admitted Gus, ushering Bill Brojan into Sterling Bank's conference room. The banker waved at the furniture with exasperation. "I mean, look at this place. Used to be like the lobby of the Ritz-Carlton. Now it's like a store display for IKEA. But even though I appreciate the feds, they're breathing down our necks. I'm not going to kid you, Bill—we're fighting for our lives. We gotta look viable before they'll give us any TARP money."

"That's why I'm here, Gus. Maybe I can help."

Gus's eyes narrowed in doubt. "Bill, I know you're charitably inclined, but I didn't know your generosity extended to banks."

"Yeah, I've got to say our giving dance card is pretty full right now," Brojan said, chuckling, "but the way I see it, we're the perfect match for Sterling right now. You've got land you don't want, and I love good land. You need cash; I've got cash. I'd like to make a deal."

"I'm on the edge of my rickety chair," said Gus, brightening.

"I've got an interest in Knightbridge Estates—at least part of it. From what I've heard, it's one of your biggest REOs."

"Sure as hell is. At one time, it was worth over forty-million—at least that's the value we used when we lent against it. Who knows what it's worth now. Maybe half, at best? The high-end wine business has crashed, and no one is buying land these days."

"No one but me."

The banker's skepticism revived. "No disrespect, Bill, but what do you know about wine? You've always been strictly apples and cherries."

"And peaches." Bill smiled. "But you've got a point. It so happens I have my eye on someone to run it for me."

It only took a few moments of mulling this over before Gus began to shake his head slowly. "You know, Bill, the FDIC will oppose any deal that involves equity from a former borrower, trying to buy back assets that secured a loan he defaulted on. Especially if he's trying to do it at a discount!"

"Yes," agreed Bill, "I'm aware of that. That's why Jess Carson, Sue, and I will be putting up all the cash."

The banker relaxed somewhat. "Jess Carson, huh? Too bad about his boy. Nathan Carson sure knew how to make wine ..." He put this thought aside and drew his chair closer to the table. "Okay, Bill, you say you only want to buy part of it. Don't know if the loan committee will go for that. What exactly did you have in mind?"

"Oh, not that much. Just the acreage in the Red Mountain appellation and the current inventory. You keep the rest of the land, all the equipment, and the buildings. With all its improvements and machinery, it's probably the best facility in the valley."

Gus tapped his pen on his pad of paper. "That's 'all' you want, huh?"

Bill rested his elbows on the narrow conference table. "That, and the label. Seven million."

Giving a low whistle, Gus scratched the back of his head. "Seven million," he repeated. "I don't suppose the label's much good to us at this point, with all the key people gone and Knightbridge going off the deep end, I hear. But seven million isn't much, compared to the loan we have against it. We went for all the marbles and loaned half the value: twenty million."

"You're keeping the most valuable parts," Brojan pointed out, overlooking the remark about Jason. "And you got a few mil back from selling his house and cars, am I right?"

"But not much on his stocks portfolio because of the crash. He was on margin."

"So say you've got sixteen mil outstanding, and you can get seven for just a portion of the place—that's got to look darn good to the feds. I'm sure you've set up loan loss reserves against the Knightbridge deal. You can show them that you've turned a big chunk of one of your most troubled assets into a bunch of cash, making your overall loss provisions look credible." Bill gave the conference room a comprehensive glance. "Should be a big push over the hump to getting that TARP money."

Gus sounded out of breath. "You've got the money in cash?"

"Sitting in US Bank, waiting for you to send the paperwork."

The banker stood up and thrust out his hand. "I'll take it to the loan committee and get back to you. The board will probably want in on this, too. We've got a huge meeting with the FDIC early next month—hell, we should probably have you come in and do the talking."

"If they want assurance, my private banker can give you any verification you need," Bill said, grasping his hand.

"Bill, your reputation speaks for itself. But I thank you," said Gus. "These days, nothing talks quite like cash."

The door to the exam room opened, and a grim Dr. Carlson entered. "Jason, I have to say I'm not happy."

"Why would that be?" retorted Jason, tossing aside the golf magazine he'd been paging through. "You're not the one with cancer."

"That's my point. You've known this is a serious problem for months, and you've done nothing."

"What do you mean 'nothing'? I had the tumor removed."

Curt Carlson rolled his eyes. "Yeah, thanks to your quote unquote 'accident.' I happen to know Dr. Wright, and you're lucky—he's an excellent thoracic surgeon—"

"And what a bedside manner! He makes you look good!"

"But as he no doubt warned you," the doctor plowed on, ignoring the slam, "the odds were that the thing had metastasized, and it has. You've let this go months without treatment."

"Okay, one: you're repeating yourself. And two: has it occurred to you, Curt, that I haven't had medical insurance for months, along with being flat-ass broke? I didn't have a way to pay you or any hospital."

"Yeah, I kind of assumed. But there's always Medicaid."

Jason exhaled with disgust. "Yeah, and I wasn't going on the dole like some illegal who just drug his ass up here from

Tijuana. But not to worry. You'll be glad to hear things have changed."

"You mean you decided to swallow that damn pride of yours?"

"Nope," said Jason. "I mean I've got coverage."

"How?"

"Doing some consulting."

"For who?"

"I'd rather not say."

"I can find out from my front desk."

Jason grinned and smoothed the crackling paper covering the examination table beneath him. "Curt, I'd like you to keep this quiet. I'm doing some work for Brojan Orchards."

The doctor threw up his hands. "Great. What's the big deal?"

"Nothing. Just keep it to yourself."

"Patient confidentiality." Carlson held up two fingers in the Boy Scout salute. "Jason, here's the straight scoop. Because of your ego and stubbornness, we're playing from behind. It's now metastatic, which means, instead of just using radiation, you'll need to undergo chemotherapy. You know what that entails, right?"

"Got a rough idea."

"Rough is exactly what it's going to be. And it might not even work." Seeing the news didn't shake him, Carlson gave a frustrated huff. "Look, Jason—dying of cancer is not the preferred ticket out of here."

"Can I tell you something, Curt?" Jason's voice was level. "One of those rare things you don't know?"

"Sure. Amaze me. What is it?"

"There are a lot worse things than dying."

Carlson gave a snort. "Yeah, right. Like what?"

Jason's eyes were serious. But they were peaceful. "Like dying wrong."

One of the first improvements Jason made when he moved

back in with Jess Carson was to get cable installed. "You still only get the same three channels you got when I was in high school," he marveled.

To which Jess replied, "Well, that's two more channels than I watch."

The cable went in, and Jason watched the Golf Channel all through his recuperation. He was taking in another tournament the day after seeing Dr. Carlson, when Jess burst in, bringing a rush of cool air and the smell of the fields.

"They went for it, Jason!" he crowed, arms high in triumph. "Sterling Bank okayed the deal!"

"You're kidding." The remote tumbled from nerveless fingers.

"I kid you not. Bill called me when I was out in the fields. I was honking the horn on that tiller and beating on the steering wheel—the gophers probably thought it was the end of the world! After all these years of prying a little wheat out of the ground, I'm finally in the wine business! I told you Bill Brojan would pull this off. He went up seven-hundred grand, but he got all the wine inventory and the label too."

Jason sagged back against the couch, eyes wide. "Damn. He really did it."

"O, ye of little faith." Still whooping, Jess gave him a congratulatory rub on the head. "Praise the Lord, we got it!"

"We got it," Jason repeated mechanically. Vistas were opening before him. He'd gotten so used to his horizon shrinking, dwindling—almost disappearing—that he could hardly take in what Jess was telling him.

He took a deep breath to steady himself, but it came out kind of ragged.

"I've got another shot."

This time, he drove up in the ancient Buick Regal that used to belong to Maria Carson. Dust from the dirt road flew up in a cloud behind him, and he stopped in front of a large, canvas-covered structure. The hand-painted sign read, "Knightbridge Cellars."

Flinging open the car door, Jason stumped up the wooden steps with his cane and entered the improvised office. It was a big room, punctuated by a secondhand table and chairs and some boxes in the corner.

"Well," he muttered, "it's a start."

Slowly, propping his cane against the metal desk, he dragged over the first box and flipped it open. Desk lamp, stapler, paper clip holder. A few award plaques.

"Need a little help with that?"

Jason's head shot up to find Marcie standing at the open front door.

"Marcie! Damn, it's great to see you."

She gave an uncertain smile. "Hi, boss."

"Does this mean you're coming back?"

"Why not? Waiting tables isn't exactly my calling in life. I've deflected more passes in the last few months than an All-Pro cornerback. Seems like everyone in the wine business is firing and no one's hiring."

Coming around the side of the desk, Jason shoved aside the paraphernalia and sat on the front of it. "Marcie, I called because I'd be thrilled to have you join me again. But before you really commit, I want you to know something."

"What's that? I'll be working for free?"

"No, thanks to Brojan we've got enough working capital." Jason chuckled. "You're not a volunteer. No—what you need to know is that I—I've got—oh, *hell*." There wasn't any subtle way to put it. "What you need to know is that I've got lung cancer."

She stared at him a minute, waiting for the punch line. When it didn't come, her eyes began to fill. "That cough of yours," she whispered. "How bad?"

"Pretty bad. Oh—hey—don't be doing that. I don't even know which box the Kleenex got packed in." The feeble joke only made Marcie's tears fall faster, and he patted her shoulder while she dabbed them with her sleeve. "Hey—save it for the memorial. I've got a decent chance. Curt Carlson is a hell of a doc, and one of his best buddies is Stu Friedman, the top oncologist in the valley, maybe even in the state. Of course, it went straight to the guy's head, and he's an arrogant bastard."

"Then you two should hit it off great," Marcie said with a sniffle, managing a watery smile.

Jason gave a roar of laughter and hugged her. "Exactly! So, what do you say? You still want in?"

"In," said Marcie. She gave him a kiss on the cheek. "But promise me—no more midnight drives in a blizzard."

13

Summer. The sun was high and warm and glorious. In every direction, rolling hills stretched like giant grass-covered sand dunes. Jason was similarly renewed. Gone were the casts and slings, the bandages and crutches. Even his scars were faded against his suntan. Instead of a cane, he now gripped a club. He could even swing full out with only an occasional twinge of pain. Everything would have been as close to perfect as things got anymore, except for the company he kept.

In a loose group around him gathered several teenage boys. Most were black or Hispanic; some were glaring at him, others were looking off into space; all were slouching on their clubs with obvious lack of interest.

"Okay, guys, here's the deal," said Jason, stepping up to a ball sitting high on a tee. "Most people make golf sound like a tough game. I'm going to show you how easy it really is."

Setting himself, he crushed the waiting ball with his powerful, trademark stack-and-tilt swing. That got their attention. The boys tracked the ball's flight and whistled appreciatively. One of them, a stocky Hispanic boy, stepped forward, hand to his forehead, to peer beyond the edge of the range where Jason's ball landed.

"Damn," he said, grinning. "I'm not goin' to be pickin' that one when we're done. That's out with the rattlesnakes."

"See what I mean?" said Jason. "Easy. Now you guys spread out a bit, tee up the ball, and just do what I did."

With shrugs and exchanged glances, the boys complied.

"Mr. Alvin never let us try to hit a driver," remarked the stocky boy under his breath to the kid beside him. "Said we weren't ready."

Jason seemed to think they were, judging by his folded arms and confident expression, a look that the boys wiped clean from his face in the next few minutes.

First the heavy-set boy took a huge swing, stepping forward into the ball. When he missed by a large margin, his momentum carried him face-forward onto the ground, just as the boy next to him heeled his shot, nailing his unfortunate peer in the backside.

"Ow! Shit, dude!" protested the Hispanic boy, struggling up. "What you doin'? This is golf, not hockey! You're not supposed to peg people, 'specially me!"

"You a damned big target," grumbled the accused.

Before Jason could intervene, another boy hit his drive off the toe of his club, shooting it between the legs of the kid next to him, who spun around and let fly a volley of cussing. That drew heated, equally colorful, retorts, which escalated into a punch being thrown. The next thing Jason knew, the two boys went for each other. Locked together, arms and legs flying, they fell grappling in the grass. That was the signal for all the remaining boys to throw down their clubs and go diving into the scrum, shouting curses and cocking fists.

Letting a few swear words of his own escape, Jason hurled himself into the struggling mass of bodies, tackling boys and prying and wrestling them away from each other. "Break it up! Break it up, you morons. Agh! Watch it, kid! Hold up—hold up, guys. I said *hold up!*"

In the pandemonium, no one noticed Rich and Alvin Williams on the porch of Rich's house, passing binoculars back and forth.

"Looks like Knightbridge knows more about playin' golf than teachin' golf," was Alvin's assessment. "Oh, man. Jamal really nailed Orlando—do we got to go over there?"

"Nah. He's breaking it up. He'll figure it out," said his brother. His smile was determined. "Might as well let him figure out what he's dealing with. He'll learn how to be a teacher."

Alvin slapped the binoculars back in Rich's hands. "He better learn fast, or we're going to have some serious lawsuits on our hands."

When Jess came in for the day and was washing up in the kitchen, he found Jason in his usual spot watching golf. But this time he was perched on the edge of the couch, pen and pad in hand, scribbling notes as fast as he could. Dropping the pen, he grabbed the remote.

"... The problems for most golfers start right at the beginning," came the TV voice. "The grip and address position. If you get those wrong, it sets off an adverse chain reaction."

"That Johnny Miller?" Jess called.

Jason gave a grunt of assent while the video went on. "First, you've got to make sure your hands are positioned so that, for a right-handed golfer, your left thumb is slightly on the right hand of the shaft, above the right hand, of course, and the right thumb is slightly on the left hand of the shaft."

Hitting the pause button again, Jason flipped a page on the pad and dashed off more notes.

"Since when have you ever watched a golf instruction video?"

Jason didn't even look up. "Since never."

"That's what I thought. So wh—"

"So today was a complete clusterfu—a complete *fiasco* with those gangbangers." He shook his ballpoint pen and clicked it a few times before throwing it aside and uttering a groan. "Who am I kidding? Maybe I should tell Jubilee to find someone else— if they aren't already thinking that themselves. Teaching this bunch of future urban terrorists how to play a gentlemen's game is borderline hopeless."

"Uh-huh." Jess got himself a glass of water from the tap. "And you can tell all that after one day, when you went in there with no preparation whatsoever?"

"I just thought—"

"You just thought if you swaggered in there and showed 'em how you do it, they would pick it up instantly," supplied Jess. He drank down his glass and set it on the counter with a *clink*. "I saw how you tried that with Nathan, years ago. Didn't work worth a damn then, and it won't work now."

Jason grimaced. "Tell me something I don't know." Sighing, he let his notepad slide to the floor and slumped back into the depths of the sofa. "This is crazy, Jess," he said quietly. "I just don't know how to work with these kids."

"Mmnh," was Jess's reply. He pulled open the fridge door and dug in the drawer for dinner fixings. "Maybe you can learn more from Johnny Miller than just the finer points of golf," he suggested, emerging with a pound of ground beef.

"What do you mean?"

"Remember the story that Miller fella told at the Jubilee golf tournament?" Jess tossed a packet of taco seasoning and a head of lettuce next to the meat. "About how he told Steve Young, when Young was quarterbacking the 49ers, that he couldn't cuss on TV? How millions of boys were watching him, and they could tell if he was shouting the F word?"

"Yeah, I remember."

"He was an example-setter when he was playing, and now you are, too."

That drew a snort from Jason. "Yeah. Somehow, I don't think ESPN is gonna be filming the Jubilee golf team or its coach. And if they did, my mouth would be the least of the problems for America's innocent youth. Hell—I could handle everyone cussing their heads off, if I knew how to turn them into golfers.

No. It's worse than that. This is going to be more like the golfing equivalent of *The Bad News Bears*."

"Always did like that movie," said Jess, turning on the burner.

Jason shook his head against the older man's optimism and clicked the play button on the remote. A minute later, he was hunched forward again, scrawling away, oblivious to Jess observing him and to the small smile curving the man's lips.

Appointment followed appointment. At least there was a new issue of *Golf Digest* in Friedman's waiting room. Reading one of the tips in the golf magazine, Jason nodded approvingly and murmured to himself, "That's a damn good idea. It could help Isaiah and a couple other guys." He gave a furtive glance right and left, before faking a cough and tearing the page out to stuff inside his vest.

"Mr. Knightbridge?" A young nurse held the door and checked her clipboard again. Her eyes widened when she saw him stand up. "Are you *the* Jason Knightbridge?"

"In the flesh—for the time being."

"Oh my God. I just love your Cab. I was so sorry to hear that ..."

"That I lost my winery?" He followed her down the hallway. "Well, don't worry your very pretty little head. I'm back in business, and if you and your boss get me through this thing, I'll give you a case of my 2002 reserve Cab that was voted top-five in the world."

"That would be so awesome!" She pointed at the exam room to his left. "Dr. Friedman is the best. If anyone can keep you—" Breaking off, she fumbled with her clipboard.

"Can keep me from croaking, he can, you were going to say?" Jason said, grinning.

She smiled. "Well, a positive mental attitude counts for a lot."

"You sound like someone else I know," Jason muttered.

Gesturing at the exam table, the nurse backed from the room. "The doctor will be with you shortly."

The walls of the exam room were lined with Friedman's degrees, awards, and honors. The man even had a few signed celebrity shots, like he was some hot television chef. Had the guy never thought of putting up something peaceful, like a picture of a sailboat? Well, hell—maybe it gave Friedman's patients more peace to know the guy was good at what he did.

The doctor gave a sharp rap before entering and thrust a hand at Jason. He was a quick, compact man who looked you in the eye. "Stu Friedman. Curt has told me a lot about your case and a lot about you. Speaking of cases, I bought my wife a case of your 2004 Cab for our twenty-fifth wedding anniversary. We're now both big fans of Knightbridge Estates."

"Like I said to your gal, if you and your team get me through this, I'll give you all a case of my finest every year that I'm still on this side of the dirt."

"That's all the incentive I need."

Jason's eyebrows quirked up. "Does that mean you're not going to charge me the equivalent of a Ferrari to pump me full of poison?"

"Well, it's not going to be a Nissan at any rate," said the doctor, washing his hands at the sink. He reached for a paper towel. "Life is pricey stuff. And isn't a Ferrari what you drive?"

"Too late," Jason said. "Don't get your hopes up. I totaled my silver bullet. But at least the bank didn't get it."

"Victory indeed," said Friedman dryly. "It's the little things, isn't it?" He dropped onto his rolling stool and pointed at the leather chair against the wall. "Wanna take a seat here? You don't need to sit on the exam table for now, unless you like sitting on butcher paper like a nice filet."

"Yeah, I hate it when people treat me like a piece of meat."

"That what you tell the ladies?" Friedman countered. He flipped a sheet on Jason's chart as he studied it. "Mm ... hate to break it to you, but in your condition, it looks like we'll be nuking you like warmed-over hash."

This got a laugh out of Jason as he took the proffered seat.

"You know, Friedman, in the old days—like a few months ago—I would've loved sparring with someone as cocksure as you are, trying to take you down a few pegs. But something's changed."

"I think I would have enjoyed the battle, from what Curt has told me," the doctor replied easily. He rolled his stool closer and leaned forward on his elbows. "So, you're not into challenging medical bravado anymore, huh? Guess that means I get to keep my inflated self-image. My lucky day. Tell me what's changed."

"*I* have." Jason hesitated, but Friedman waited him out. "Doc, you probably heard about my accident."

"I heard you had a very, very close call."

Jason gave a short nod. "Uh-huh. And ever since then ... well, I look at life differently."

"Understandable."

There was a silence. They could hear the nurse talking to someone in the hall and a muffled response.

Jason said, "You've been an oncologist for a long time. You must have seen a lot of people die in your career."

"Of course," Friedman admitted, holding up his palms. "Some. But not all that many. I'm actually really good at what I do—which, I say again, should be welcome news for you."

"It is. Don't get me wrong." Jason flashed him a grin. "I'm glad you think you got it all figured out. I know for a fact that's a good feeling, for as long as it lasts. But has anyone ever told you about going over ... to the other side?"

Friedman rolled backward an inch, his gaze steady. "I take it you're not referring to the other side of the clinic. Or batting for the other team, huh? You're asking me, has anyone ever told me about dying?"

"I guess, based on your training, that's what you'd call it."

The doctor tried for an offhand tone. "In my line of business, it comes up, from time to time."

Now it was Jason who leaned forward. "But I'm curious, Doc—very curious. In all your years of dealing with dying and nearly dying people, has anyone told you what it's like to pass across and come back?"

"Ah." The doctor shifted uncomfortably.

Undoubtedly, in all his years of med school there wasn't any class on the woo-woo side of things, Jason thought.

"Well, sure," said Friedman, scratching the back of his head. "Sure. I've heard lots of stories, but nothing I believe. The mind does strange things when it's on the edge of death. Besides, there are almost always large quantities of drugs involved."

"So there's never been an incident that caused you to think there might be more to it than hallucinations?" pressed Jason.

The doctor drew back at his intensity, frowning. "Look—it's natural to be worried, but I don't think this is where your focus needs to be, yet. Let me do my dog-and-pony show and talk to you about your treatment—"

"Friedman, I'm going to tell you something I haven't told anyone else," Jason said, cutting him off. "I need you to buy me at least a year with that skillset you're so proud of."

"I hope to do better than that," said the doctor, trying to regain his footing in the conversation. "Why a year, though?"

"Because I've been to the other side," Jason declared. "Not once, but twice. No—hear me out. The first time was when I nearly drowned as a kid. The second time was my so-called accident. Friedman, it wasn't an accident. I tried to kill myself. And while I lay there, my body hanging on by a thread, I met someone." His voice dropped lower. "Someone came to me. Someone who told me—with love but firmly—what a huge mistake I was making. She taught me a lot of things—things I know are in my mind that explain so much, but that I can't pull up. But what I remember, beyond vividly, is that I need to make things right here. And to do that, I've got to have time."

The doctor's lips parted, as if he were about to speak. Then it snapped shut again. He rolled further away and took up his clipboard, making a random notation. "That's all very interesting," he pronounced. "But now let's talk about your treatment options."

Jason shook his head decisively. "Not until you tell me, Doctor, if you have any clue what I'm talking about—if you've ever had a situation that you and all your limitless knowledge can't explain. It looked like, a moment ago, you were holding out on me."

Again, Friedman looked like he would brush him off. But his hands had tightened around the clipboard. He dropped his gaze to the floor, thinking. When he finally spoke, the words came with reluctance.

"You know, there was one time, several years ago ... we were doing a chemo procedure." He cleared his throat. "I usually don't do those, but in this case, there were some complications ..."

Friedman saw himself again, the nurse beside him, next to a bed with a woman in it. She was hooked up to various IV bags, her eyes blank. And then she began to jerk violently, as if she were experiencing a seizure. Grabbing her shoulders, he tried to hold her down, even as the nurse lunged for the alarm button, but the patient's movements grew even more violent. The heart monitor went crazy, adding to the chaos, and then, just as suddenly—it flat-lined.

"I was yelling," Friedman muttered, by this point more to himself than Jason. "'We're losing her! Adrenaline! Fast!' The nurse gave me a syringe. I jammed it in her heart. Nothing. I sent the nurse for the cardiac crash unit, while I started pumping the woman's chest. I'd never lost a patient that way, and I sure as hell wasn't going to start! I was yelling at her. I told her, 'You can't die! We are *not* losing you! I won't let that happen. Think of your children—think of your husband—think of anything that keeps you hanging on.' It didn't matter. I was yelling to myself. Nothing was doing anything. Then the crash guys busted in and pushed me away. They slapped the paddles on her and gave her a jolt. A million years passed. They did it again. I was watching from the corner, panting.

"And then, finally, there was this one, reluctant beep. And then another. And another." Friedman's face was ashen, recalling the moment. "It was the heart monitor. She was back." He passed a hand over his eyes. "She'd had some rare allergic reaction to the chemo cocktail we were using. It was very, very close."

Sweat stood out on the doctor's forehead.

"Yeah." Jason nodded. "That must've been a bad day at the office." He made an impatient movement. "But—you're a doctor—you must've seen stuff like that before. I don't see why it made such an impression."

"Not that," said Friedman. He pulled a handkerchief from his pocket to swab himself. "I mean, yeah, it was stressful as hell, but you're right—I've seen worse. No. It was—it was what she told me when she woke up that got to me."

Jason straightened. "What was that?"

The doctor rose abruptly from his stool and ran fingers through his dark hair. He gave Jason a guarded look. "You need to understand that she was totally unconscious that whole time. There was no way she could know what was going on."

Jason found he was holding his breath.

"She told me," Friedman went on slowly, "that after her heart stopped, she felt herself rising out of her body and going up to the ceiling in the corner by the window."

Jason started breathing again, fighting a twinge of disappointment. "Yeah, I read some neurologist saying that kind of out-of-body thing wasn't that uncommon. That it could be explained by the brain hallucinating or dreaming, in response to stress."

This time it was Friedman shaking his head, his brows drawing together. "I know what the literature says. It wasn't that that stuck with me. It was that she was able to describe everything that happened—precisely. She even repeated exactly what I'd said to her. No one could have known that! There were just the two of us in the room—and she was gone."

Jason got to his feet, meeting the doctor's sheepish expression with a growing smile. He put a gentle hand on Friedman's shoulder.

"Welcome to my world, Doc. A strange and beautiful place. Now—*now*—we can start talking treatment options."

The dozen boys gathered around him again at the driving range tee area regarded him with skepticism.

Jason took a deep breath. "Listen, guys. Last time wasn't exactly our finest hour."

"No shit!" muttered the heavyset Hispanic boy to the kid he'd punched a few days ago. "Mr. Alvin said he'd make us run to the Tri-Cities if that happened again." He jerked his chin over his shoulder at a grizzled older man, perched on a riding mower and watching from a distance. "And there's Mr. Alvin, Sr., keeping an eye out."

"The fact of the matter is, it was my fault," Jason went on.

Heads snapped up at this admission. One boy narrowed his eyes in puzzlement.

"I wasn't ready to teach you. But I won't make that mistake again." He made a point of looking at each one in turn, whether or not they made eye contact with him. "This is a great game, a game you can play all your life. It might even help you get a job. You meet a lot of quality people playing it. In fact, learning golf when I was about your age changed my life. Made me what I am ..." His voice tailed off, and only the boy nearest him might have heard Jason add, "Or at least what I was."

He held up his hands. "Okay—enough apologizing and philosophizing. Let's get specific. How many of you play football?" When all of them raised their hands, Jason's mouth popped open. "All of you?"

"Mr. Jason," said the stocky boy, "we're only thirty-five

dudes right now. Almost all of us are needed, spite of bein' only in the eight-man league." He grinned. "But even though we're the smallest school, we won the state championship at our level last year."

"That's what I heard. And I'll tell you what: we're going to win a state championship in golf, too. It may take time—maybe even a lot of time—but we can do it." A shadow crossed his face as he considered the irony of making long-term commitments at this stage in the game, but he gave himself a shake. "First, though, we've got to work on the basics. It's going to be the golfing equivalent of blocking and tackling. Now, what's the first thing Mr. Alvin had you work on in football practice?"

"Where we stand and how we stand," volunteered the smallest boy.

"Exactly! Your stance. We're going to focus first on how we stand. 'Cause if you get that wrong, you're fu—you're screwed," he amended. "So, let me show you how to address the ball."

"Address the ball?" a boy echoed, his face skeptical.

"Like, hello, ball!" joked the heavyset kid, to a chorus of laughs.

"Very funny. Just for that, kid, you're going to be my role model. Come up here, and the rest of you spread out. What's your name, son?"

"Orlando."

"Orlando," Jason repeated. "You're going to show your buddies how to prepare to hit a golf ball." Handing him a club and putting a ball down for him, Jason took him by the shoulders to maneuver him into place. "First, assume an athletic position, like you're going to shoot a free throw. Bend from the waist with a straight back. No hunching over." He corrected Orlando's slump. "You want your feet slightly more than shoulder-width apart." Seeing the boy's death-grip on the club, he intervened. "Hey, hey, don't strangle the club. You're not trying to choke it to death. Look, you guys milk cows around here, right? Hold the club as gently as you hold Bossie's teats."

That got a wave of laughter out of them and a few cracks at Orlando's expense, and Jason smiled in return. "I knew you knew what I meant. Okay, guys, I want to see you all setting up just like Orlando. Orlando, hold that pose for a while so they can imitate you."

Orlando gave a come-hither wiggle of his backside.

"Oh, yeah—check out this booty if you wanna achieve greatness," he crowed.

After their laughter died down, he resumed his model stance, and they obediently lined up on either side of him, throwing him glances as they adjusted their own positions.

The sound of a riding mower engine starting up and rumbling away reached Jason's ears, and he gave an inward smile as he went from boy to boy, making adjustments.

Maybe Alvin, Sr. would have better news for his sons about the Jubilee Golf Team this time out.

His golf-instructor-to-hoodlums career wasn't the only thing that looked like it just might be making progress.

"I like what I'm seeing," said Jason as he walked down the row of grapes, Marcie tagging along behind him. He stopped again to inspect some of the fruit. "A cold winter creates the best grapes, at least for the vines that survive, and most of ours made it."

"Boss, what about the customers?" Marcie asked, tucking her clipboard under her arm. "Do we have any left? They obviously all heard you lost the winery."

"Yeah." His hand dropped. "We've got our work cut out for us in that regard. I'm going to head over to the coast soon and meet the head buyer at Costco. If we get them back, we're off to the races. And I've always had a good rapport with the buyer."

Marcie snorted. "You certainly have."

Jason favored her with a stern look, but he couldn't keep it up. He laughed. "She might not be quite as friendly as in the past." Whipping off his Titleist golf cap, he revealed a newly bald head.

"Oh, I don't know." Marcie gave him a gentle punch to the shoulder. "I think baldness becomes you."

"Yeah, I'm a regular Bruce Willis. If I don't come back, Marcie, it's because I got the lead in the next *Die Hard* movie."

Swoop ... *thwack* ... hiss. Swoop ... *chunk* ... silence. Swoop ... *pop* ... ssss. All up and down the row, the boys of the golf team were hitting balls while Jason walked back and forth between them.

"Remember, guys, it's crucial to be on your front foot at impact. That's right, that's right." Jason paused to admire an adept swing and then shook his head over the next. "Deshawn, this isn't baseball. You can't fall back when you hit the ball. Okay, okay—hold your fire for a bit."

The clubs went still as eyes turned to him.

"Did you watch those DVDs I gave you last time? Good. Tell me—whose swing did you like the best?"

"John Daly!" called out Orlando.

Jason did a double-take. "John Daly? Why him?"

"Because he hits the crap out of the ball," the stocky boy explained, "and he dresses like he's in the circus ... and 'cause he's fat like me."

The other boys erupted in laughter, but Jason, seeing the flicker of uncertainty in Orlando's face, managed not to join them. "I wouldn't say you're fat, Orlando," he said. "You just haven't had your growth spurt yet."

"Except for his belly!" cracked one of the smaller kids, drawing more hoots and laughs.

"All right, all right." Jason held up a hand. "From what I understand, Orlando was your star offensive and defensive lineman last season, so give him a break. Plus, he's got a point. One of the reasons I wanted you to watch the Daly DVD was so that you realize you don't have to be built like Tiger Woods to be a good golfer. But I also wanted you to watch it so you can see the dangers of over-swinging. Daly could win a lot more tournaments if he swung under control. Let me ask you guys: where is his club at the top of his swing?"

Taking a driver, he lifted it back smoothly until the club was above his shoulders and horizontal with the ground. "Is this where his club is, when he finishes his back swing?" No one replied, but he saw some heads shaking. "Right. So, where is it?"

"Way past that!" piped up a small white kid.

"Exactly, Reese! You were paying attention to something besides Daly's beer belly and ugly pants." Jason extended the club even further, twisting his upper body. "He goes way beyond parallel. Parallel is what it's called where your club stops here." He returned the club to horizontal. "Anything beyond this and you're asking for trouble." Dropping his pose, he pointed to one of the older teenagers. "Isaiah, you love Tiger. Where is his club at the top of his swing?"

Isaiah lowered his gaze and chewed his lip.

"Come on, Isaiah. Don't overthink it. Overthinking is never good in any sport, especially golf. Just see his swing in your mind and tell me where his club stops."

The boy's face lit up. "Tiger stops before he even gets to there—to parell—to prellell!" He ignored the burst of ridicule the boys gave him when he mangled the word. "I remember wonderin' how he can hit it so far when he doesn't take it all the way back."

"Good! Very good," crowed Jason. "You guys are paying attention. I'm proud of you." He ignored their startled, exchanged glances and pressed on. "Even though Tiger's club doesn't get quite all the way to parallel, the next time you watch his DVD, check out his shoulders. They're fully turned and behind the ball. So, he's got plenty of power but a lot more control than Orlando's favorite golfing clown. Now, all of you spread out again. Get in the proper address position, and then slowly take the club back around to parallel—but no further."

They obeyed, letting him run up and down the line to check each of them while they took more swings. It wasn't until the ball buckets were empty and they were putting their clubs away, talking excitedly, that they pushed Isaiah forward as their spokesman.

"Mr. Jason," he began in his low voice, "when can we play on a real course?"

Pushing his cap back, Jason scratched his bare head. "Not yet, fellas. But it won't be much longer. I'm going to take you all out to the country club before summer's over."

With the cheers the boys let fly, no one heard him mutter, "Once I rejoin it myself."

"Look out, John Daly," whooped Orlando. "I'm gonna be crankin' it past yo fat ass 'fore you know it!"

"What you talkin' about?" another boy challenged. "I been hittin' it at least thirty yards further 'n you."

"Oh, right? No way—you see as bad as you golf."

Laughing and jostling and ribbing each other, the golf team dispersed. Jason watched them go, smiling, before bending over his notebook to scrawl a few lines for the next practice.

A shadow fell across the page.

Glancing up, Jason saw Daman standing there, eyes narrowed and chin raised. Jason gave a nod of acknowledgment, which drew no response. After waiting another beat, he shrugged and went back to writing.

"You think you could teach me this pussy game?"

Hiding a grin, Jason shut his notebook and snapped the rubber band around it. "Yeah, I guess so. It's a hard game, though. Much harder to learn than it looks."

Daman didn't look fazed. "If those bitch-ass punks can hit the ball after a couple months, I should be playing on the tour by next year."

Jason gave a silent chuckle. "I see your time on Mr. Alvin's shit list hasn't diminished your opinion of yourself."

"Can't nothin' do that," Daman replied amiably.

Looking over, Jason saw the boy was smiling, and he found himself smiling in return. "For once, you *are* telling it like it is."

He threw a nod at his golf bag and then laid his hand on the kid's shoulder. "I think I've got a few clubs in here that just might work for you."

14

Among the things Costco knew how to do right was parking lots, even at their corporate headquarters, Jason thought as he swung Maria's old Buick Regal wide to pull into a spot. None of that "compact space" BS for the warehouse store—those narrow slots that didn't fit more than some kid's skateboard. Grabbing Sam's black doctor bag from the backseat, Jason checked his watch and headed inside.

The woman who came to greet him was dressed well and good-looking. Jason had often thought Linda Fiorini's confidence one of her best features, and he thought it again as she extended a hand to him.

"Jason, so great to see you again. It's been too long." The twinkle in her eyes told him she meant it. "Please come in."

Sparing a glance at her shapely rear end swishing in her tailored pantsuit, Jason took the seat she offered him in the corner of her spacious office.

"Can I get you any coffee or water?"

"No thanks, Linda. I'm fine. Well, almost fine." Seeing her gaze drawn to the golf hat, which he hadn't removed, he gave her a sheepish grin. "Here it is—the big reveal."

He lifted his cap and watched her give the slightest wince, her smile faltering briefly.

"I heard about your condition. I'm so sorry."

"No worries," said Jason easily, replacing his hat. "My treatment is going really well."

"Great, that's great." She seemed glad to hear it, even if he wasn't sure she believed it. Linda crossed her legs, dangling her foot in its leather pump. "Your health was one of the things I wanted to chat with you about. You've had a really tough year, haven't you?"

He took a deep breath. "Only if you call losing everything tough."

The foot swung back and forth. "But I hear you've got your winery back and you're up and running again."

He'd forgotten that little habit she had, of running the tip of her tongue along the bottom of her very white teeth. He also hadn't remembered that red, red lipstick she wore.

"Well, sort of," said Jason. "We're definitely back in business, but I don't actually own the place anymore. Bill Brojan—you know, of Brojan Orchards, a huge Costco vendor—and another guy I know over there, they control all the equity. At this point, I'm just on a profit-incentive basis." He gave her a little wink. "Which is the bit you need to remember, if the FDIC ever calls you about us."

The darting tongue disappeared, and she cleared her throat. "That's what I heard, and it's one of the things I wanted to talk to you about. Frankly, Jason, it's a bit of a concern."

"How so?"

Her legs uncrossed. She was all business now. "Costco likes continuity and stability in its partners. The reality is, Knightbridge Estates is not the same company it was."

It was Jason's turn for the charm offensive. "True, but Brojan's got pockets almost as deep as your founder Jim Sinegal's, and it's the same killer wine. In fact, as part of the deal with the bank, we got all the juice we had fermenting from the last four harvests, plus all the bottled but unsold inventory from earlier vintages. The 2005 is already drinking really well." Reaching into Sam's bag, he pulled out a Reidel wine goblet, sheathed in a Titleist driver head cover.

Linda laughed. "I love your glass protector."

He flashed her a smile. "Nothing but the best. And you're going to love this Cab. It's from one of our Red Mountain vineyards."

"That's where your greatest wine always came from."

"That's right. And we got all the Red Mountain acreage back from the bank. We kept the best and let them have the rest."

Taking the glass Jason handed her, she gave it a swirl and held it to her nostrils.

"Same great nose your juice has always had ..." She held the goblet up to the sunlight from her office window. "And lovely legs, too."

"You know me," said Jason. "I've always been a fan of lovely legs."

Linda gave a most unbusinesslike giggle, and their eyes met.

A half-hour later, he was back in Maria's Buick dialing his cell phone.

It rang a few times before Jess picked up.

"Hello?"

"Hey, old man. I just wanted to let you know that I'll be home in time for dinner. How about grilling up some New Yorks?"

"That's all you've got to say—placing your dinner order?" demanded Jess. "What happened with Costco, dammit?"

Jason tsk-tsked. "Now, Jess. It isn't right for a good Christian man like you to be cussing."

"Look here, Jason—you quit trifling with me, or I'll treat you to some cussing," Jess retorted. "Despite my rude health, at my age, stress—"

"We're in like Flynn!" Jason whooped. He grinned like a fool to hear Jess start hollering on the other end.

"I knew it!" Jess said, cheering. "They've always loved you at Costco."

"Correction! Linda's always loved me at Costco. And at a lot of hotels around here, too," he added under his breath.

"Eh? What about the hotels?"

"I said, my favorite hotels around here are booked, so I really will be home for dinner."

"New York steaks it is, then," agreed Jess. "Dad gum, I can't wait to tell Bill you got Costco back."

"Hell—invite him to the party. And maybe if you get him and Sue to join us, you might even break out a better wine than your usual Two Buck Upchuck."

It had been years since he had been so hands-on during crush. There had been Head Winemaker Kim running things, of course—the turncoat. Not to mention Jason's many distractions—the women, the awards, the high life. All the things which had fallen away.

Now it was just him overseeing every step of the process and directing the workers, Marcie trailing after him. Other wineries in the valley had snapped up Jason's employees when Knightbridge looked to go belly up, but with persistence, he had been able to lure back a few—ones like Miguel Rosario, who had little experience running the equipment but who spoke adequate English and who learned quickly. The day after Jason reprimanded one worker for throwing grapes around like unclaimed luggage at the airport, he found Miguel delivering another such lecture in rapid-fire Spanish, while demonstrating at the same time the proper handling, placing grapes in the bin with precision and even tenderness.

Miguel showed similar aptitude for the mysteries of the machinery—the destemmer, the press, the fermenter, all the pumps and plungers. He was learning to read the gauges on the vats and to decipher the secrets revealed about the young wine within.

Jason clapped a hand on his shoulder. "You got this, my

man. In years to come, they might be slapping labels on *Miguel Cellars*—or *Michel Cellars*, if they want to be fancy about it."

Marcie found Jason in his hut office later, legs kicked up on the desk, looking mighty pleased.

"Boss, that may have been our best crush ever," she declared. "We lost even less fruit than we first thought."

He beamed at her. "Have you seen the juice? It has the deep purple look that tells you it's going to be a great vintage. Robert Parker's going to have an orgasm when he tastes this one."

His admin shook her head, laughing. "You do have a way with words, boss, in an X-rated manner of speaking."

"Rate my language whatever you want, my dear Marcie. But I assure you this vintage is straight-up AAA."

He was back making wine, and he was back at the country club. Though the company he kept nowadays had changed.

"This is what I call arriving in style."

Jason gripped the dashboard of the passenger van as Alvin Williams misjudged the corner of the driveway entrance and jolted them over the curb. "Easy there, Junior—you clip the club sign, and that's more than this piece of junk is worth."

Pushing up the bill of his Titleist golf cap, Jason turned in his seat to eye the boys.

"Okay, guys. This is the day you've been dreaming of, so don't blow it. Shirts tucked in, no F-bombs, no sagging, and talk in whispers—if you talk at all—at least until we get out on the course. The only way I was able to get you on here is that it's a Monday. Which means there'll be just a few ladies and some retired geezers playing today, but if you screw up at all, this will be the last time you and your wonderful assortment of tattoos will ever set foot on Walla Walla Country Club grounds."

Even following his instructions, they were a sight to behold in their baggy shorts and flat-billed caps, piling out of the van with "Jubilee Ranch" emblazoned on it. Several older club members froze on the putting green, watching the cavalcade approach the pro shop. To say the old guard was curious would be to put the most positive spin on their expressions. The boys were hardly less amazed as they looked out from the elevation of the clubhouse to the fairways below.

"Man, you ever seen grass this green?" whispered Orlando to Jamal.

"Dude, look—they got a swimmin' pool over there. Them rich kids sho' got the life."

Orlando nodded. "I could get used to this, real easy."

"Right. You do one cannonball with yo' fat ass in that pool and they be showing you the door." But Jamal's voice lost its scathing note when he added, "Maybe we can get a job here someday."

"Maybe."

Jason waved his arm at them. "Okay, crew, let's head to the driving range. After that, three of you are going to play with me, and the others are going with Mr. Alvin. Daman, you're in his group. Remember—no screw-ups!"

For the first three holes, the boys suffered from timidity. Their swings were apologetic, their ribbing of each other nonexistent. Only Jason charged around, delivering instructions at his usual volume. "What was that, Jamal? I've seen better swings on a kids' playground set."

"I ain't used to having strange people watchin'," muttered Jamal, his eyes sliding to the group of stylish women in their Nike and Adidas skirts who had stepped aside to let the hoodlums play through.

"Like no one watched you guys play football?" Jason challenged.

"Not many folks," put in Deshawn. "And the ones that did didn't look like those ladies."

"We had uniforms then," said Jamal. "We were lookin' like a football team should look."

"Well, I hate to break it to you," Jason answered dryly, "but even if Jubilee had budget for it, you guys would look terrible in golf skirts, so quit fantasizing."

The boys gave a cursory laugh, their shoulders still slumped, and he felt a flare of indignation for them. "Deshawn, it's your shot. And straighten up! That's not the posture we've been practicing all this time. In fact, all of you—I want to see the shoulders back and the focus in your eyes. We paid our fees, and we met the dress code rules. We've got every bit as much right to be on this course today as anyone else out here. One thing that *will* make it hard for you to fit in here, however, is if you play like crap and don't give it your best effort. We've worked hard. Let's let it show."

The pep talk helped. The boys began to relax somewhat, even beginning to crack some jokes by the fourth hole.

At the fifth tee, Jason led off with his usual booming drive, cutting the dog-leg and almost getting on the short par four in one shot. The boys whooped appreciatively, and when Orlando stepped up, his enthusiasm got the better of him. He took a huge swing, his club going well past parallel, resulting in a monster slice that sent the ball flying straight for the expensive houses that lined the course.

"That was the Daly swing, Orlando!" groaned Jason as he followed the ball's trajectory. "C'mon," he said, coaxing it, "hit something cheap."

Intent silence fell. They cupped their hands to their ears and just caught the *thunk* of the ball bouncing off a hard surface.

"Phew," Jason said with a whistle. "A roof. No glass, no foul. Now listen, guys: I want you to swing under control, not like maniac-boy here. Orlando, no more shelling the locals. Put the big dog away until you can dial it down."

As the foursome walked down the right rough of the

sixteenth hole, closer to the houses, they attracted onlookers of a different sort. Several Hispanic men were doing work by a backyard pool, which Jason recognized, with a quirk of his mouth, as the same pool into which he'd sunk the golf cart. The men lowered their blower and clippers and hose, taking in the parade of multiracial, tattooed boys with surprise.

It wasn't the boys who garnered all the attention, though. Presently the sliding glass door flung open, and out came the maid Jason had defended on that ill-fated day. She didn't appear to have forgiven him for it, because she no sooner caught sight of him than she let loose a torrent of shrill, excitable speech, pointing her finger at him as if it were a dagger she would gladly thrust between his ribs.

Giving a mock shudder, Jason turned to Orlando. "You speak her lingo, Orlando. What's she saying?"

The stocky boy's eyes were enormous. He shook his head. "Mr. Jason, she's talkin' 'bout you. My older brother has called me some really nasty things in Spanish before, but I've never heard all those bad words at the same time, so close together."

Jason sighed, but he was almost smiling. "As they say, no good deed goes unpunished."

Bent over his desk, he went over the figures for Costco again, checking them against the ones in Linda's e-mails. He was scrolling downward when the door to his office banged open and Marcie burst in.

"Boss," she cried breathlessly, catching at the papers her entrance sent flying. "You've gotta come quick! It's Miguel. He's passed out! He was working on one of the vats when he lost consciousness!"

Jason jumped up so fast he banged his thighs on the desk. "What? It's gotta be the CO_2! Damn, that could kill him—didn't the alarm go off?"

"No," Marcie said as she scrambled after him. "I've called 9-1-1. They should be here any minute."

Miguel lay motionless on the concrete floor, a group of workers clustered around him. Jason and Marcie charged through the door, Jason shouldering the others out of the way.

"Get back! Give him air." He flipped off his cap and put his head to Rosario's chest.

No motion, and no sound.

Jason looked around wildly. Over the faint whine of a siren approaching, he barked, "Why the hell didn't the alarm sound? Marcie, grab the oxygen bottle out of the case on the wall."

The workers parted again to let her through, and she quickly returned with the bottle and connected mask. Cradling Miguel's head in one massive hand, Jason worked to fit the mask on with the other, while Marcie read the dials on the tank. She frowned, weighing the bottle in her hand.

"Okay, got it. Turn the valve on."

She obeyed, still frowning at the meter. She shook the bottle, but the damned arrow was still pegged on the E.

"Boss, I think this thing is empty—"

But he wasn't listening. He was muttering to Miguel, *urging* him. "Come on, buddy. You got this. This isn't how this is going to go. You got this, Miguel! Listen to me—you're coming back."

"But we have a spare in the shed," Marcie said, dithering. "Julio, *vaya—oxígeno! Mas oxígeno! Almaçen*—is that a shed? Never mind—I'll go get it—"

Before she could do more than thrust the empty bottle at the worker nearest her, there was a wave of gasps.

Miguel's eyelids flickered.

Staring, Marcie watched the man's eyes slowly open and his mouth move. She saw puzzlement dawn as he recognized Jason hovering over him.

"He's back," she whispered.

"There you go, champ!" hollered Jason. "Hey—you're going

to be just fine." He sat back on his heels as the doors of the ambulance slammed outside and paramedics rushed in.

"We'll take it from here," said the first EMT. His partner was donning his stethoscope. Seeing their victim already struggling to sit up, the paramedic added, "Looks like you did a good job of reviving him."

"Yeah, we got him oxygen right away. I think that did the trick," Jason explained. "He must have ingested CO_2 from the vat and passed out."

The EMT nodded, giving his partner a questioning look as the second listened to Miguel's heart.

"His heart rate is fast but regular," the second paramedic announced. "Strong. He seems okay, but we'll take in him anyhow to be checked out."

By this time, Miguel was okay enough to look embarrassed at the crowd gathered and the fuss made over him. Over his mild protests, they helped him onto the gurney and wheeled him out.

It was some time before the excitement died down and the workers returned to their tasks, leaving Jason and Marcie alone. He shot her a relieved grin. "Don't see that every day, do you?"

"No," she agreed. Her voice was thoughtful. "Boss, there's something I need to tell you."

He gave her a sidewise glance. "I don't like the tone of that," he said warily. "What? You think Miguel's gonna sue?"

She shook her head and tapped the oxygen bottle with her fingernails. "Not that. This. This bottle. There was no oxygen. It was empty."

He frowned. "You mean it's empty now."

"No, I mean it was empty when I got it out of the box."

"That's impossible. How the hell else did he come to? There must have been just enough left in there."

Marcie only gave him one of her steady, measuring looks and shrugged. She handed him the bottle. He shook it. Bounced it up and down. Fiddled with the valve.

"The dial says it's empty," said Jason.

"Do I hear an echo in here?" she asked dryly.

It was his turn to shrug. "Well, it could just be a busted dial. You know—there's oxygen in there, but it's not registering."

She sighed. "Boss, I'm the one who orders these things. They're never this light when they're full. I'll get the spare from the shed, and you'll see—unless they sent us *two* defective ones."

Jason mulled this over, weighing the bottle again in his hands. "This is how it was when you first took it out of the box?"

"Yup."

"Huh." He handed the apparatus back to her. "Well, I say we get a refund on that one and just chalk the whole thing up to one of life's many mysteries."

"Or miracles."

Ignoring his skeptical laugh, Marcie tucked the bottle under her arm and marched off.

15

The hospital only kept Miguel Rosario for a few hours, and the next day he was back at work.

"My man," Jason greeted him, clapping him on the shoulder. "Welcome back to the land of the living. You and your lawyer will be happy to hear Marcie replaced the batteries in that damned CO_2 alarm—in fact, in every alarm we've got on the place. We can't have another scare like that."

"Mr. Jason," began Miguel, his voice giving an uncharacteristic quaver. "I want to thank—"

"No time, no time," Jason said, cutting him off, backing away hurriedly from his thanks. "Have to head over to Jubilee. Don't want to be late for golfing with gangsters. Text me if you run into any issues."

What was there to thank him for, anyhow? That he kept defective CO_2 alarms around the place and tried to revive people with equally defective oxygen bottles? The less said about it, the better, in Jason's opinion.

He put the incident from his mind over the next couple of hours as he supervised the team practice. The boys were just shagging balls when Rich Williams approached.

"Hey, Jason. Can I borrow you for a few minutes?"

"Sure." He tucked his pencil behind his ear and slapped shut his notebook. "What's up?"

"There's something I'd like to show you in the gym."

A minute later, Rich let them into the pitch-black building, and the door swung shut behind them.

"Is it a new skylight?" Jason ribbed him.

On cue, the gym lights blazed on, and the men found themselves surrounded by dozens of people and tables burdened with food. Decorations were strung everywhere, and hundreds of balloons bobbed. "Surprise!" everyone shouted.

Jason's mouth popped open. "It's not my birthday," he uttered.

"Nope," said Rich.

The crowd—men, women, and children—burst into "For He's a Jolly Good Fellow," slightly off-key and with a decided Latino accent. A banner unfurled: *"Muchas Gracias, Señor Jason!"*

It looked like Miguel Rosario might let Jason escape being thanked, but the rest of his family and friends sure wouldn't.

"Well, I'll be damned," Jason said under his breath, giving an uncertain wave to the gathering.

Rich Williams grinned. "Most likely."

"That was some event today," Rich said a few hours later, handing him a beer.

The two men were kicking back in the rocking chairs on the executive director's front porch, taking in the view of the Ranch and the driving range, fifty feet or so below the home.

"Yeah." Jason ran a finger through the condensation on the bottle. "It was. But I have to admit, I feel guilty."

"Guilty? Why?"

"Because I didn't *do* anything. Unless you count jeopardizing his life with faulty equipment."

The porch creaked as Rich halted in his rocking. "Didn't you give Miguel oxygen when he was out?"

"Mm." Jason took a big swig of his beer before replying. "That's just it. Here's the really strange part, Rich. The oxygen bottle was empty. I didn't realize it at the time, but Marcie told me she could tell immediately there was nothing in it. Then, when she turned on the valve, *nada*."

Rich nodded, rocking back again. "Uh-huh. That's what I heard."

Jason looked at him sharply. "You did? How did you hear that?"

"Marcie must have told someone. Anyway, the word has gotten around among the Brojan Orchards workers at the speed of light in a vacuum."

Almost choking on his beer, Jason set the bottle down hard. "Damn. She shouldn't have told anyone. That's not like her."

"I think she only told Jess Carson, and then he told Bill, and then Bill mentioned it to Sue …"

Jason threw up his hands. "And the rest is history—or more accurately, mythology." He sighed. "Right! What do I look like—some kind of faith healer?"

Grinning, Rich said, "I've got to admit, no one would ever accuse you of that. Come on, calm down. Enjoy your beer."

But no sooner did Jason take up his bottle and try to do just that than Rich added, "But God does work in mysterious ways. And through the most unlikely people."

Jason gave a bark of a laugh. "Damned straight. If healer is the job description, there's no more unlikely candidate than me."

He wasn't the only one in uncharted territory.

According to Jubilee's athletic director, Alvin Williams, Daman was spending less and less of his free time on the basketball court and more and more of it at the driving range. Jason found him out there often and usually joined him when he did.

"You better watch it," he told the boy one fall afternoon, after Daman hit the ball with his lithe, powerful swing. The contact sounded like a gunshot. "You might get good at this game. And let me warn you—it can get addictive."

Daman put another ball on the tee. "That's okay."

Another booming shot followed.

"But it might interfere with your NBA career." Jason delivered this line with a slight rap cadence, jerking his chin to an imaginary beat.

Daman didn't dignify this mock effort at hipness with a response. He only placed another ball.

"I wouldn't mind being the next Tiger."

And damned if he just might not be, thought Jason, the next time he took Daman to the country club.

And the time after that.

The kid improved steadily. Jason started reflecting on his own rapid improvement almost thirty years earlier. It didn't take much memory-searching for him to realize Daman made him look almost developmentally challenged.

Jason knew it raised eyebrows at the club whenever he brought the Jubilee golf team out, and it didn't seem to be any less eccentric if he played rounds with only Daman. For all the years Jason had spent in the spotlight, courting attention, he suspected he drew even more notice now, when he wasn't even trying. Well, hell—why not? His life was a gossip goldmine: bankruptcy, cancer, divorce, hanging with hoodlums, trying to resuscitate Knightbridge Cellars.

Come and get me, Jason thought. *Let 'er rip.*

One time on the course, when Daman got outside his own teenage head enough to ask a few desultory questions about "the wine biz," Jason cut short their round and drove him out to the vineyard. Under Marcie's bemused gaze, he walked the kid up and down the rows, pointing out different varietals and talking drainage and slope and soil and exposure. Daman absorbed the knowledge like he did everything else—with apparent indifference and total mastery.

It didn't surprise him, therefore, when Rich Williams called him into his office again. Jason suspected it would be about the boy and the time he was spending with him.

"There's the man," said Rich, swinging away from his

computer keyboard. "Please have a seat. Thanks for coming out here late in the day."

"Sure. What's up? You said it was important."

Rich chewed his lip.

Here it comes, thought Jason. Maybe Jubilee heard about Daman's time at the winery and thought it wasn't a good idea—promoting future alcohol abuse, or something.

"Yes, it is important," Rich said. "But, frankly, I've been hesitant to bring it up to you."

"Why?" He tried to keep the defensive note from his voice.

"Because I know you're busy, and I also know that you've never ... never—uh—done anything like this."

Jason held up questioning palms. "You've certainly got my attention. What is this 'this'?"

Clearing his throat, Rich tented his fingers together. "Several women would like you to join a group with them—and me."

Something else entirely, then.

Relaxing, Jason sat back in his chair. "Rich, my man—I didn't know you were into group sex."

"I thought I said you'd never done anything like this," Rich shot back. Then he gave an uncomfortable chuckle. "That's not exactly the group I had in mind. This one would be a prayer group."

Jason stared. "A *what*!"

"A couple of their husbands are very ill," added Rich, as if this made it comprehensible.

"That's a bummer, but it's not my business," snapped Jason. "Look—if this is about that thing with Miguel Rosario, you need to tell these people I didn't do anything. It was just some kind of weird coincidence."

Uncowed, Rich leaned forward. "Jason, what you need to realize is that 'these people,' as you call them, don't believe in coincidences. They believe in miracles."

Jason was already getting up. "That's ridiculous. No way. I won't do it."

But there he was, a few days later, sitting in a circle in a darkened room with a bunch of middle-aged Hispanic women and damned Rich Williams. Votive candles and rosary beads and an undercurrent of murmured prayers, for crying out loud.

"Let's take each other's hands," said Rich, like he did this every day. Maybe he did.

He reached out to the women on either side of him, ignoring Jason's appalled look. Jason didn't move an inch, but the women next to him took hold of his hands, and he could hardly yank them away.

"*Los manos son muy grandes!*" uttered the woman to his right, holding Jason's oversized hand up to the woman on his left.

"*Muy, muy grandes!*" marveled the other.

Yeah, and Rich Williams was going to be in *muy, muy grande* pain after this was done, Jason told himself. But Jubilee's executive director just bowed his head and shut his eyes, followed by the women, and Jason had no choice but to do the same, squirming.

"Lord," intoned Rich, "the eight of us are gathered here in prayer to ask that your healing touch be placed on Hernando and Julio, husbands of Carmela and Guadalupe. Even though we don't speak the same language, and I don't understand the prayers of these ladies any more than they understand mine, you do. You know the cries of our hearts. We worshipfully ask you to hear the pleas we are making on behalf of these men, to restore them to health."

The words were hardly spoken when the women flanking Jason jumped and began speaking urgently to each other in Spanish so rapid he could catch none of it.

"What are they saying, Margarita?" Rich asked a heavyset woman with braided hair.

"They both felt a shock from Señor Jason's hands," supplied Margarita breathlessly. "They believe God has given him unusually large, strong hands—*muy macho*—and that they have special powers. Healing powers."

"What?" echoed Jason, aghast. This time he did snatch his hands from the women, while Margarita continued to translate. "They're loco!" he told *Rich*. "*Muy loco!*"

Rich only raised his eyebrows. "They're asking, Jason—begging, really—that you lay your hands on their husbands."

And looking from one face to the next around the circle, Jason didn't need an interpreter to understand the pleading eyes and suppliant hands.

"Do I have a choice?"

Rich couldn't hide his smile. "Not really."

The only way to recover from scenes like that and the one that followed—stuffy, darkened rooms, hands pushing him from behind, fevered brows hot under his touch, awkward mutterings of God-knew-what issuing from him—was to get out to the range again and shag balls with the golf team. After scenes like that, Jason thought, spending his time teaching thugs how to swing a club properly sounded relatively painless. Given the choice between listening to cussing and posturing or urgent, expectant Spanish praying directed at his head, he'd take the cussing and posturing—any day and twice on Sunday.

Which was how he was out with the team some days later, making adjustments to Jamal's posture and grip, when Rich Williams came striding over.

"Hey, Jason. I've got some good news for you—both Hernando and Julio are doing much, much better."

Tapping the back of Jamal's hand to get him to slide it up a hair, Jason said, "That's great. Who the hell are they?"

"The two guys you laid hands on last week."

That got Jason's attention. He dismissed Jamal with a nod and walked some distance away from the boys.

"Really?" His surprise quickly gave way to dismay. "Now,

look, Rich, I'm telling you: you've got to explain to these people that this is all just—just some kind of spiritual placebo effect."

Williams laughed and thumped him on the shoulder. "Well, any good doctor would tell you that the mind is at least as important as the medicine."

Jason shrugged this off impatiently. "I'm really glad you find this all so comical. I'm telling you, this thing is starting to get out of hand."

"You mean, out of 'hands,' right?" Rich answered, still grinning.

"Chris Rock has nothing on you, Williams," said Jason wryly. "But, seriously—I don't know what you all think is going on, but have you thought about what's going to happen when these 'miracles' quit happening? When it's time for the angry mob to run the witch doctor out of town? I don't need more trouble in my life."

The executive director looked him straight in the eye. "Have you thought about what will happen if they don't?"

So back to golf. Whatever the hell was going on with freak healings and people thinking magical thoughts, Jason put his head down and focused on the game.

The division championship tournament rolled around. Leaves fell; balls flew.

Alvin Williams Sr. studied the scoreboard alongside Jason, nodding. "Uh-huh. That's right. Jason, you've got to feel good, real good. Quite an improvement for the team, going from dead last the previous year to fourth place this one."

"They've worked really hard," Jason answered. He was beaming.

The old man pointed. "And Daman shooting a seventy-nine!" He gave a low whistle. "That's incredible, considerin' how recently he started playin' the game. And that he's still on the football team."

"I'm proud of him. I'm proud of them all. Hard work," Jason said again.

"They weren't the only ones puttin' in the time and effort," Alvin, Sr. replied. "Truth be told, I never thought you had it in you to stick with the program. It was pretty ugly in the beginning."

"More like totally fugly," Jason replied in agreement. "But we did it."

He turned to find the team in a semicircle behind them, gawping up at the results. "Okay, guys, I promised to take you to Dairy Queen if you came in seventh, and you did way better than that. So, I'll drive you there, and then you can have anything you want ... because Mr. Alvin is paying."

Whoops and laughs greeted this, and Jason put an arm around the old guy as they headed for the parking lot.

Yes, sir. Golf was predictable. Golf was good.

But even taking fourth in the division championship couldn't make the weirdness go away. It wasn't like Miguel Rosario was weird with him—after that first day, the guy went back to work and was all business, though Jason caught the occasional look in his employee's eye that told him all was not forgotten.

For the most part, however, things went on at Knightbridge. He and Miguel were talking filtration one afternoon in front of some of the big vats when Marcie found them.

"Boss, there are some people here to see you."

"Oh, good," said Jason, thrusting his clipboard at Miguel and straightening his cap. "It must be the camera crew from *Wine Spectator*."

"Not exactly," Marcie replied, poker-faced.

Not exactly turned out to mean *not at all*. When he followed her into the office, he discovered the small room crowded with people: four adults and seven children, all Hispanic, all crammed into the limited space.

"What's this all about?" Jason muttered under his breath.

"You know, boss, I'm not exactly fluent in Spanish, and they're talking some kind of Indian dialect, but it's something about sick children." She bit her lip. "And they're not the only ones."

"What do you mean?"

"Look."

Leading him to the side window, she scooted over to let him peer out. By the picnic table under the cottonwood trees milled dozens more people. Maybe thirty or forty, altogether. Some were standing, some sitting. All were waiting.

Jason wavered on his feet and gripped the window sill. Probably no one in the cramped office required a translation of the oath that burst from him, English or no English.

"Look, Williams, I mean it. You gotta stop this insanity! This is way out of control. These people are treating me like I'm some kind of miracle worker! Dozens of them showed up at the winery earlier today."

Jubilee's executive director pushed away the keyboard he'd been typing at and got up to shut the door Jason had flung open. Smoothing his tie, he sat down again. "Did you pray with them?"

"Did I—did I pray with them?" Jason echoed, his volume dropping. He slumped into the seat across the desk from Rich. "Well, sort of. Marcie gathered them all in a circle outside by the creek, and I said a few things, which she translated. Then they brought some sick babies and kids forward, and I put my hands on their heads. You know—I had to get rid of them. Arguing about it would have taken longer! We barely got them out of there before the writer and camera crew from *Wine Spectator* pulled up. This can't go on!"

Rich nodded slowly. "As long as you keep praying, and it keeps working, they'll keep showing up."

"This is crazy." Jason removed his cap to run a hand over his scalp, now bristling again with the beginnings of hair. He slapped his cap back on. "Who knows what the hell is going on. All I know is, I can't deal with it." Leaping up again, he began pacing. "I could use a drink. I don't suppose you hide any Maker's Mark in that file cabinet of yours?"

"Jason, did you ever think that maybe this is what you were meant to do?"

This drew no answer but a scoffing sound. Rich watched him pace back and forth a few more times before spinning his chair to pull out the file cabinet's upper drawer. "Sorry, man. I don't have any liquor stashed away, and any garbage we confiscate from the kids isn't good enough for the drain we pour it down." He shut the drawer. "But I wonder if all this business—what you call crazy—"

"'Crazy' doesn't begin to cover it," Jason replied snappily.

"I wonder, Jason, if this isn't your real Maker's Mark."

16

"*Feliz Navidad*, ladies," Jason called to the group of women inside Brojan Orchards' main office. They were hanging Christmas decorations, laughing and chatting in Spanish, while festive music played. "Are the boys in the conference room already?"

"*Si, Señor* Jason," answered the receptionist, waving a candy cane in the direction he should go. "They are expecting you."

For all the impressiveness of the Brojan Orchards processing facilities and storage warehouse compound, the conference room was barebones. Jess and Bill were seated at the simple table, doctoring their coffee as Jason walked in.

"Greetings, gentlemen." He placed Sam's old black doctor's bag on the table. Removing his cap, he ran fingers through his minimal hair. "Things are looking pretty merry out there, but I think I can make this an even merrier Christmas for both of you."

Jess beamed at him, already having his suspicions from Jason's mood around the house lately, and Bill Brojan put down his mug to give an encouraging nod.

"I'm pleased to announce," Jason began, "that we cleared over a million this year, even though ownership of Knightbridge Cellars didn't transfer to you until June 30. The juice we'd stored up for the last five years was huge. Thank you, Sterling Bank, for letting us get that for a song."

Slapping his hand on the table, Jess crowed, "Bill, you knew how valuable that would be, early on."

"Yeah," Brojan admitted shyly. "But frankly I thought we'd have to sit on most of it for several more years. Jason, you did a great job of restarting the distribution almost immediately."

"A team effort. You got us a great deal from the bank, Marcie busted her cute little butt—and I underestimated how many female buyers would go for a bald-headed guy. You're looking at about a thirty-percent annualized return on investment." He unzipped the black bag and pulled out two checks, sliding one to Jess and the other to Bill. "Don't spend it all in one place—unless it's on our website."

Jess Carson's eyes widened as he surveyed the amount. "Good *Lord*—and I don't use that term lightly. If this doesn't beat working twelve-hour days in the hot sun or blowing snow, just to coax a little stubble out of the ground!"

"Sue will be really pleased," said Bill in his understated way. "Thanks for your hard work, Jason."

"Knowing you and Sue, you'll probably just give it to Jubilee or some charity down in Mexico, but that's your business. Mine is to make and sell great wine. The rest takes care of itself. But I should warn you both, 2010 is going to be a year of investing in the business. We've got to build out the facilities. So even with a full twelve months of sales, I wouldn't expect much more than this next Christmas. It might even be less."

Brojan pressed his hands flat on the table. "No worries. We're in this for the long haul. We'll keep upping your share of the profits as time goes by. Eventually, we'll start transferring you the equity."

Jason's mind bounded at the term "long haul." He gave Bill an appreciative smile before shrugging. "We'll worry about that later. For now, I'm just ecstatic to be back doing what I love. I didn't realize how much I missed it, especially the wine-making."

"Speaking of wine-making," said Bill, "how's your chief winemaker-in-training doing, Miguel Rosario?"

"Totally fine," Jason assured him. "Like the accident never happened."

There was a little pause, in which Bill went for the coffee pot to top them off. Jason had a sinking feeling he knew where the conversation was headed, but before he could do more than cast about for another topic, Bill was saying, "I've heard you helped quite a few other folks since then. Including a number of our associates—"

"Now, don't you start with that nonsense, Bill," Jason said, cutting him off, over his accelerating heart. "I don't know what Williams has been telling you, but this whole 'healing' thing is just a figment of Rich's fertile fantasy factory." He gave an uncomfortable laugh. "Matter of fact, I wish I had vineyards half as prolific as his imagination."

He saw Brojan and Jess exchange a glance, Jess even smiling. But when Jess saw Jason's mouth tighten, he took pity on him and changed the subject. "Hey, speaking of profit-sharing, Bill tells me you got yourself a new rig. Hope this one handles snow better than your last one."

A few minutes later, the two of them were in the parking lot, admiring the shiny, blue metallic Lexus SUV next to Jess's old pickup.

"That's another thing I owe Bill," said Jason. "If he hadn't co-signed for it, the dealer would never have leased it to me—not with my credit score that makes Argentina's look good."

"Pretty soon you'll be able to pay cash for your cars," Jess replied absently. He chewed the inside of his cheek for a minute, and Jason got a creeping feeling the man had something else on his mind.

He did.

"Jason, there's something I'd like to chat with you about that's got nothing to do with cars or business."

Bracing himself, Jason said, "Why do I get the feeling it's got everything to do with *my* business? Out with it, old man."

"Well, I heard you're going to Hawaii."

"Yup."

"And takin' Daman."

"That sure sounds like my business and none of yours," Jason replied huffily. "Look—I've been killing myself for the last six months, and I need some sun, golf, and beach time. And I want company. Someone who can play golf well. It should appeal to your Christian instincts that I'm taking a kid from the Chicago projects to Hawaii, instead of letting him go back to that hellhole over the holidays, like a lot of the Jubilee kids do. Rich tells me that sometimes they never come back."

Jess held up placating hands. "Don't get me wrong. I think it's wonderful what you're doin' for that young man. Better than takin' some woman, and if the other boys don't mind and Jubilee signs off. I'm all for mentoring. In fact, it reminds me of a situation I witnessed thirty years ago, when Sam Steele took you under his wing."

He stopped and waited to see if Jason would say anything.

He didn't.

Jess rang a finger along the side mirror of the SUV, dashing off droplets. Clearing his throat, he forged ahead. "But the difference between you and Sam Steele is that you have a son of your own."

If he thought Jason was quiet before, that was nothing to the deafening silence that greeted this statement.

Looking down at the shallow layer of snow on the ground, Jason moved it around with his shoe. He scraped the grains to the left, then spread them flat, and then scraped them to the right.

Jess gripped the side mirror, feeling the cold metal burn on his skin. "Jason—when's the last time you saw J.J.?"

At that, Jason blew out a steaming breath. He looked up at the gray sky and then down at the ground again. His voice came out rough, uncertain, un-Jason-like. "Rich Williams once said to me that we're all like snow-covered dung. He had that right. In my case, though, it's more like a mountain of manure. It would take one helluva blizzard to cover up all of my shit."

He didn't expect Jess to contradict him, and Jess didn't.

After a while Jason went on. "Honestly, Jess, I'm ashamed to see J.J. There was ... a bad scene last year at the house. Nate even saw it."

"I heard about it," Jess said shortly. "But you have to get past it, and most importantly, you need to help J.J. deal with it. He saw things a boy should never have to see. He might be mad at you, but he needs you, warts and all."

Jason snorted. "Would that be genital warts and all?"

"Whatever." Carson rapped a fist on the hood of the Lexus. "For the first time, Jason—before it's too late—act like his dad."

Digging in the pocket of his jeans for his keys and backing away, Jason nodded. "I hear you, I hear you. It's on my bucket list."

Jess caught him by the sleeve. "What *number* is it, on the bucket list?"

Finally, Jason looked straight at him. Jess couldn't remember the last time he'd seen him with his defenses so down. Maybe when Jason was a boy? Maybe that day at the river, when he came to, sputtering and wondering where on earth he was.

"You wanna know the truth, Jess? Here it is: I'm afraid to face Sarah."

The grip on his sleeve loosened, but Jess still held his gaze. "I know it. And you should be, for what you put her through. But it's time to man up."

He let his fingers fall away.

"You go along now, son."

Thank God for voicemail. First contact and time and place could all be established without genuine interaction. If Sarah's voice in her messages was anything to go by, a hard winter lay ahead.

His ex-wife's new place was entirely unlike their former home, as if Sarah had tossed out all her old design ideas along with her husband. Gone were the semicircular driveway in front and the porte cochere, to be replaced by a modern structure that could have been designed by Frank Lloyd Wright, or Seattle's hot new architect, Tom Kundig. One thing stayed the same though: the new place was as meticulously kept as the old. His mouth twisted wryly. That's right. Ditch the husband and the starter dream home, but keep the crew that plowed the snow into those tidy little bumpers. Good help was hard to find.

Only the thought that she must have seen him pull up got Jason out of his car. He would have preferred to take another five minutes blowing the heater and working up his nerve. But he did get out, and he made it up the slippery steps in front of the ten-foot wooden doors with no mishaps. Flexing his fingers, he pushed the doorbell.

There was a muffled clicking of heels on tile, and the door swung open.

Sarah.

The old Jason might have cracked that she looked like a million bucks—twenty million, to be exact. But the icy look in her narrowed blue eyes froze any words in his throat.

After a moment it became clear, however, that if he didn't speak, she wasn't going to either. Nor was she going to invite him in, even if she had to heat the whole frozen Walla Walla Valley through the open door.

His mouth worked a moment before he managed to blurt out, "Hi. Is J.J. ready?"

"How nice of you to put in an appearance." Her voice was cool and steady. "What's it been? Over a year?"

He shifted his weight from one foot to the other, cleared his throat to dislodge what felt like a golf ball. "Things have changed. I've changed."

Without acknowledging this, she said, "I hear you've become quite the ... healer."

She made him sound exactly like the televangelist charlatan he dreaded, and he made no answer.

"Too bad you can't heal your relationship with your own son."

Grasping at this, Jason overlooked her hostility. "Yes. I mean, no. I mean, that's why I'm here."

"Hm." Throwing him one last skeptical look, she backed up a step and opened the door a bit wider. J.J. stood behind her, his eyes huge. To judge from his face, the boy wasn't looking forward to this rapprochement any more than his mother. He seemed to have grown a couple inches, and his hair was longer. When J.J. was a baby, Sarah never wanted to cut his hair.

It took a second for Jason to tear his eyes from his son and notice that J.J. wasn't alone. He had a death-grip on Ringo's collar. The dog, at least, was happy to see him. When Jason looked at him, he gave a whining bark and lunged for his old master, yanking J.J. to his knees. Ringo leapt on Jason, planting huge paws on his shoulders and knocking him off the front stoop into one of the snow bumpers.

"Hey, hey, old fella. Hey there, Ringo," Jason said with a laugh, writhing away from the dog's enthusiastic tongue, even while he petted him.

As J.J. tried to haul the bull mastiff off his father and Jason managed to scramble back up, brushing snow and crazy dog off, the boy started laughing too.

There might even have been the hint of a smile on Sarah's face.

It would take more than a dog's antics to make things right with his son, but Ringo's presence gave them something to look at that first outing, besides each other, and something to laugh about.

"Mom doesn't like him out in the snow," J.J. said at one point, when the bull mastiff was romping through deep white piles while they stumbled along behind, plastic toboggan sleds bouncing against their backs. The dog stopped periodically to shake whole daubs and clods off, before bounding and lolloping into new drifts. "She says he makes a mess, even if I wipe his paws with a towel."

"Yeah," Jason agreed, sweeping snow off the front of his jeans. "She's right about that."

"But she was the one who suggested he come along today. Wasn't that funny?" J.J. glanced at him sidewise.

"Yeah," Jason said again. He remembered as well as J.J. how Sarah would roll her eyes when Ringo tracked anything through the house: snow, mud, dust. She'd be right behind him, wiping or sweeping. Sarah liked a clean floor.

She must have relented in this case because she thought J.J. would be more comfortable with a familiar companion. Not that she was wrong about that, he admitted to himself. That was Sarah—insightful. Hadn't she always seen right to the heart of things? No BS about her.

He had liked that—loved that—once.

It occurred to him that maybe Sarah let Ringo come along today, not just for J.J.'s sake but possibly for his own. She would've known that Jason missed the damned dog.

"It was nice of your mom to let Ringo come," Jason said. "Even though he'll be a mess when he's done."

"I don't know about nice," J.J. answered dubiously, puffing a little as he staggered along in Jason's tracks. "She said at least the worst of the snow and wet would trash your car and not the house."

Ringo chose that moment to fly past them over the edge of the bluff, diving headfirst into a large mound of snow that built up in a swale. When he emerged, the lower half of his black muzzle was covered in a beard of snow. J.J. burst out laughing, and Jason laughed to hear him laugh, while Ringo froze, his expression like he'd been caught with his paw in the cookie jar.

Jason put a mitted hand on J.J.'s shoulder and gave it a

tentative pat. "Well, then—mess, here we come. Let's stop here. I think this is high enough."

Unlooping the toboggan from his back, J.J. threw his father a grin. "Race you down!"

Sarah had her wish granted, about the snow and wet and destruction in Jason's new car afterward, but he didn't care a bit. The backseat was piled with discarded damp snow gear, across which slumped Ringo, wiped out and contented and radiating waves of wet-dog smell. The windows fogged moistly until Jason ran the air-conditioner and the heater full-blast, and J.J. even had his socked feet on the dash at Jason's prompting, to warm them. In his hands was his second cup of hot chocolate.

The snow was coming down hard now, but Jason wasn't driving the Lexus anywhere near its limits, and they might as well have been on hot asphalt in summer, the way it handled. He still missed the Ferrari some days, but hey—this wasn't so bad. Come spring, he could throw a few Jubilee thugs in and hit the country club, instead of having to invite them one at a time or giving in and driving the piece-of-crap school van.

He looked over at the boy, who was blowing on his cocoa and watching the white scenery pass.

"Hey, J.J. In the spring, what would you think about learning to play golf? You're the perfect age right now."

Surprised, J.J. looked right at him, eyes wide.

"Golf is fun, and I've got some practice now, teaching kids to play," Jason added.

He wondered if Sarah had poisoned that particular well—told the boy golf was for weenies, or bastards like his father. Not to mention, he had no idea if she would even allow J.J. to hang out with him that much. Golf took time, God knew.

But her enmity must not have extended to her ex's sporting pastimes, because a big smile spread across the boy's face. "That would be awesome ... Dad."

It wasn't like he tried to keep J.J. and Daman a secret from each other. It was just that what Jess Carson had implied stuck in his craw: Had he taken Daman to Hawaii not just to have a golf partner and do a good deed, but because it was easier to build a relationship than to rebuild one?

Not that it was easy building a relationship with someone as prickly as Daman. The kid had a mouth on him and an ego that never took a day off.

The evening after Jason only beat Daman by one stroke, they were lounging on the lanai of their room, Jason sipping a cocktail and Daman springing up every other moment to point something out or to check out bikini babes below.

"Jeez, take it easy," Jason said, mocking him. "You're gonna sprain your neck, whipping it back and forth like that."

"We don't have no views like this in Cabrini Green, I got to say," Daman said. "Though we got an alley where you can see drug deals goin' down pretty much twenty-four-seven. I'd be watchin' too, if the dealers looked like some of these ladies." He raised a hand in answer to one of their waves. "If you wasn't such a broken old man, you'd know what I was talkin' about."

"This broken old man hasn't played thirty-six in one day in at least ten years," Jason said defensively. "And that last chemo round was a bitch. Even playing in a cart, I'm whipped."

"Yeah, you got your sob stories ready. All I'm sayin' is, at my age, the testosterone is flowin' freely, and I've been stuck livin' with a bunch of ugly dudes. In your case, I'd be suggestin' you ask them for some Viagra in your IV, next time you go in for chemo."

"Ha, ha, very funny. It may astonish you, but I haven't ever needed much help, chemical or otherwise, when it came to women."

Daman gave an appreciative whistle. "Oo-ee! Listen to the bald guy swagger! Swagger, swagger. You better let me see some of these historical moves of yours. When we goin' down for dinner?"

"Didn't I just say I'm done for today? Plus, Rich Williams made me swear on a stack of his precious Bibles I'd keep you out of trouble. What do you say we just order room service?"

"That like where they bring the food to your room?"

Jason grinned at him. "Never had it before, huh?"

Dropping into the lounge chair next to Jason's and leaning back with his hands behind his head, Daman said, "Let's just say Jubilee hasn't started that amenity yet for its guests."

Another amenity Jubilee didn't offer was pay-per-view movies.

"You mean, you can just push a few buttons and watch it?" Daman marveled, scrolling through the menu.

Jason grabbed the remote before the kid could select the Adult category. "I've got to have a serious chat with Mr. Rich. If he's not careful, they could lose their four-diamond rating."

They ended up watching *The Blind Side*, which Daman found interesting for the football and Michael Oher, and Jason—

"Man, what are you doin'?" demanded Daman at the end, peering over and frowning at Jason as the figures on the screen crowded together, hugging and joyous. "Are you *cryin'*?"

Setting his wineglass down, Jason dashed away his tear and grumbled, "They're a family. His surrogate family. They're a real family now."

"Uh-huh." Daman only exhaled slowly, shaking his head.

Sun, golf, swimming, food, and movies.

Their final night they watched *The Treasure of the Sierra Madre*. It had been one of his favorite movies growing up. He couldn't remember how many times he and Nate watched it at the Carsons'. It took some pressure to get Daman to watch the old black-and-white classic.

He'd completely forgotten the healing scene.

The Indian villagers surrounded Humphrey Bogart and his two comrades, Walter Huston and Tim Holt. With machetes drawn, they indicated that Huston should go with them. As drums beat softly, the villagers presented Huston with a seriously ill young boy. Huston lifted the boy's arms up and down. He put his ear to the boy's chest and then raised his arms again. Women prayed rosary beads. The resuscitation attempts continued until, at last, the boy began to stir. Huston slapped his face, gently at first, and then harder. Finally, finally, the boy opened his eyes and the village burst into rejoicing, crossing themselves. Huston smiled.

"You ain't gonna start cryin' again, are you?" Daman asked, interrupting Jason's spellbound trance. He had paused the movie and was studying him again.

Blinking slowly, Jason surfaced. "What? Crying? No. It's just—just that—"

"Just that you're losin' it," Daman supplied. "I thought this was one of your favorites."

"It is, but I forgot about this part," said Jason lamely. "Never paid much attention to it before."

He settled back against the couch cushions and nodded at the screen.

Still frowning, Daman started it up again. But Jason couldn't say he saw much more of the film that night. He was too lost in thought.

On the plane ride home, Jason whipped the issue of *Golf Magazine* from Daman's fingers.

"What would you think of helping teach my kid J.J. to play the game?"

"You got a kid J.J.? Let me guess—that stand for Jason, Jr.?"

"I got a kid J.J. Yes, J.J. stands for Jason, Jr. He's nearly fifteen." Jason felt his face grow hot. "I'm not super close to him because—I worked a lot when he was little. But he says he wants to learn."

Daman cocked his head at him. "You thinkin' you're Golf Yoda all the time. Why do you want me to help teach?"

He didn't answer for a minute. To be honest, part of the reason he wanted Daman along was for the Ringo Effect: things would be less awkward with J.J. if they weren't one-on-one. Daman would break the ice. And it wouldn't be bad for Daman, either, to have someone around who wasn't an authority or a peer or a semblance of a mentor. It might soften him, get him to think outside himself.

Tossing the magazine onto Daman's tray table, Jason only said, "As Golf Yoda, I've learned, the best way to learn something is to teach it, and since I beat you by four shots our last round, I'm thinking you need remedial lessons. But, hey—I'd appreciate it if you helped me out with him. You've become an okay kid, especially when you've got your smart-assness under control. And, you know, I think J.J. would hit it off with you. Kinda like you and I have hit it off."

"Aww, Cheese Whiz, old man," drawled Daman. He turned his head away to look out the window, but not before Jason had seen the funny look in his eye and the way he bit his lip.

Jason punched him in the shoulder. "You aren't gonna start crying again, are you? Honestly, I can't take you anywhere."

17

"You been out on the range again?" Jess hoisted Jason's golf bag from where he'd left it leaning in the hallway and propped it in the corner.

"Yup."

"Golf team getting in some early work? I should have known you'd be right back out there, the second the snow was gone."

"Not the golf team yet." Jason muted the television and rolled to a sitting position. "Though Daman was with me. We, uh, were showing J.J. the basics."

Jess gave a whoop and clapped his hands together. "That's right, that's right." Throwing himself into the armchair, he kicked his boots off. "Getting J.J. out there. Well, how'd it go? Did he like it?"

Brow furrowing, Jason reviewed the morning in his mind. "He's awkward. Almost as tall as Daman, and hasn't grown into his limbs yet. He's got to work on finishing on his front foot. When we got him finishing forward, things improved. With more practice—"

Jess moaned. "I don't mean his golf swing, for crying out loud! I mean, how did he and Daman like each other? How was it, having your son out there? You know—was he ... resentful ... that it was Daman who got the R&R trip with you? That it was Daman and the other Jubilee kids who got all the golf lessons and time with you, up to now?"

"J.J. doesn't have a resentful bone in his body," declared Jason. "Unlike his dear mother."

But Jess wasn't in the mood for wisecracks. He just sat back and waited, and eventually, giving a sigh, Jason went on. "It was a little weird, at first. I mean, J.J. knew I coach the golf team, and I'd mentioned Daman before. But you know how Daman is—cocky as all get out and busting my ass any opportunity he gets—all in good fun. You could tell J.J. was kinda uncomfortable with it. He's still shy around me."

Jess nodded. "Daman isn't just that way with you, you know. Seems to be his MO. Was he hard on J.J. too?"

He shook his head slowly. "That's the funny thing. It's like, when Daman saw how it was, he toned it all down. He was … great with J.J. Patient. Even encouraging."

Jason fell silent, remembering one particular time when J.J. was struggling to make contact, falling back after each swing. Daman had been hitting balls next to him, his usual grace and power on display, textbook swing after textbook swing. But he stopped after a minute and approached the other boy. "Don't sweat it, J.J.," Daman advised. "Last year, when I first started, I was struggling just like you. But your dad knows the game and how to teach it. You'll be hittin' it real good, real soon."

The relief and appreciation on J.J.'s face had been almost painful for Jason to see.

Of course.

Didn't every boy need to hear he had what it takes? How did a kid like Daman know that instinctively, when Jason had to be clubbed over the head to get it?

"Good for Daman," said Jess, interrupting Jason's reverie. He slapped a hand over Jason's knee and gripped it, almost as if he knew what he'd been thinking.

Jason cleared his throat. "I managed to get J.J.'s swing straightened out, and by the end Daman was even telling him how much he'd improved."

"Good for Daman," Jess repeated with emphasis. He gave Jason's knee a shake. "Not only that. Good for you and J.J."

The older man's eyes flicked to the frozen television screen. "*The Blind Side*, huh?"

"Yeah. Daman and I saw it in Hawaii. I thought it was a good one."

"I'll say. Not like most of the trash Hollywood puts out these days. But, hey—that reminds me." Jess reached over Jason for the remote. "I recorded something the other day I thought you might like to see."

Accepting the change of subject gratefully, Jason jeered, "Don't tell me you actually figured out how to work the DVR."

"Miracles do happen, occasionally!" Jess said, chuckling. "In fact, more than occasionally, lately." He hit a few buttons, and Oprah appeared on the screen, seated with a fiftyish-year-old man in a suit and bow tie. Seeing Jason's doubtful expression, Jess conceded, "Actually, I was trying to record something else but got this by accident. Almost deleted it because I'm not much of an Oprah fan, but for some reason I hung around long enough to hear this guy. He had quite a story."

"So?"

"So, you need to hear what he has to say. This guy got some rare kind of meningitis that left him totally braindead. Clinically. But while he was out, gone, he had this experience."

"Aw, come on, Jess," Jason complained, though there was a wary note in his voice. "Look at the purple shirt and the bow tie. He's like a carnival barker. Did he dream he was on the midway again?"

"The guy happens to be a neurosurgeon, Jason, not some bozo. And I'm telling you, he was braindead for nearly a week! But he had this experience he couldn't explain, even with all his education and brain experience. Just listen to some of these bits."

"Initially I was in this kind of vague, foggy, murky underground. It was like being in dirty Jell-O," the bow-tied neurosurgeon was saying in a soft drawl. He had dark, earnest eyes.

"Initially when?" asked Jason.

"When he was out," Jess replied impatiently. "When he was braindead. Shhhh ..."

"There was a pounding, mechanical sound, deep, deep, somewhere off in the distance," the doctor went on. "Every now and then, there might be some grotesque face of something that would boil up out of the muck and chant or roar and then go back in the muck. And it was kind of a hideous place, yet I remembered nothing else."

"Oh my God," whispered Jason. "Turn it up! I've been there. That place, Jess—it was like that."

But Oprah was looking dismayed. "What you were describing felt like hell ... a form of hell."

Her guest explained that it was more a state of mere existence. He didn't know any better—couldn't remember any other state of being.

"Yeah," muttered Jason. "Yeah."

"And then?" she prompted.

"And then I was rescued by this spinning white light. This very slowly spinning—moving toward me had all these fine filaments ..."

Oprah interrupted again with another question, to Jason's mounting irritation. If she would just let the man tell his story!

"Initially it was just very bright," the guest answered her. "It came with the most gorgeous melody. After all those eons of hearing this pounding mechanical subterranean sound, there's this lovely melody, a perfect melody as it came toward me."

By this point, Jason was leaning so far forward Jess thought he might fall into the screen.

In answer to another of his host's prompts, the doctor continued, "As it got closer, it expanded. And it was a rip in the reality around me. It was a portal in to this brilliant, lovely, vivid, verdant valley, going up steeply into this brilliant light ..."

Jess shifted his weight on the armchair to watch Jason. He probably could have dropped a book on his foot and gotten no reaction.

Too soon, the interview clip ended, and after a dumbfounded instant, Jason whirled around, scrabbling for the remote. "What? That's it? It's over? I wanted to hear more about what he saw next."

"I thought you would," said Jess. Holding the remote clear of Jason's grabbing hands, he clicked to the next segment of the interview.

"In his book, Eben provides a vivid description of his passage into this new dimension," Oprah was saying, over a background of mystical universe imagery and glows. "There he meets a guide, a woman who leads him on his journey, Eben says on the wings of a giant butterfly, into another world of inexplicable beauty."

"*What did she say?*" Jason said in a choked voice, succeeding in snatching the clicker from Jess. He ran the recording back again, not trusting his ears.

"A guide," said Oprah again, "a woman who leads him on his journey, Eben says on the wings of a giant butterfly, into another world of inexplicable beauty." The universe shots gave way to a scene of nature, a monarch butterfly flying above it.

As if she had spoken magic words that froze him, spellbound, Jason hardly blinked, every muscle locked in concentration.

"You've had flying dreams before," said Oprah. They were still seated in the same studio, wearing the same clothes. There was the purple shirt and bowtie. "How was this different than a flying dream?"

"It was that it was so much more real," Eben replied. "I mean it makes sitting even here, in this wonderful studio, seem dreamlike by comparison. It was so sharp and crisp. You could see all around, and above us were these kind of billowing clouds that had beautiful colors in them against this blue-black sky. And there were these arcs of shimmering beings, of these orbs of light that were shooting through the sky, leaving these trails. And the music that they were putting out—indescribably beautiful. That would be crescendo after crescendo after crescendo, higher and higher, in response to any kind of questioning in my mind—"

"So, this woman," she interrupted. "You were escorted by this lovely woman—"

"Right. And she was beside me on a butterfly—"

"Did you recognize her? Did you know her? Was it somebody you'd seen in this life?"

"No. She was very beautiful. I remember her face perfectly, and she was looking at me with the most loving smile—"

"What is the message you received?" Oprah pressed. "Tell us that."

The woman had no patience, Jason thought, kicking the couch in frustration. He would have liked to hear a lot more about the woman and the music and the butterfly.

The guest, however, was unruffled. "You are loved, deeply cherished. Forever. There is nothing you have to fear. You will always be loved ... Nothing to worry about. You are taken care of. So, this was the most comforting, wonderful news that she could give me. That pure love. Don't worry."

"Thought you might find that interesting," said Jess when the second segment wrapped up. Rising with a grunt, he went over to the set and shut it off.

"Wait—that was all you got recorded?"

"Yup. But I'd already read the guy's book. It's called *Proof of Heaven*. That's why it caught my attention."

"Does it say in the book who the beautiful girl was?"

Jess nodded slowly, wonderingly. "Yep. It does. That's another amazing part. So Dr. Alexander had no idea who this girl was in his experience or what have you, just like he told Oprah. Maybe heaven is just full of pretty girls. But then, months later ..." He broke off, scratching his forehead. "Maybe I can go find the place in the book."

"Forget the book," Jason ordered. "Just tell me. Months later, *what*, old man?"

"Well, it turns out this Dr. Alexander was adopted as a baby, and he never knew his birth family until just a couple of years before he got the meningitis. But in this birth family, he had a sister who died before he ever reconnected with them. So, along about a few months after his near-passing, the doctor's surviving birth sister sends him a photograph of the sister who died. He looks at it and looks at it, thinking he's seen her before, but he can't place her. So he puts the picture on his dresser and goes to sleep. When he woke up the next morning, it hit him."

"*What* hit him?" he pressed, already guessing, but wanting to hear Jess say it.

"The sister who died was the beautiful girl who rode with him through heaven."

Jason felt a run of goosebumps on his arms and neck. He let out a long breath and stared up at the ceiling. It was an old popcorn ceiling, with little chunks broken off, from where he and Nate had been playing ball indoors and things got out of hand. It was when you damaged the popcorn that the asbestos leaked out, wasn't it? Maybe if Nate or Maria had lived a little longer, they would've gotten lung cancer too. Wouldn't explain Jess's perfect health, though.

"Jess," Jason said, after another minute.

"Son?"

"Listening to that guy—you're not gonna believe it, but I realize—I'm positive—that what I was flying on was a butterfly too. In my experience. Vision. Whatever it was. I'd forgotten that part. But there were the wings and the color. It had to be one."

"Huh," grunted Jess.

"And there was a girl with me too, who was familiar. I know I know her, but just like the doctor, I can't place her either."

Shaking his head to clear his thoughts, he gave one of his old grins. "I mean, I think I must know her. Power of suggestion, right? But who knows? Maybe I don't. Maybe Dr. Alexander's dead sister has to fly everyone around."

Perhaps it was because he spent the rest of the evening trying to grasp at his vision and the mystery girl that, when he fell asleep that night, they both returned to him, almost as vividly as when he was comatose after his "accident." He'd had these dreams before, starting right before all the healing stuff, but never with such clarity and intensity.

He was soaring again. Against and through that tapestry of vibrant colors. Flying, moving up and down with a gentle, rhythmic pulse.

He looked over at his companion, the one who had been with him after he tried to kill himself, and felt once more that sensation. He *knew* her. She was familiar, her eyes, her golden hair.

They rose and rose, drawn straight upward toward something that was like the sun, only brighter, piercing a sky so blue it was nearly purple. The luminance grew. It seemed to gather them in, to swallow them up.

And then they were standing in a place of total whiteness. Glowing figures surrounded them, and he heard again the music, the melody his waking mind could never recall. It came from the beings around him. They were singing, softly at first, and then growing louder, until, at the very crescendo, they fell back. He thought they might have fallen away, but then he realized they were bowed down. A larger figure had descended among them, shining so brightly that Jason tried to shield his eyes, but it was not the kind of radiance that could be obscured. As it drew even closer, his companion bent low as well.

He should bow too, shouldn't he? But he wanted to know—had to know. He stretched his hands toward the presence, half in wonder and half in dread. And the presence, now directly before him, responded with a surge. Something that reached for his two hands, meeting them in an explosive electric arc. He felt it—whatever it was—rush over and through him, bathing him in the same radiance. The figure grew, loomed, as the singing rose again, as the music and the light enveloped him.

And then it was gone. Vanished.

The light. The ethereal beings. His companion. The music. The radiant Other.

He awoke in darkness and confusion, clutching at the

bedcoverings as he became aware of a rapping noise, sharp and persistent. Someone at the door?

The clock read 2:39 a.m.

Jason heard stirring from Jess's room and a grumbled question. They met in the hall, rumpled and squinting.

"What the hell is going on?" Jason demanded.

"Your guess is as good as mine."

Jess cracked the door to find a young Latino woman on the step, looking very cold and very scared. Instantly he stepped back to let her in. "What's wrong, young lady? What happened?"

"*No hablo ingles. Mi hermano* ees *muy, muy enfermo. Usted*—you—*debe venir deprisa. Andele! Andele!*"

"My Spanish still sucks, but I get the idea," Jason answered. "*Si, si. Uno momentito.* I need to get dressed. *Yo* put on clothas—I mean *ropas*." He slapped at himself in pantomime, and the woman nodded and burst into tears.

"I'm coming with you," Jess said. "I'll drive."

Then they were jolting over potholes through a trailer park, following an old Chevy Impala missing its hubcaps. The darkness couldn't hide the dilapidated state of the trailer they pulled up to, and the whole scene made Jason feel sick to his stomach. He hadn't been in a place like this since—since he had fled it, decades earlier.

"This sure brings back memories," he grumbled to Jess under his breath. "*Muy mal* memories."

The inside of the trailer was cramped but neat, however. A Coleman lantern illuminated the interior, where an older woman sat by a bed, fingering her beads and murmuring prayers. In the bed lay a young man, shivering and sweating under brightly colored blankets. The young woman spoke to the older one, and they both made way for Jason to approach.

He held up his big hand. "*Hola.* I'd say *como estas*, but I can see it's more like 'coma' *estas.*"

The young man's voice was weak but clear. "No worries. I

speak English. I'm sorry my sister dragged you here in the middle of the night. I told her it was a waste of time."

"Looks like you need to see a doctor."

With a faint shrug and a shudder, the young man said, "No job, no money, no doctor."

Jason chuckled ruefully. "I know that drill. But I'll take you to the ER at Walla Walla General. They'll have to treat you."

The young man gave a nod and translated Jason's words to the two women. His sister let loose a stream of urgent words, to which the older woman added, slapping a vigorous hand on the mattress. That made the young man almost smile. His glazed eyes sought Jason's and he said, "They agree with you. But they insist you pray with me first, and then lay your hands on my head. They have heard the stories of your healing powers." Ignoring Jason's sputtering, he lifted weak fingers. "They say they have more faith in you than in the gringo doctors."

Jason groaned. He felt Jess's hand on his shoulder.

"Look," said Jason, "I have to be honest with you. This whole healing thing is a farce, but it's taken on a life of its own, kind of like some biblical version of the Frankenstein story."

"I can see you're no monster," the young man whispered. "And that you're not trying to fool anybody."

"That's for damn sure. But the more I try to squelch this thing, the bigger it gets."

"Maybe because it's bigger than you. Much bigger." He gestured at the women, who waited and listened uncomprehendingly. "But I think there's no taking me to the ER until you pray for me, so I'd ... appreciate it."

Jason's gaze traveled to Jess and the two women. Then he blew out a resigned breath, grimacing. "Okay. But I just want you to know I'm in way over my head."

"That makes two of us."

"What's your name, son?"

"Ricky."

He placed one massive hand over Ricky's trembling, damp

forehead, and the young man shut his eyes. Their heads were bowed. Jason saw the women grasp for each other's hands and felt Jess's grip on his own shoulder tighten.

Clearing his throat, he began tentatively. "Uh, over these last few months, I've heard lots of prayers directed to the Father, Son, and Holy Spirit. But, honestly, God—or whoever you are and wherever you are—that's information overload to me. It's hard enough for me to pray to one of you, much less all three. So, I just want to ask You—one of You—I don't know who—to help this young man Ricky who looks to be in really tough shape. In fact, if I didn't know better, I'd say he's dying."

His voice trailing off, Jason opened his eyes and looked intently at Ricky. He didn't know what to expect, if anything. All the other times people claimed his praying had an effect, all the healing happened out of his sight, other than that first time, with Miguel. Which is why people were nuts in the first place to think it had anything to do with him—anything at all to do with the few clumsy, muttered words he came up with.

Ricky was shivering even harder. *That's done it*, thought Jason. *I should've called 911 the second that girl knocked on Jess's door. Now this craziness is not only wasting time, but it might be the only time he has left.*

He didn't know why, but he took the young man's face between his hands, staring at him. He inspected the dark lashes on the pale cheeks, the beads of perspiration, the mouth cracked, with lips pressed together. The women were still praying, praying, but their murmurings faded as Jason felt the urge to bow his own head again.

Hell. What the hell.
Go for it.

18

Maybe one thing comes at the cost of another—one gift for another.

Not that Jason had ever wanted to be known as some kind of faith healer in the first place.

He heard through the grapevine that Ricky, the young man with the fever, recovered. It was not in the way other "victims" of Jason's stumbling prayers recovered, restored to health in a burst and a glow—no, Ricky healed slowly, with one step forward and two steps back.

Some three weeks later, Jason was yanked out of bed to pray for a matriarch who could no longer speak, but only grasped his hand weakly, her rosary beads digging into his palms.

She died a few weeks later.

He received flowers nonetheless, gifts of food, murmured *gracias*, but he felt the guilt and embarrassment of being unable to do what was expected of him, even if the other half of his brain knew the expectations were ridiculous. He had never failed before—if it was even him failing.

His next call came two months on from there, one morning while he and Jess stood in the sleek, modern tasting room being constructed around them, talking budget overruns and timelines. At the appearance of the urgent family members, pleading for his attendance in broken English, Jason threw up his hands in resignation.

Surely it was becoming obvious that, whatever bizarre power had healed those early cases, it had nothing to do with him—not with his abilities or lack thereof, his willingness or unwillingness, or even the size of his hands, which the hopeful found so marvelous. The power had come from outside him and gone back to wherever it came from. The middle-aged man he prayed for that morning didn't die, at least. But he didn't improve much either, remaining unable to work, to his family's dismay. Jason ended up hiring on the wife and the oldest son, telling himself the winery was growing and needed more staff.

Which was true.

But while his mysterious power to heal seemed to have leaked away, the rest of Jason's life surged with new growth. The winery's case volume rebounded to pre-crash numbers, and with the reduced overhead, Jason found the money rolling in like breakers off the Washington coast. Hence the build-out of the new tasting room and offices, a project that moved glacially, mowing down all deliverable dates and cost estimates in its path, but that came along in any case. And whether or not Jason felt compelled to hire family members of those he was helpless to heal, the original skeleton crew grew monthly.

As Knightbridge Cellars returned to health, so did Jason. His hair grew back in; he gained color and put some weight back on. Was this how it worked? Had he somehow hogged what remained of his healing hooha, hoarding it like a bearded survivalist did his burning ember?

He didn't know.

Daman looked skeptical the first time Jason suggested going without a golf cart for their round. "Come on, man. See reason. J.J. and I don't want to be draggin' your sorry cancer-ass around when you get tired."

"J.J. would love nothing better than his old man leaning on him, right?" Jason slung an arm around his son's shoulders.

The boy was getting taller. "And I told you I had lung cancer, not ass cancer."

It had taken J.J. a while to get used to how his father and Daman were always trash-talking each other, and he positively blanched the first time he heard Daman rib Jason about his illness, but repetition had its effects.

"I wouldn't complain for a hole or two," J.J. said, "but, after that, we'd just lay you down and leave you somewhere and tell the folks coming after to play through."

"Works for me. Just pick a shady spot," Jason cracked. Releasing J.J., he reached for his golf bag. "Let's go, you wimps. Don't make me have to carry your crap, too."

He made it through the round that day. And the one later in the week. And the ones in the weeks after that. He made it through running the winery and showing the boys the basics. He made it through the endless facilities build-out.

He made it through his second season with the Jubilee Golf Team. Daman was eighteen that year—eighteen, going on thirty, Jason liked to say—and his last season playing for the school was a memorable one.

When they gathered around the giant scoreboard that year, surrounded by the young golfers and coaches from all across the county, it was Daman's name circled in red, as was his score: seventy. Scrawled in the space beside it was the word *Medalist*. The team as a whole took second, and Jason and Alvin, Sr. near to broke their hands off, high-fiving the young men and slapping each other on the back.

Rich went all out with a celebration, inviting parents and community members and the entire school roster and staff to partake. Jason ponied up for gleaming trophies and spent a few nights, tongue clamped between his teeth, trying to write something meaningful to each kid, and he had an envelope to hand each boy as he climbed onto the rostrum to have his picture taken under the *Congratulations, Jubilee 2010 Golfers!* banner.

There was another celebration around Christmas, when the new Knightbridge facilities were at long last complete, and he and Marcie presided over the ribbon-cutting. Where the old Knightbridge Wineries had been modeled after classic chateaux, the reborn version was gleaming and modern. Copper and stainless steel, rich wood and granite. Not intentionally, Jason thought, but it had turned out a lot like Sarah's new home.

"Merry Christmas to us," Jason said, grinning at his lieutenant.

"You must have been a good, good boy," Marcie said, laughing.

She wasn't the only one to think so.

Despite the unusually cold and snowy winter, one great iceberg in his life had begun to melt.

Jason's SUV swooped up the curving driveway of Sarah's home, pulling up to the front door. The door to the house was garlanded with evergreen, and after pressing the bell, Jason slid the wreath he was carrying down his arm and hung it on the waiting nail.

The door opened and Sarah glanced from him to the wreath and back again, a smile spreading across her features.

"You rang?"

"Walla Walla Wreath Delivery, ma'am." He saluted and then threw a wave over her shoulder at J.J. and Ringo barreling down the staircase.

"It's perfect. Just what I had in mind." She backed up to let him in. "And you're right on time."

Winter yielded to spring, another glorious one in the Walla Walla Valley. Unlike the western side of the state, the southeastern corner, where Washington's wine country tucked into the right angle bordered by Oregon and Idaho, enjoys early springs, extended falls, and abundant sunshine. The wine grapes weren't the only ones to love it.

Once the snow vanished from the club course, Jason and the boys were back out there, including J.J. And it wasn't much longer before dropping his son off led to sticking around for dinner. Half the time, Daman joined them, and he was there for one memorable dinner in March. Pushing his chair back from the table, Daman rubbed his gut and sighed.

"Miz Sarah, I got to say, that meal more than made up for the fact that you were once married to this joker."

"It'll take a few more meals than that," Jason cracked, throwing his napkin at him. "But you sure ate your share. All that food in your gut must go a ways to balancing that swollen head."

"Which'll help your swing," suggested J.J.

"Ain't nothin' that can balance this head out today," said Daman, unabashed. If anything, his grin grew more unrepentant. "It's bigger than ever. I recommend somebody ask me about my future plans, 'fore I get so swelled up I bust."

"I thought high school seniors got tired of that question," Sarah said with a laugh. "But I'll bite: what are your future plans, Daman?"

"Funny you should ask." Rising from his seat, he left the room, leaving them looking at each other in puzzlement. In a moment he was back, a big white envelope in his hands. He tossed it on the table. "Had that stuffed in my jacket all day. Surprised you didn't hear it crinklin' each time I swung the club."

Jason lunged for the envelope. "Is that what I think it is?"

"Uh-huh. Y'all give it up for the class of 2015."

"Whoa!" J.J. whispered. "Whoa. UW!"

Pandemonium greeted this announcement, with Sarah clutching Daman again and Jason whooping and pounding him on the back, while J.J. hammered his fists on the table. When they all settled down, Jason found his cheeks were wet, and even Daman turned to dash a hand at his eyes.

"You got in!" Sarah shrieked and clapped her hands, springing up to throw her arms around him.

Jason found himself speechless, swallowing hard so he wouldn't choke up. If he did, he'd never hear the end of it from Daman, that was for sure. But his eyes were bright and his voice shook a little anyhow.

"Proud of you, kid, even if you're going to be a damn Husky."

"Uh-huh," said Daman again, when Sarah released him. His voice wasn't completely steady either. He cleared his throat. "Thanks to goin' to school out here in cow country—not to mention havin' a coach of questionable ability—they only gave me a partial ride. I gotta come up with the rest, but that won't be no problem for a man of my many talents."

This.

Jason looked around him, feeling his throat swell as he took in the faces at the table.

It doesn't get any better than this.

Spring gave way to summer.

Jason wouldn't have believed the changes of the past year if he hadn't lived them. Wouldn't have believed the winery could not only get back on its feet but could *boom*. Wouldn't have believed Sarah and J.J. would let him back into their lives—even back into their hearts. Through all the time spent with him, or with him and Daman and the other boys, J.J. had lost that tentativeness with his father. And Sarah—well, Jason hadn't wanted to put words to what was happening there. Not yet.

He almost forgot about the whole wacko healing thing. The nighttime summons and stray phone calls trailed off, and while it had been embarrassing to be considered a faith healer—for lack of anything better to call it—Jason found it equally embarrassing, for a time, to be a has-been faith healer. But the embarrassment, too, passed.

One thing for another.

On the whole, he wasn't sorry for the exchange.

Another round of golf, another drop-off at Sarah's.

"You better watch out, Daman," J.J. said, waving the scorecard at him from the backseat. "I'm going to be beating you soon. You shot sixty-nine, but I shot seventy-five. A year ago, you needed to give me a stroke a hole."

"That's right," Daman answered mildly. "I don't have to baby you all the time no more. But you ain't the only one gettin' better. You'll find it's hard to catch a movin' target."

Sarah was in the driveway, toweling Ringo off from a hose bath, and no sooner did they pile out of the SUV than the dog bounded toward them, planting his paws and giving a great shake, sending water droplets and drool flying all directions.

"Thanks, Ringo," drawled Daman. "Man, that dog's better at watering than the sprinklers at the country club."

"Come on, Daman," J.J. said with a laugh, wiping his forearms off on his khakis. "I recorded the Open."

The boys disappeared inside, trailed by Ringo, and Sarah smiled at Jason. "Good day?"

Before Jason could change his expression, she saw the grimace on his face. He gave a tight nod, his hand going up to massage his armpit.

"You okay?"

Jason took a shallow breath. "Fine, fine. Just some achiness. Probably I've caught a summer cold from Isaiah. That kid's been coughing up a lung for a couple weeks now. I told Rich he'd better get him in to the doctor before Isaiah coughs himself inside out." He tried to roll his shoulder, wincing again. "It's that, or I pulled something. Too much golf."

"I never thought I'd hear those words come out of your mouth," Sarah said, laughing. But when his answering chuckle brought on another twinge, her brow furrowed. "Maybe you and Isaiah ought to go in together. Let me get you an ice pack or something."

"Wait, wait, wait." He caught her wrist before she could turn away, though the quick movement made him flinch again.

She gave him a questioning look, but he felt her pulse quicken.

"What would you say to dinner tonight, Sarah? Just me and you. The boys order pizza and watch the Open while we go out?"

Something flickered in her face, but she didn't pull away. "That's ambitious of you. Don't you think two Ibuprofen and an early bedtime might be a better idea, in your condition?"

He grinned at her. "You mean my lovelorn condition?"

"You're unbelievable!"

But she laughed again, and Jason might have pressed his luck then, except she saw the tightness return to his jaw. This time Sarah folded her arms over her stomach and shook her head. "Sorry, Casanova. Your aching armpit is undermining your charm offensive."

"Damn."

"Better luck next time."

"I *do* have my usual follow-up appointment with Friedman this week," Jason replied. "And once I beg some painkillers and antibiotics off him, I'll be back to storm your castle."

"I'll have the boiling oil ready." Leaning in, she gave him a kiss near his ear. "J.J. and I will take Daman home later. You go on and get some rest."

One thing for another. An exchange.

The good news was, Isaiah hadn't given him the flu or TB. He wasn't even contagious. The bad news was, Isaiah had some kind of lung disease, and more tests were needed to determine how serious.

That would've been enough bad news, but there was more: Jason's cancer was back.

"It's metastasized into your lymph system," Friedman told him, his face as gray as Jason's.

Just hearing this made it suddenly harder to breathe. For a minute, all he could hear was his panicked heartbeat, the whir of the clinic's AC, heels going down the hall outside the examination room.

"How long?" he managed.

Friedman exhaled slowly, rocking on his heels.

"Jesus, you're gonna say it—"

"It's only a matter of time, Jason."

There it was. *A matter of time.* And not much more, at that. How had it been that the first time he went through this, Jason had only wanted another year? But what a year it had been! Now, like all human beings, once he got it, he wanted more.

He got in the car and drove—like the first time, but not like the first time. This time it was summer, and he just drove and drove, with no idea where he was going. He ended up on I-84, running alongside the Columbia River, his eyes narrowed against the summer sun.

His phone rang, Marcie's name flashing on the caller ID, but Jason didn't move to answer it. Outside Boardman it rang again. Sarah. Again, he let it go to voicemail.

He kept going. Arlington. Rufus. Biggs Junction. The Dalles. Chenoweth. Rowena. Mosier. He drove until the road ran out and the mighty river emptied into the Pacific, where its surging waters seemed to stall, as if it was resisting being swallowed up by the vast and endlessly churning ocean. The Pacific won in the end, of course, but Jason felt like one of those trillion or so tiny water droplets, fighting to exist, to remain intact.

He'd gotten more time than he asked for, but had he done enough? Changed enough?

High above the river he sat on the bluff, breathing. The muted roar of the waves blended with the ebb and flow of his own blood, the rhythm of his heart.

Here.

Now.

Here.

Now.

Enough.

He didn't know when he became aware of voices—young ones, calling and laughing below him. Shaking his head, Jason looked down and saw two boys playing on the sand bars. They ran through the shallow water of the wide delta, up onto the sand, and then back into the river. On the far side of one bar, the current ran deeper, faster, and the boys splashed on its edge, kicking water at each other.

"Nate!" yelled the one. Or it might not have been Nate—Jason couldn't make it out clearly. "Check this out!" He plunged into that deeper current, only to have it whip him around and steal his foothold. Arms thrashed and water flew.

"Whoa!" he gasped. "It's deep here!" His head disappeared, bobbed up again. The boasting voice turned to alarm, loud enough that Jason could hear him clearly now. "Max! Help! *Help!*"

Jason found himself on his feet, stumbling around, searching for the path down to the river, just as Max below was scrambling toward his buddy. But before Max could reach him, the other boy hooted, jumping out of the water, back onto the sandbar. Max laughed too, after chucking a clod of mud at his friend. Above them, Jason sagged with relief. He sat down hard and let the tension drain from him. *Little bastard.*

It hit him then—like the echo of memory had broken something loose where it had lodged, a seam of silver in a vein of quartz. Boys horsing around in the river. Yes. He remembered.

It was that one time, over thirty years earlier and three hundred miles to the east, when he and Nate were goofing off in that same river. That time when he'd gone under for real, cheated death for real.

"All these years," Jason muttered.

They were borrowed time, time that never belonged to him in the first place.

His hands grasped at the weedy grass beside him, and a few

pebbles shook loose, tumbling off the bluff and plummeting into the river far, far below.

"You should have taken me back then," Jason told the Columbia. "In 1978. You sure tried. But Jess—crazy, stubborn, never-say-die Jess—he had other ideas."

The indifferent waters below him made no response. Nature rolled on, the river losing itself in the foam and swell of the wider ocean. The river that had almost stolen his future.

He'd been given an incredible gift—decades more of life. Hell, he'd mostly squandered them, but they'd been given him all the same. And there was still a bit more time.

Maybe just enough.

Out of the back hatch he pulled his longtime companion: Sam's old black doctor's bag. Running his fingers one last time across the grain of the leather, Jason walked slowly to the edge of the cliff. The boys' voices carried to him, and from his perch he watched them another few moments.

Then he took a step back, swinging his arm behind him, letting the weight of the bag rock him onto his heel. The pain under his left arm knifed through him. Damn, the thing was heavier than he remembered. Clenching his teeth, he let the momentum throw him forward again. He planted his foot six inches from the verge and followed through.

With a mighty heave, he let it go.

19

"Darling, I have something important to tell you."

Sarah rolled onto her back to smile up at him. Her head lay in his lap, his hand in her hair. They were relaxing on a blanket under cloudless skies, an emptied picnic basket nearby and the sounds carrying to them of Ringo galloping after a ball while J.J. laughed and called to him.

"You just did say something important," Sarah murmured. "You haven't called me 'darling' since before we were married."

Jason gave a rueful grin. "My mistake." Drawing her hair through his fingers, his hand came to rest lightly on her shoulder. "And a damned lot of time wasted. Because, unfortunately, this isn't the wonderful kind of important."

Her breath catching, she sat up. "What do you mean? What is it?"

"It's me."

The wary look returned to her eyes, and he rushed on. "It's my cancer. It's back, and this time Friedman says there's nothing that can be done. No—listen, babe—I'm sorry to dump it on you like this. But I wanted you to know one thing. I know I was a terrible husband—I've been way better at being your ex, pathetic as that is—but what I want to say is, one day I want you to marry again—"

"Jason—" She was gasping, but he barreled on.

"Someone who will give you everything I didn't, Sarah. I

don't mean money. I mean all the things that really matter. The things I held back on. The things I should have given you. But you've got to warn this guy, whoever he is: when you get to heaven, you're going to be mine again. And then I'll be the husband you deserve."

She threw herself at him then, burying her head in his chest, the sobs choking her. He put gentle arms around her, rocking and soothing her wordlessly. Over her head he saw J.J. now standing with his hands hanging down, staring at them, Ringo nudging the ball at his feet.

"Mom," the boy ventured uncertainly, "what's wrong?"

Jason bent his head to whisper, "I need to tell J.J. now."

Numbly she released him and gave a nod, trying to smooth out her ragged breathing. But before Jason was halfway to their son, he saw the dread in the boy's expression, and it lanced through him. How could a kid that young look like that, unless he'd already been hurt so many times by life that he knew to brace himself?

Jason felt his steps drag, but the arm he put around his son's shoulders was firm, and J.J., after standing stiffly another moment, yielded, letting his father lead him further off.

Hell, thought Jason. A year ago, he didn't have a relationship with his son. A year ago, he couldn't have put his arm around him. A year ago, J.J. wouldn't have trusted him to lead him anywhere.

So, there was that.

That and Sarah forgiving him.

Life might not be a picnic, but that didn't mean there weren't a few picnics in it—a few instants, before the clouds gathered, of sun and blue sky and everything right with the world.

"I'm surprised you picked this place," Jess Carson rumbled, "given the history. Not to mention, I've never heard you order soda water before."

They were at the Blue Mountain Bar and Grill, pulled up at the same bar where Nate and Jason had their big brawl. They were even seated on the same damned stools, if Jason remembered right.

Jess gave Jason a skeptical look before he took a sip of his beer.

"I've got my reasons for both," answered Jason. "The more I've thought about what happened here, three years ago, the more I realize how right Nate was."

As always, when his son was mentioned, Jess got that hollowed-out look in his eyes. Jason suspected something of the same look came into his own eyes, for that matter.

"Nate felt what was coming," he went on. "For both of us."

Jess sighed heavily, taking another deep draw of his beer. "Yes, Nathan always had a special gift that way. Lord, I miss him."

A silence fell between them, broken only by the strains from the jukebox that neither one noticed. The barkeep ran a rag down the length of the counter, checking the status of their drinks.

"Jess," he began again, "one of the many things I'm grateful for, over these last few years, is how we've reconnected. I've come to appreciate what a fine man you really are, and to admire how deep your faith is."

Something flickered over the older man's craggy face, and he set his beer down. "That ... means a lot to me, Jason, to hear you say those words. It truly does. But, I have to admit, a chill just ran down my spine."

"Yeah. I'm thinking Nate might have gotten his intuition from you, Jess. You're going to need to call on that unshakeable faith of yours one more time." Jason let out a slow breath. "I'm terminal."

Jess said nothing, but Jason saw his hands tremble. He didn't gasp or pepper him with questions; he only sat, stunned. Jason might have thought the old man turned to stone, except for the lone tear he saw, winding its way down Jess's cheek.

"I'm so sorry to do this to you."

Jess dashed the tear away. "You're sorry to do this to me," he echoed, head bowed. "You're the one who's dy—who's—" His words broke off as if someone had knocked the wind from him. His hands clenched and unclenched. "Good Lord—I don't know—I don't know how I can go through this again, after Nathan. Go through this alone—"

"You're not going to be alone," Jason interrupted, gripping Jess's wrist. "Not this time. Listen to me: you've got two young men who need you. Neither of them has really ever had a father. Jess, I'm asking you to take J.J. and Daman under your wing. Do for them what you tried to do for me."

Jess was shaking his head slowly, still staring at the bar. "Yeah. You know, I don't know just how many years I have left."

Moving to clap an arm around his shoulders, Jason gave him a shake. "Remember that rude health of yours? Don't give me that old man act. Something tells me you have many, many miles to go before you sleep."

The teasing, the lack of pity, rallied Jess. He managed a half-smile, his eyes meeting Jason's. "I'll do my best, Jason. They're both fine boys. J.J. just needed to know you gave a damn about him. And Daman—I got to admit, I never thought Daman would change like he has."

"It's going to take some money, I know," Jason went on, swirling his glass of soda water. "Sarah will provide for J.J., of course, but she's even offered to help out Daman. Wouldn't you know it—she took half the money she squeezed from me and put it into stocks back when they were crushed in 2009." He grinned. "She's made back everything I lost. She always was a smart one. Now I just have to figure out what to do with the winery. Bill and I need to chat."

But Jess was shaking his head again. "Doesn't seem fair, Jason. You've built things back up. Not just the winery—your life, too. You deserve more time. And you've ... changed." Downing the last of his beer, he slid his pint glass away. "Got to say … I'm proud of you, son. Proud. And Nate would be, too."

His voice choked on the last words, and Jason patted him, his own voice not entirely steady. "Whatever good is in me, I learned it from you, Jess. You and Nate both. But there isn't much more time left, and I've got a lot to do."

"Shouldn't you just take it easy?"

Jason shrugged this off. "There's no point in that. This thing's going to get me either way. I want to go out on my own terms. Besides making sure J.J. and Daman are taken care of—by Sarah and you—and settling the winery, there are two other things I have to do."

In answer to the question in Jess's eyes, he said, "Rich has told me that Bill is giving Jubilee three more years of funding at a decreasing amount. Weaning them. Jubilee has got to come up with at least a million a year to offset that. Bill and Sue are right to feel they've carried the ranch long enough to lay a good foundation, and now they've got other causes to support."

"Mm-hmm." Jess waved away the bartender who came to clear his glass. "And what's the second thing?"

Jason grimaced at his soda water. He could use a beer himself. "It's Isaiah."

"From the golf team? He still got that cough?"

"Not just a cough. He's really sick. Turns out it's a terminal lung disease, pulmonary fibrosis. Jess, he needs a transplant."

Jess only sputtered at this, his hands splayed against the bar. Then he turned sharp eyes on Jason. "But—but—have you—"

"Laid hands on him?" Jason guessed wryly. "Sure I did. I was desperate enough to hope the gift I was always eager to get rid of might visit me one last time. But he hasn't responded." He peeled the napkin from the bottom of his soda water glass. "He doesn't have much time. Less than me, probably. He's on an organ recipient list, but there's no way he'll get one in time."

This time Jess raised a finger at the barkeep and tapped the counter in front of him, running his other hand through his stiff gray hair. "What are you saying, Jason? You want to give him your lungs? With your condition?"

"Ironically, my lungs are clear," Jason replied. "That was just the original site, but Dr. Wright got that tumor out after my accident."

"Well, that may be, but you're still usin' 'em, as far as I can see. What exactly are you going to do?"

Jason gave a deep sigh and reached for Jess's refill. Not much harm one good pull could do him, at this point. Then he pushed it back toward the old man.

"I wish I knew."

It wasn't the entire truth. He had an idea what he needed to do; he just wasn't sure exactly *how* to get it done.

But first he would talk to Rich Williams.

The gym at Jubilee Ranch rang with voices and laughter and the sounds of cutlery. The boys from the golf team and some of the school staff were gathered for an early banquet, and the long table sagged under plates of food. Along the wall hung the handsewn banners boasting the team results from the past couple years, and a riser at the side of the room held a heap of wrapped packages, all the same size and shape. Over his mild objections, Jason held the place of honor in the center of the table, flanked by Rich on one side and J.J. on the other, the team members fanning out from there. They had also insisted he say the blessing, which turned out to be not as horrific as he anticipated, given all the experience with awkward-prayer situations he now had under his belt. Nonetheless he was happy to sink back into his seat after pronouncing the final, "Amen and dig in!" And as good as the food was, it couldn't beat the satisfaction he felt as he looked out over each of the boys on the team.

"Gentlemen," Rich Williams began some time later, rising from his seat and raising his arms to quiet the gathering. "Normally, we wouldn't hold an event like this until the end of the golf season, but Coach Jason wanted to do it at the beginning this year, and I think it has something to do with all those presents there. While we're all finishing up eating, the coach has something to say to you and something for each of you."

Through the clamor of cutlery being laid down so the boys could cheer and hammer on the table, Jason stood slowly, swallowing a few times as he waited for the noise to die down.

"Okay, guys. I promised all of you who were on the team last season that I'd get you all new Nike golf shoes if you won the whole enchilada this year. But then I realized that you'll have a lot better shot at winning in the first place if we just go ahead and get rid of those ratty things you've been calling shoes."

The words were barely out of his mouth than the boys were scrambling from their seats, shouting, charging the stack of boxes on the riser. Ripped paper and ribbons flew, and a few elbows connected with rib cages before Rich Williams threw himself into the melee, bellowing, "Gentlemen! Sit down *immediately*. If you don't, no one will get any shoes, so help me."

Knowing he was as good as his word, the boys reluctantly set the boxes back on the riser and slunk back to their seats, not without a few shoves and muttered accusations.

"Let's do this right," Jason began again, biting back a laugh. He nudged his son beside him. "J.J., you've got our list. Just tell me who gets which size. And, Daman, you play Santa and help me locate the right boxes."

J.J. unfolded the sheet of paper in his shirt pocket. "Orlando has the size thirteen pair."

"Of course he would. And is the width P, as in pancake?"

Taking the box Daman handed him, Jason strode over to where Orlando had risen uncertainly to his feet. When Orlando held out a hand for the box, Jason laid a firm hand on his shoulder and pressed him back down on the bench. Then he knelt carefully and began to untie Orlando's shoes.

"Mr. Jason," the big boy said, squirming, "I can do this."

"Of course you can. But I want to do it."

A half-horrified, half-amazed hush fell over the gathering as Jason removed Orlando's old shoes. No one even thought to crack a joke about foot odor, they were so unprepared. Taking the new shoes from their box, Jason slid them onto Orlando's feet and fastened them.

It took less than a minute, but when Jason rose again, he was a little out of breath. "J.J., who's next?"

"Isaiah, size nine."

"Perfect. Just the man I want to take care of."

In the few weeks since his diagnosis, Isaiah's condition had deteriorated, and he now had to sit at the end of the banquet table, to make room for his oxygen bottle. Again, Jason knelt. As he had with Orlando, he carefully untied and removed Isaiah's shoes and tied on the new pair. When he looked up, he saw tears stealing down the boy's face.

"We're going to beat this thing," Jason said under his breath. "You're going to be back playing golf before you know it, so don't be selling these shoes on eBay."

Even if he could have caught his breath properly, Isaiah wouldn't have known what to say, and Jason couldn't think of any more either. For all the thousands of words he'd given those boys, the coaching, the razzing, the glib zingers, the pep talks—all he had now was a growing lump in his throat and fingers that trembled as they did their work.

Thirteen boys in all.

Thirteen pairs of shoes.

It was dead silent by the time Rich Williams stood up again. "Gentlemen, while you all deserve congratulations for your fine season last year—a season, I have to confess, I never thought I'd live long enough to see—this evening is meant to be about much more than you. More than collecting on a bet." He glanced over at Jason who, guessing where his thoughts were tending, shook his head and tried to forestall him with a grimace. But Williams forged ahead.

"This evening is also about a man who has helped you all

tremendously and who has become a great friend—and a great inspiration—to me—"

That was as far as he got before the collected gathering was applauding and hooting and beating on the table again. Jason, not trusting his voice at all by this point, stood briefly to acknowledge their cheering, before Rich grabbed him in a bear hug. Another roar of approval met this, and when Jason finally broke free, he gave the boys a go-along-with-you wave and dropped back onto the bench.

No, there weren't words for this.

But the memory of it, the sounds, the faces, the *joy* of it, would stay with him to the last.

Rich Williams's own gift from Jason wasn't long in coming, though neither one had planned on it.

It arrived quietly enough, with Jess tossing an envelope on the counter one afternoon.

"Howdy, Jason. Lookie what's been bouncing around at the post office for you. From all the marks on it, I'm guessing they tried to deliver it a few times to your old address until Sandy down there got wise to it and knew to send it along here."

"Probably the IRS wanting to bleed me some more," said Jason. "It's almost worth dying, to tell them they can kiss my—"

"It's not the IRS. It's from an insurance company."

Frowning, Jason reached for the envelope to inspect it. "Pacific Life Insurance Company? Pacific ... kinda rings a bell." He stuck a finger under the flap and ripped it open, pulling out the sheet within.

"I'll be damned," he said, chuckling ruefully. "It's that policy I took out eight years ago to pay our estate taxes. Not that I've got an estate to worry about anymore. How is it that vulture Gus didn't get his grubby talons on this? It's got almost a million of cash value and $10 million face." He looked up sharply, tapping the envelope against his palm and studying the wall as if it contained figures.

"Does seem strange old Gus would miss an asset that large," agreed Jess. "Are you sure it's still in your name?"

Jason ran a hand through his hair. "That's what just hit me. This was intended to pay our estate taxes when I died, so it was held in an irrevocable trust to keep it out of my estate." He skimmed through the sheet of paper again, to convince himself it was real. It was.

"I even paid more to have it based on just my life, in case Sarah and I split up. So, I don't actually own it. I never did."

"I know Bill and Sue Brojan have a whopper one of those, so their family won't have to sell the orchards and businesses when they die," said Jess. He poured himself an iced-tea refill and got a glass out for Jason. "So, who *does* own your policy?"

"The trust." Jason stared blankly at the glass Jess slid toward him, his mind still racing. "I can't access the funds, which is why Gus couldn't either, but ..."

"But what?"

A slow smile dawned on Jason's face. "But I can change the beneficiary. As long as it doesn't go to me."

"You mean you can leave it to anyone?"

"I mean I can leave it to anyone." He gave Jess a gleeful sock in the shoulder. "But don't get your hopes up, old man. It also means I can leave it to any *organization*." He took a deep drink from his iced tea and slammed the glass back down, beaming.

"Two down, one to go."

"Huh?"

"Jess, my man, we're going to have a party—one big, frolicking, rollicking, joyous party. I'll call Sarah. We'll have it at her place, out by the pool. We're going to invite *everyone*. And the first name on the guest list is gonna be Rich Williams."

20

Jess Carson stood at the edge of the patio, looking down on the groups milling around the pool deck. There were over one-hundred people gathered in Sarah's backyard, clustered in bunches or sprawled in the chairs and lounges around the pool. Others chatted under her covered patio, laughter breaking out occasionally. He saw Jason buzzing around, pushing food and drinks on the guests. He saw their hostess chatting with the Brojans and Rich Williams, the latter of whom kept glancing at the Pacific Life statement Jason had earlier handed him. He saw hordes of Jubilee boys, including some lured into the water by the warm fall sunshine. Isaiah was drawn up to the edge in his wheelchair, Daman seated on the lip of the pool beside him.

Reaching inside his vest, Jess drew a photo out and studied it for a moment. He didn't need to; heaven knew he'd looked at it plenty lately, trying to decide what to do. He put it away again.

"Hey, Jason." Jess caught him on his next pass into the kitchen. "I know you're busy helping out and all, but there's something I need to talk to you about. And show you."

Jason waved his empty tray. "Can we do it later? Gotta keep the barbarians fed, and I haven't had a chance to catch up with Bill. Wait'll I tell him I've convinced Kim to dump Leonetti and come work for Knightbridge again!"

"The key was that you and Bill gave her half the equity." Jess replied. "Without her—or someone like her—that stock would be almost worthless." Jason winced slightly at hearing that word.

"Frankly, I've waited longer than I should have to show you this," Jess said firmly. "It won't take too long, and this time just seems right. Can we go inside?"

Shrugging, Jason gestured toward the twenty-foot-wide opening where the sliding glass doors had been slid back into the flanking walls. He expected Jess to stop in the kitchen, but the old man kept going, past the nook and the formal dining room, through the family room and finally on into the study. The sounds of the guests were muffled from here.

Jess settled onto the leather sofa and slapped the armchair on the other side of the coffee table.

"Well, you got me," said Jason, taking the seat offered to him. His face was wary. It was a great day—a wonderful day—and he didn't think he wanted any bad news delivered just then. What could it be? The old man looked healthy enough.

As if he'd read his mind, Jess gave a snort. "It's not about me, Jason. I'm not showing you my CAT scans, or anything like that. Just a picture. But you'll probably find it even more shocking." Fishing it from his vest pocket again, he pulled out his reading glasses and inspected it once more.

"This here picture was taken back in sixty-five. My golly, I forgot how pretty she was. She'd gone over to the coast that summer to work, and while she was in the big city those few months, she fell in love. Head over heels."

"Who did? Maria? Let me see that."

Jess let him take the photo. "Not my Maria."

Jason whistled. "She's gorgeous, all right. But who is she? She looks sort of familiar."

"Her fella played for the Chieftains—that's what they called the Seattle U team back then, when they had a basketball team. It was just a few years after Elgin Baylor's glory days, when he made that little school a national powerhouse."

"You don't have to tell me," Jason chuckled. "Sam Steele

had plenty to say about Baylor being one of the greatest NBA players, all time. He was proud he came out of a Washington school. I only vaguely remember the tail-end of his career, when he was with the Lakers. But you didn't answer my question: who is she?"

Jess took a deep breath and exhaled it slowly, falling back against the sofa cushions. He pulled off his reading glasses.

"That would be your mama, Jason."

Jason jerked like he'd been stung, the picture fluttering to the floor. He gave Jess a sharp look, but when the old man merely returned the look, unblinking, Jason's mouth dropped open. After a long moment, he leaned down and retrieved the photograph, holding it gingerly by the edges, as if it might slice him. He placed it on the corner of the coffee table.

"It ... can't be," he muttered. "This woman—she's beautiful. And she's—happy."

Tapping his fingers on the coffee table, Jess stared at the fireplace. "Yes, sir. She was both of those at the time. You know, her pappy Willie and I were good friends, almost brothers, even though he was almost ten years older than me. He was a fine man, but he had a powerful thirst and a wicked temper when he'd been drinkin', which was most of the time. Maria and I, we'd gone over to Seattle that summer to see the old World's Fair site, and we stopped in to visit her. That's when I took that picture—and met David."

"Her ... lover?"

"Uh-huh. David was what we used to call a mulatto, a very light-skinned black man, with green eyes. He could pass for white. Handsome too, and extremely intelligent. We met him a few times. He wanted to become some kind of scientist—a physicist, I think." Jess's gaze returned to Jason. "That isn't all I remember about him. Like I said, he played for the Chieftains ... and he had four finger joints."

Jason went very still.

"Your mama got pregnant," Jess went on. "David was the

father. In those days, out-of-wedlock births were scandalous enough, but when it involved a white woman and a black man ..."

"Are you telling me what I think you're telling me?" Jason whispered. His hands had begun to shake. He thrust them under his arms.

"I am. Jason, David was your real daddy."

Jason grunted softly, as if he'd had the wind knocked from him. He nodded once, then sprang to his feet to pace back and forth in front of the fireplace.

"Well, that explains a few things." He swallowed hard. "I never could believe Leon—that slimy piece of white trash—was related to me." Halting suddenly, he slammed a hand against the stone mantel. "But what happened? Where did ... this David go? Does he even know I—? How did I—?"

Jess's eyes were soft, regretful. "I tried to find out what happened to him when you had your first go-round with the cancer thing. Turns out he was gone himself, some years past. Leukemia, I think. I'm sorry."

Jason pulled a face. So was he. Whoever this David was—his ... father—he'd lost him twice in the space of a minute. It was all such a roller-coaster he couldn't even say if he was sorry or just stunned.

"You can imagine how your grandpappy reacted to the news of her pregnancy," Jess went on in a quiet voice. "Willie wanted your mama to have an abortion. But I gotta give her credit. It would have been a lot easier, but she would have none of it. I helped arrange to have her move up to Vancouver, BC, where the whole thing could be kept on the QT. Had—still have—some family up there. David wanted to marry her, but Willie said he'd see 'em both dead first. He didn't much like me marrying a Mexican woman, but black marrying white was a whole 'nother kettle of fish! Your granddad figured he'd take things one step at a time: first he'd get rid of the boyfriend, and then he'd pressure your mama to give you up for adoption."

"Too bad Old Willie died when I was little," Jason said with a snort, throwing himself down in the armchair again. "Sounds like I would've loved the guy. But you didn't answer my question: what happened to David, all those years in between? If he knew about me—knew about a baby coming, at least—why did he never try to get in touch?"

Shoulders sagging, Jess shook his head. "Only your mama knew the full details of that. And she wasn't going to share that with her dad or me, that's for sure. I can only guess that she had to choose her battles: keep you or keep David. She picked you. Everything has a price, though. She might never have forgiven her dad for making her choose. Or David, for letting himself be driven away."

"Or me, for being the one she gave him up for," muttered Jason. He said it under his breath, not wanting Jess to hear him, but the old man did. Jess put a bracing hand on him.

"You may be right about that, son. Though, if it makes any difference to you, I don't think she forgave herself, either."

A brief silence fell. Jason could hear the music being dialed up on the stereo outside and wondered if it was Daman at the controls. Abruptly he got to his feet again and crossed the room, his long fingers fiddling with the bronze candlesticks on the mantel.

"So, in addition to being part black, I'm also a Canuck, you say? That's something. Do you have any more surprises up your sleeve? Any more secrets you've been sitting on for a few decades? Like maybe my name isn't even Jason?"

Swallowing hard, Jess stared down at the floor, provoking a sharp laugh from Jason. "Jeez, I was kidding! But clearly there's more. Come on, Jess ... your silence is breaking my eardrums right now. Let's have it."

Jess took a slow breath. "Actually, your given name wasn't Jason. It was David. David, Jr. David Howell, Jr. I always thought it was appropriate when you named J.J. Jason, Jr. Of course, your grandpappy wasn't on board with the name, either.

Dead set against it, as a matter of fact. He arranged a quickie marriage to Leon—"

"That worthless SOB!" cut in Jason, knocking one of the candlesticks over, clearly startling himself in uttering that detested word.

"Willie gave Leon some money to get him to do it."

"Of course he did. And, of course, Leon was game. Sounds just like Leon the Loser. He probably pissed it away at an Indian casino."

Jess had picked up the photograph again and studied it, his head cocked to one side. "Maybe your mama should have given you up. It was a hard choice, one she probably regretted more than she should have. No doubt she blamed you for the way her life turned out. It's an old, sad, familiar story. Though, you know, I can still see her right after you were born, in that little Vancouver hospital room, rocking you and smiling down on you like you were the Baby Jesus himself."

Jason made an impatient movement. "God, did that ever change! She always made me feel like the son of Satan. The bad seed." He shut his eyes and gripped his head. "I need to lie down. Everything is spinning."

"You take your time," Jess soothed. Vacating the sofa for the armchair, he let Jason hurl himself down and stretch out. "So, this picture ... Did you want to keep it, or have me put it in a safe place?"

A "safe place"? Jason almost laughed. There clearly was nothing safe about the past, about the truth.

Jason finally spoke in a soft, halting voice. "It never occurred to me why she didn't keep any pictures of her youthful self around."

He hesitated. How could it be that he had never seen a picture of his mom when she was young? Maybe because she couldn't stand the sight of how pretty she once was, or how she looked when all of life lay before her.

Jason held out a hand for the photograph, resisting the urge to crumple it—and all it stood for—in his fist. What would be the point? History was already rewritten. His grandfather Willie had managed to obliterate every whisper of David Howell's existence, and Jason's own anger toward his mother had—until now—tried to do the same to her.

He gave another mirthless laugh. *That's right.* From his newly discovered dad he got the extra finger joints and impeccable athletic chops, and from his mother's side ... well, the ability to be a world-class asshole and to nurse a grudge to its last, bitter, bitter drop.

He had blamed her for shaping him—for warping him. But she was gone now. And it had never occurred to him to ask what or who had shaped her.

Jason let his eyes run over the picture of his mother again. The beautiful, smiling stranger he never knew.

Or *did* he?

"I must be crazy," he said slowly.

"It's a lot to take in," Jess agreed.

"No—I mean, yes, it is. But that's not it, Jess." Sitting up, he flicked on the floor lamp and bent over the photograph. "It's that—this young, happy face—it shouldn't look so familiar."

"Well, life hit her hard, you know," said Jess, "but it *is* your mama in there. Before the smoking and drinking and regret and all."

But Jason wasn't listening. He had shut his eyes again and was nodding to himself, even humming snatches of something.

Then he took a sharp breath, his eyes popping open. "That's it! My *God*! That's her!"

"What's it? Who's her?"

"That's her!" Jason whooped, throwing up his hands and then raking them through his short hair as he fell back against the sofa. He did laugh now. "God, I can't believe it. Jess—it's the girl I've been dreaming of. You know—the butterfly girl! The one from my little foray into who-knows-where—the time I wrecked the Ferrari and I thought I was dead for sure. That beautiful girl who came and met me. We can rule out the brain doctor's sister now. I had my own guardian. I couldn't stop wondering about her, afterward. She started to pop up sometimes, when I fell asleep. All this time—the butterfly girl—all this time I've been dreaming of my ... my *mother*!"

Jess made an indeterminate sound, rubbing his hands back and forth over his knees like he wanted something solid to clutch. His eyes were blinking rapidly. When he spoke, his voice was choked. "You ... you don't say. Imagine that."

"Imagine that," echoed Jason.

Clearing his throat a couple of times, the old man sat forward, his knees almost touching Jason's. "Look here—I'm not sure what that last thing on your punch list is, Jason, but what I think this all means is that you're gonna need to forgive her. Forgive your mom. For everything."

Jason threw him a glance before returning his gaze to the picture. "That so, huh?" He tucked the photo in his chest pocket and folded his arms behind his head, chuckling softly. "God sure does have one helluva sense of humor."

The party showed no signs of winding down when Jason and Jess finally rejoined everyone, and Jason had to rap on a glass with a spoon to get everyone's attention—that, and fend off a beach ball that Jamal pitched at him from the pool.

"Okay, okay," he said, grinning. "Thanks for your attention, and I'll let you all get back to celebrating very shortly, but I wanted to say just a few words. First off, thank you all for being here today, and for messing up Sarah's house and eating all her food—"

Applause and hollering broke out in response to this. Sarah tossed a napkin at Jason and gave the boys a wink and a wave.

"And since you've been enjoying this hospitality, you've got to hear another one of my speeches. I promise, no golf pointers today. No—in fact—what I want to say is, uh, I just want you each to know how much I care about you—all of you."

Hearing some of the boys groan, and seeing others of them shift uncomfortably, he forged ahead. "Don't worry, guys, I'll try not to get too sappy on you. Well—maybe just a little sappy. You mean a lot to me. I had my own limited ideas about life, the universe, and everything, and you've played a huge role in changing my focus away from me, which was once my favorite subject." He continued to speak over a smattering of tepid chuckles. And I wanna say, guys, don't let the world slap its labels on you, like I did before I knew you all. You showed me up, and I'm glad you did. I'm proud to say I know you.

"But, look—because I care about you guys, there's more you need to hear." And they would hear it all right, he thought wryly. The whole gathering had fallen dead silent. You could hear the bubbling of the pool pump and Ringo chewing at something on his back haunch.

He took a deep breath. "As most of you know, I shouldn't be standing here with you today. I just about drowned when I was your age, and then, just before I met you all, I tried my damnedest to die in a car wreck. What that all means is that, twice in my life, I've been across the Great Divide." He made air quotes here, which didn't make anyone look more comfortable with the topic. Gritting his teeth, he went on. "It took me two times probably because I was such a slow learner, at least when it comes to matters of the heart...and of the soul." But I've caught on now. And I realize I'm the least likely person to be telling you this, but I'd be missing a huge opportunity if I didn't say something now. See, it's because I care about you so much that I'm speaking up. About how this life, what we're living right now, is definitely not as good as it gets."

If he thought telling the boys what they meant to him made them fidgety, that was nothing compared to this. They were all squirming by this point and avoiding eye contact with him and each other. Only Rich, Sarah, Jess, and the Brojans seemed dialed in to his words, but Jason had been working with the teenagers long enough to know they were still listening.

Grinning, he went on. "What I'm trying to say is, there's another world out there, beyond this one. Actually, countless worlds. I know because I've seen them. And there's a God. God *is*. He really *is*. And God is love. He radiates love like the sun radiates light and heat." He found Sarah beside him, and he put an arm around her waist to pull her closer. "As most of you guys did, I grew up dirt poor, and maybe like some of you, in a love-free environment—at least until I moved in with Jess Carson and his family. But even then, I took that for granted, like a fool. It's taken me almost all my life to learn how to be in synch with God's love and to figure out that, really, nothing else matters."

His gaze swept the gathering, a few of the boys' eyes flickering up to meet his and then to look away.

"I don't want you guys to have to wait that long," he said. "What I'm saying is, don't be stupid like I was."

Isaiah was watching him, although he, too, looked down when Jason's gaze found his. He saw the boy's hands were trembling in his lap.

Yeah, thought Jason, *you get it. You know what I'm getting at.*

Maybe it always took standing on the very edge of the abyss.

Well, Isaiah wasn't going to go over before he did. Not if he could help it.

It didn't take long to clean up afterward, with J.J. and Daman and Sarah's maid to help them. When the last chair was folded and put in the shed and Jason returned from dumping bags of garbage in the bin, he found Daman hunched on a lounge chair, staring at the ground.

"Hey there."

"Hey."

Unspooling the hose, Jason turned it on and dropped it into the pool. "You guys must have been having naval battles. The water's way down."

Daman merely grunted.

Jason nudged him with his foot. "When are you heading back to the coast?"

"Guess pretty soon."

"Think maybe you should wait till morning?"

"School's starting soon. They got some kind of orientation for freshmen."

Jason put a hand on his shoulder. "Hey. I know you're scared, but it's going to be okay."

He thought Daman would shrug him off. Maybe make some crack. But he didn't. He only seemed to draw even further into himself. And if it hadn't been dead silent, Jason wouldn't have heard him answer.

"How can it be okay?" he breathed. "You were the closest thing I ever had to a father."

God.

Sad, but true. Three years of trading jokes, with a little lecturing on Jason's part and belligerence on Daman's. Three years of golf games and meals and random trips and outings. That was the closest Daman got.

Jason shook his head slowly. Well, hell. If it hadn't been for Jess Carson, that would've been more than Jason himself had. Though Sam Steele tried his best, in his warped way.

Lord. However much Jason had fallen short as a surrogate, at least he'd spared Daman the booze, gambling, and whores.

So, there was that.

He gave Daman's shoulder a shake. "Easy on the past tense, fella. It's going to be okay," he said again. "Because now you're going to have a father ... and a mother. Jess and Sarah are going to be there for you. You're part of their—*our*—family now."

"Won't be the same."

"No, it won't. But in some ways, it'll be better. You're going to have your own bedroom right here in this beautiful house whenever you come back from the U. And I've set it up so you'll be working at the winery during your breaks and summer. Kim is going to teach you everything she knows about winemaking. And—only imminent death could drag this from me, you understand—she might even know more about it than I do. J.J. will be working there too. Your brother from another mother."

Daman nodded. He stretched out a foot and pressed on the hose to stop the flow. Then he released it.

Jason socked him gently in the ribs. "And ... last but not least, did I mention I'm leaving my golf membership to you?"

At this, Daman finally looked up. His eyes were glistening, but there was a twinkle in them. "Oh, yeah? That's nice. Thank. How long did you say the doc gave you?"

Jason roared with laughter and rubbed the kid's head. "Come on. Let's go for a walk with J.J. and Ringo. It's a beautiful evening."

No sooner did Ringo's acute canine ears pick up his name and the magic word than he abandoned the plate of table scraps he'd been licking clean and bounded over to them. They found J.J. stuffing a last bag of trash into the bin, and the three of them managed to ram it all down so the lid would shut.

It was the last time he saw Daman before the *last* time. But it was how he liked to remember him, loping with that loose stride of his, teasing J.J., and making cracks about the dog as the sun set, orange and blazing, over Sarah's little vineyard.

21

No one remembers the first dream he ever has, but Jason would remember the last.

The morning after the party, he woke before dawn. Sitting on the edge of the bed as the light grew brighter around him, he played and replayed what he had just seen. It ought to have filled him with trepidation, but instead he only felt the uncanny *rightness* of it—a peace settling over him like a loving hand on his shoulder.

This.

And this was the day.

He beat Jess getting up, for once. The old guy only slept till five a.m. on a good day, but when he ambled into the kitchen that morning, he found Jason already dressed, making coffee.

"You're sure up early."

"Yup." Jason got two mugs out. "I had a dream that woke me up around four."

Taking the cup offered to him, Jess nodded his thanks. "Good dream or bad?"

Jason considered. "Good. Real good, I'd say. Something I never could have come up with on my own. Just look at that sky—it's going to be a beautiful day for a swim."

"Say again?" Jess frowned. "The caffeine hasn't kicked in yet. You dreamed you were gonna go for a swim?"

"Uh-huh. That's how I know: not only am I gonna go for a swim in the river, but I want you to come with me."

Jess choked on his coffee, and Jason gave him reassuring thumps on the back. "But you won't have to go in, old man. Just be sure to bring some rope."

Here Jess set his mug down firmly on the counter. "Jason, you're making no sense," he accused when he could catch his breath.

"You've got plenty of rope, right?" Jason said, persisting. "I've never known you to be without any."

"Sure, I've got plenty of rope," Jess retorted. "A man should always be prepared. Matter of fact, I've still got the rope—"

When Jess broke off, Jason cocked an eyebrow. "Go on. Your Alzheimer's acting up? You've still got *what* rope?"

"I've still got the rope I used to pull you out thirty years ago," Jess replied. "And if you haven't grown any more common sense in the in-between times, don't talk to *me* about losing *my* mind."

Jason only grinned. "Of course you still have that same rope. 'Cause if it ain't broke, don't fix it, right? Okay. Grab that famous rope, but bring some more too. You'll need to tie them together, if I'm not mistaken."

Releasing a slow breath, Jess shook his head. "I don't know if I like the sound of this." He studied Jason's face a minute, finding only calm determination there. Then he shook his head again, shrugging. "Whatever it is, this is all about that dream you had."

"The coffee is taking effect, I see, because your sixth sense is waking up." Jason put an arm around Jess's shoulders. "You're a pillar, old man. Let me make you some breakfast, for once, and then we'll get on to the day's activities."

They drove in Jess's old GMC along the river until houses hid it from view. Back and forth, down Harris, up Newcomer, back along George Washington Way, taking a right on Saint to get back to the river. Jess was whistling an old Hank Williams tune, "I'm So Lonesome I Could Cry," as he made the big circle. He looked over at the passenger seat a few times, but Jason was staring out the window. Finally, Jess cleared his throat. "We lookin' for anything in particular?"

Jason took a measured breath. "I'm not sure. I think I'll know when I see it. At least, I hope I do. Let's just pull over on the next go-round."

As soon as they approached the entrance to the riverfront park, a 1990s vintage Camaro came racing down the road from the opposite direction. It was souped-up and emitted an angry growl as the gears downshifted and the engine revved. It suddenly turned right in front of Jess, forcing him to brake hard and swerve to avoid a collision.

"Good Lord, what a fool," he growled. "I could have T-boned him! Guy must have a death wish."

Nodding, Jason said, "That would be our man now, Jess. Follow him in."

The morning sunrise was casting its light upon the land, and a deep bass sound thumped from the still-running Camaro when the two of them made their way to a bench overlooking the Columbia. They took a seat, the long rope coiled beside Jess. A man was fishing from the dock.

"You're not really going in there, are you?" asked Jess. He pointed at the warning sign posted by the dock, indicating dangerous currents. "It's beautiful, like you said, but look at that water. You know how many folks drown each year, at this very spot? They think they can make it out to the little island, but the water's too high and cold and fast this time of year. Goin' swimmin' in there would be like suicide."

Jason stretched his arms along the back of the bench. "Don't worry. Never again. Offing myself is really not my thing anymore."

The fisherman reeled in his line and detached the sock that had become hooked to it. Then, with a smooth, whipping motion, he cast his lure again.

"There's nothing that would make me take my own life now," Jason went on. "Not after what I've seen ... and learned."

"Taking your own life is one thing," agreed Jess, "and I'm glad to hear that you wouldn't do it. But *risking* your life is a whole 'nother deal. If you aren't planning on going for a leisurely swim, I can only guess you're thinking you're gonna haul somebody else out."

Jason gave him a sidewise glance.

"What else is all this rope for? I suppose you'd risk your life," Jess said, "if it came to saving someone?"

"Mm," grunted Jason. "What someone would that be?"

On cue, the distant thump of the car stereo cut off abruptly. The doors of the Camaro flew open, and three teenage boys jumped out. Shouting and whooping, they began to run over the grass toward the dock, peeling off their Richland Bombers Football sweatshirts as they went.

"All right, you wusses," yelled the largest boy. "We're swimming to Nelson Island. If you wanna be a Richland Bomber, consider this part of your initiation."

Thundering onto the dock, they began to kick off their shoes. The fisherman scowled at them, not least because their noise put paid to any hopes he had of catching something. Reeling in his line, he said, "I just want to tell you young fellas that if you're fool enough to jump in that water this late in the year, I'm not coming in after you."

"Shit, I've swum over there a bunch of times," countered the ringleader. "I'll show you guys how it's done."

"I wouldn't do that," warned the fisherman again. "They've released a lot of water from the dams upriver. It's moving faster than it does in July and August, and you know the Columbia is never warm. There's a reason they built those nuclear cooling towers at Hanford."

Ignoring him, the young man dove in. When he bobbed up, gasping and spluttering, he began to swim toward the island, goading the other boys, who were now hesitating on the dock.

On the bench, Jess heaved a sigh, more resigned than alarmed.

"Idiot," said Jason, but without harshness. Standing up, he turned toward his companion. "You're right, Jess. I wouldn't throw my life away, but I'd sure risk it now to help someone—even a dumb someone, like that kid. What can I say? I learned from the best. That dope can't be any more hopeless than I was at his age, and you risked yourself to get me."

Jess's jaw was trembling, but he reached for the rope and began to wrap it around Jason's waist.

"Make sure it's good and tight."

"Don't tell me how to tie knots," Jess grumbled.

"In case anything goes wrong—or maybe I should say, in case this all goes right—I've set everything up with Friedman," said Jason. "He's going to make sure Isaiah gets my lungs, for what they're worth. Carlson will take care of the rest of my—I guess you could say—my recyclable parts."

Jess nodded tightly. "You can do this, Jason," he protested. "Don't talk like this'll be it for you. I might've risked my hide once for your fool head, but I lived to tell the tale."

"You did." Jason grabbed the old man in a hug. "And I didn't say it *was* it, for me. Didn't I tell you I've learned a lot?" He released him, and a moment later, Jess reluctantly let him go.

"See you soon, Jess."

"Take care, son."

"And pull hard, dammit!" Jason said, grinning.

Jess picked up the coils of rope, but before Jason could head off, Jess grabbed at his shirt. "Son," —he twisted the cotton material in his fist and hung on— "I just want to tell you again how proud I am of you."

For the first time that morning, Jason wavered, his eyes lighting up. He looked about to say something, but nothing emerged. He swallowed and nodded once.

Then he gently pulled himself free from the old man's grip and started for the dock.

"Glad some of you have some brains in those heads," the fisherman was saying to the two boys who remained beside him. They only looked embarrassed not to be following their buddy and tried not to make eye contact with him or each other.

"You never can tell these kids anything," muttered the fisherman, turning to Jess and Jason for support. "Oh—yep—there he goes. Like I said, more than he bargained for."

Sure enough, the teenager, who was halfway to the island, had begun to flounder. His skin was bright red across his back but turning blue toward his extremities. He flipped onto his back to conserve energy but began to sink in any case, his cries of increasing alarm piercing the air.

"I guess he's gonna have to learn the hard way," said the man angrily, but Jason already had his shirt off and was pulling off his shoes. The other two boys made feeble motions toward jumping in, but Jason pushed them back.

"You guys stay right here. I'll get out to him and try to circle around him with this rope. If you help Jess here, you can pull us both in."

"Have you ever tried to save someone drowning?" demanded the fisherman. "It's a lot tougher than you think. Odds are, you'll both go down." Digging out his cell phone, he held up an arm to halt Jason while he speed-dialed with the other hand. "Let the professionals deal with this."

Jason only nodded at Jess, who was tying the rope to the cleat at the end of the dock. They both knew 911 would be too late—much, much too late. Stepping around the fisherman's outstretched arm, Jason dove in.

The water hit him like an icy wall. Jeez, you'd think all that winding through British Columbia and Washington State would give the water time to warm up, but this felt fresh off the snowmelt of the Canadian Rockies. Jason wasn't as strong as he used to be, either. He'd lost a lot of muscle mass and weight in the last few months, and if it weren't for the rope around his waist, he thought the current might have borne him away before he even reached the kid. Some rescue that would have been.

But he drove through the water, forcing his numbing arms to churn, and following the panicked cries, he felt a surge of determination. *That's right. This is how it went.* This was how it was supposed to go.

He tried to come up behind the flailing swimmer, but the boy saw him approach and spun around desperately to clutch Jason around the neck and shoulders, trying to climb him in his terror.

"They're both going under!" shouted one of the boys on the dock.

"We've got to move fast now," Jess urged. "Get behind me and start pulling."

Even with their combined weights on the rope, the river was overmatching them. They saw Jason and the boy struggling, coughing, disappearing, and reappearing. Jason was yelling something hoarsely, probably trying to snap the boy out of his blind panic, before they went under again.

"You gonna help us?" Jess yelled over his shoulder at the fisherman, who stood gawking. "You rather be right or rather save some lives?"

"But my line—"

"Damn your line! No fish is gonna come anywhere near it, with all this hollering and thrashing going on in the water."

Grimacing, the fisherman wedged his pole between the boards of the dock and took hold of the end of the rope. The four of them hauled and strained, sweat beading and running down their faces, the cords in their arms bulging. The river fought them, unwilling to give them back an inch. It was like all their efforts only slowed the water's efforts to sweep the victims even further downstream.

In the distance a siren whined, but they didn't heed it in their concentration. Jason and the boy were nowhere to be seen now. If not for the dead weight at the end of the rope, Jess would have thought they were both lost.

With a squeal of rubber and last wail of siren, an ambulance screeched into the parking lot, and two EMTs vaulted out, running to join them.

"What's the story?" the first one demanded.

"We've got two in the water," Jess panted, the rope cutting into his palms.

"Two?"

"Yeah," he gasped, "my friend went in after their buddy. He's tied to this rope, but the boy's hangin' on to him in a death grip, so they're both goin' down."

The second paramedic was already calling for backup, but the first joined them in pulling on the rope. Slowly, slowly, inch by painful inch, they began to reel it in.

"This is what almost always happens," the one EMT said, grimacing with effort. "One guy goes in to help another, and one tragedy turns into two. It's a good thing you thought to tie a rope around your friend."

"Yeah," panted the fisherman. "You always bring a hundred yards of rope when you go to a park?"

"I did this time," Jess said tightly. "Had it right next to us on the bench. All because ... my friend—the one in the water—he had some kind of ... premonition."

In their surprise, they almost let go of the rope, and Jess had to dig his heels in so it wouldn't play out again. But no one asked him any questions. They only gave him funny looks and went back to pulling.

An eternity passed. Most of the line now lay on the dock beside them again, and Jess saw the two paramedics exchange a grim glance. But then—

"Look! There they are!" he shouted.

Two limp figures bobbed up, close in to the shore. Neither was moving, but they could see the rope was looped under the teenager's arms, cutting in to his colorless skin. With a splash, the two EMTs scrambled into the water, grabbing the rope for balance. With a few almighty heaves, they succeeded in dragging Jason and the boy onto the bank, where they immediately began CPR.

They were all silently counting the compressions, the teenagers wincing at how firmly the paramedic pumped their friend's chest. Twenty-six, twenty-seven, twenty-eight ...

Before they reached the end of the first set, the boy's head rolled to the side, and vomited up a painter's bucket of water, to his friends' cheers.

"This one's going to make it, Guy."

The first paramedic didn't pause in pumping Jason's chest. "He'll live, at least. Too early to know about brain damage."

"If you ask me, he was brain damaged to jump in there in the first place," said the second.

"That's called adolescence," Guy said. "Weren't you brain damaged, when you were his age? I don't know about this fella here, though. He's not responding."

Jess stood over them, his face shadowed.

With a cough and a groan, the boy opened his eyes and tried to sit up.

"Whoa—just lay back down, young man," the second EMT ordered. "You okay?"

"Y-yeah."

"What's your name, son?"

"Shane."

"That's a good sign," Guy said. "You're one lucky dude, Shane. You owe this man here your life. I sure hope you get a chance to thank him."

The second crew of paramedics blared up in their ambulance and came pounding down to the dock a minute later. After the first EMTs delivered rapid instructions, they began lifting Shane onto a gurney.

Jess lost count of how many sets of compressions Guy performed on Jason, but when he finished another, Guy put his head to Jason's chest again and then sat back on his heels.

"Damn, Chuck. I think we've lost the hero. God, that's not fair."

No sooner had the words left his mouth than Jason erupted with a blast of water of his own, his head rolling weakly to his side on the sloped bank.

"Holy shit!" yelled Guy. "He's still with us. Come on, bud. Wake up."

"Still alive?" Jess echoed, crowding in closer. "That wasn't part of his plan."

Guy and the other paramedic whipped around to look up at him, their faces a mix of shock and disgust.

"What are you talking about?" Guy snapped. "What plan? Was this some kind of set-up?"

"N-no," Jess reared back. "*No!* I didn't mean like that."

"You almost seem disappointed he's not dead."

Jess retreated another step, holding up his hands. "No, no, nothing like that," he said again. "It's a long story, young man. And I'm certainly not disappointed. You just do your job. I'll explain it all when we get to the hospital."

With another glance at the second paramedic, Guy turned back to Jason, who remained unconscious. "He's still got a pulse, but it's very faint. Give me your smelling salts, Chuck."

Waving them under Jason's nose brought no response. "Let's give him some adrenaline." This, too, yielded no response.

Quietly, Chuck and Guy loaded Jason on the second gurney and wheeled him to the ambulance, with Jess following behind, the coil of wet rope under his arm. The younger boys had mumbled to each other and shaken Jess's hand before picking up their clothes and shoes and sheepishly asking if they could hitch a ride with him to the hospital.

Jess spared the fisherman one last glance, and the man gave him a nod before turning and casting his line in again, as if nothing had happened—as if Jess's whole world hadn't been upended.

The last thing he heard before the paramedics shut the ambulance doors was Guy.

"I hope we haven't saved the guy's body and lost his brain."

22

Was he alive or was he dead?

He couldn't tell.

He was lying there anyway. There was steady beeping and a hum. Attachments. But he couldn't raise his arms or open his eyes to investigate further.

There was sleep. There was unconsciousness. There were the memories.

"Brain dead." That was Friedman speaking now. He recognized the matter-of-fact tone that masked any uncertainties.

This pronouncement was met with choked sobs, a grappling for his hand. Jason tried to move his own in response, but it refused to cooperate.

The urgent grip resurrected a memory: Jess taking him by the hands, the arms, untangling him and hauling him from the water.

Rescue.

Lifeline.

But which time was it? Which rescue was he remembering?

Darkness closed in again.

When he came to, just about everyone was there. Sarah, Jess, J.J. He heard Rich Williams and Daman and the golf team boys. No Isaiah.

"God's timing," Rich was saying.

Jason heard a scoffing sound, felt weight shift on the end of the bed. He didn't need to be able to open his eyes to know it was Daman. The boy wasn't having it. He could picture Rich going toe-to-toe with him.

"Jason knew he didn't have long," Williams said. "And he knew Isaiah doesn't either. That's why he put this living will in place."

Footsteps. More weight on the bed. "I don't want to see him go either," Sarah told Daman. "And I don't want to unplug that respirator either, but it's what Jason wanted. He told Jess—he had some kind of premonition that morning—a dream. He knew he could save Isaiah this way. Not to mention that teenager down at the river."

Daman took another sharp breath. If it had been any other kid, Jason might have thought he was choking up. There was murmuring, more shifting weight. Then Sarah got up again.

"Thanks for coming back, Rich. I think we're almost ready. Friedman will be here any minute."

"Are you sure you don't want an ordained minister for this?" Rich questioned. "I mean, I've never done one of these before."

"You're exactly the person he would want to have do this," Jess assured him. "You know, his folks never had him baptized, and by the time he came to live with us, it was too late. He hated church."

"Okay. I'll do my best. I guess now I know how Jason felt when people wanted him to pray with them. At least no one is expecting a miracle from me. You wanna wake J.J. up for this, Sarah?"

Jason felt them draw closer around him. Then there was cool water running down his forehead.

"With this water," Rich intoned, "I consecrate you, Jason Knightbridge, as a child of God. You belong to him, now and forever."

More water was sprinkled on him. A big hand patted him

on the head. Other hands were on his arms and hands and legs. Then Rich began to sing. Other voices swelled with his, even Daman's, low and reluctant. How did that kid even know this song? "Baptized in water, sealed by the Spirit, cleansed by the blood of Christ our King ..."

When the notes died away, the room fell silent. Even the humming of the machinery seemed muted. It was so quiet that Jason thought he heard a faint thumping. Soft, soft.

"It's that butterfly again," Sarah said wonderingly. "I saw it on the sill earlier. It's crazy, but I almost imagined it wanted to come inside."

The tapping continued. Then he heard her stride away from the bed and caught the click of her fingernails against the window. "Oh!" she breathed. "Look—it didn't even fly away when I touched the glass."

"It's like it wanted you to try to touch it," Jess marveled.

Another silence fell. Then Sarah murmured, "How peaceful it looks."

"Have you said your goodbyes?" Friedman's voice broke the spell. The doctor sighed heavily as he strode in to stand beside the bed, and Jason smiled to himself. Good old, know-it-all doc. Having to unplug dying patients most likely didn't rank high on the guy's list of favorite activities.

"Yes, yes, just one moment, Dr. Friedman," Sarah replied. There was a rattling as she cranked the window open. "I knew it! Look at that—it wanted to come in."

Jason had no trouble picturing Friedman's expression: it was time to unplug the family vegetable, and these people were having some kind of *nature encounter*? If Jason could have laughed out loud, he would have.

The doctor cleared his throat. "Sarah," he began again. "We've discussed this. If we're going to carry out the terms of the living will, we have to take steps now."

"Of course," she agreed absently. "But look, Doctor."

Jason felt it then. With his heightened senses, he felt the

brush of the butterfly's wings. He felt the infinitely light pressure of its weight as it landed in his hair. He felt the stillness of the room as those around him seemed to hold their breath.

And then everything changed.

He was flooded.

Alight.

Dazzled.

His eyes flew open, and he saw all around him the vision. It was the *place* he had been twice before—the indescribable center of it all, rushing, spinning, whirling toward that one, glowing presence.

His body was sitting up, as those in the hospital room drew back in astonishment. Jason didn't even register them. He was shouting, unable to contain what he saw, *who* he saw.

"Oh, wow! Oh, *wow!* Oh my God, it's all so beautiful. And ... Mama. You came for me. Yes, let's go. I love you! I can't wait. Come on—"

He fell back against the pillows. A last breath, a glow, issued from him, rising above his body, circled by the butterfly. Jess would say later he thought he heard singing. Sarah would say she heard Jason laugh.

The light and its companion escaped through the open window, remaining just visible for several more moments before vanishing.

It was Dr. Friedman who sat hard on the bed then, as if his legs would no longer support him. "Good God," he muttered. "What the hell just happened? What the hell did we just see?"

"I don't think it had anything to do with hell, Doctor," Rich murmured. "Quite the contrary."

Friedman almost glared at him, before bewilderment overtook him again. "So he—Jason—he was ... right, after all?"

Daman shook his head. There were tears running down his face, but he was smiling. "Wherever he is now, I hope he can't hear you, Doc. It'll surely go to his head."

Turning to regard the young man beside him, a slow, answering smile grew on Friedman's face. "I'll risk it. I can't say I'm sorry to be wrong, in this case." Quietly, he drew the coverlet over the body.

"He ... he told me he wasn't afraid to die," ventured J.J. "He used to be, but he wasn't anymore." Sarah put an arm around her son's shoulders, and the boy's voice grew stronger. "It was the last thing he said to me. That, and he told me ..."

"Told you what, son?" Jess prompted, nodding at him.

J.J.'s eyes met his.

"He said, 'Don't be afraid. Only believe...and...'"

"And what, son?"

"And believe that we will all be together again."

The old man smiled, nodded, then put his still strong right arm around J.J., pulling him tight against his chest.